This book should be returned to any branch of the
Lancashire County Library on or before the date shown

		N M0
2 8 APR 2018		

Lancashire County Library
Bowran Street
Preston PR1 2UX

www.lancashire.gov.uk/libraries

LL1(A)

SOLID CITIZENS

*Marcus Corvinus investigates the murder of a
prominent local politician in the latest
intriguing mystery*

December, AD39. While enjoying the Winter
Festival holiday at his adopted daughter's
home in the Alban Hills, Marcus Corvinus
discovers that an outwardly respectable
pillar of the community, local politician
Quintus Caesius, has been discovered beat-
en to death at the rear entrance of the town
brothel.

Questioning those who knew the victim,
Corvinus is dismayed to find Bovillae a
place of small town secrets, bitter feuds,
malicious gossip and deadly rivalry: a world
away from the sophistication of Rome. As
he is to discover, there are several suspects
with reason to bear Caesius a grudge. But
who would hate him enough to kill him?
And what would a supposedly solid citizen
be doing visiting the local brothel?

SOLID CITIZENS

David Wishart

Severn House Large Print
London & New York

This first large print edition published 2014
in Great Britain and the USA by
SEVERN HOUSE PUBLISHERS LTD of
19 Cedar Road, Sutton, Surrey, England, SM2 5DA.
First world regular print edition published 2013 by
Severn House Publishers Ltd., London and New York.

British Library Cataloguing in Publication Data

Wishart, David, 1952- author.
  Solid citizens. -- (Marcus Corvinus series)
  1. Corvinus, Marcus (Fictitious character)--Fiction.
  2. Murder--Investigation--Fiction. 3. Rome--History--
  Empire, 30 B.C.-476 A.D.--Fiction. 4. Detective and
  mystery stories. 5. Large type books.
  I. Title II. Series
  823.9'2-dc23

  ISBN-13: 9780727897152

Severn House Publishers support the Forest Stewardship Council™
[FSC™], the leading international forest certification organisation. All
our titles that are printed on FSC certified paper carry the FSC logo.

MIX
Paper from
responsible sources
FSC® C013056

Printed and bound in Great Britain by
T J International, Padstow, Cornwall.

Dramatis personae
Only the names of characters appearing or referred to more than once are given.

Castrimoenium
Bathyllus: Corvinus's major-domo
Marilla: Corvinus's adopted daughter
Clarus, Cornelius: Marilla's husband
Lupercus: Clarus and Marilla's major-domo
Perilla, Rufia: Corvinus's wife
Priscus, Titus Helvius: Corvinus's stepfather
Vipsania: Corvinus's mother
Phormio: Vipsania's chef

Bovillae and elsewhere
Andromeda, Opilia: owner of the Bovillan brothel
Anthus: Quintus Caesius's major-domo
Baebius, Quintus: an antiques collector
Caesius, Lucius: the murdered man's brother
Caesius, Quintus: the murdered man, Bovillan censor-elect. His wife (now dead) was Vatinia and his father (also dead) was Marcus Caesius

Canidius, Sextus: the current quaestor
Carillus: head slave in the Bovillan brothel
Decimus: Manlius's rod man
Dossenus: a mentally-defective vagrant
Garganius, Sextus: a former night-watchman
Libanius, Quintus: a Castrimoenian senator
Lydia: a prostitute
Manlius, Marcus: one of the current aediles
Mettius, Aulus: Quintus Caesius's nephew
Nausiphanes: an elderly freedman
Nerva, Publius Silius: a Bovillan senator
Novius, Publius: a lawyer
Opilia Lucinda: brothel owner in Tibur; Andromeda's former mistress
Roscius, Quintus: a farmer
Ulpius, Marcus: a carter
Vatinia Secunda: Mettius's mother

The story is set during the first half of December AD39.

ONE

I like the Winter Festival.

Oh yeah, sure, it can be a complete pain in the rectum, and it's really a time for the bought help. Still, there isn't much to beat the simple pleasure of coming downstairs on that first Winter Festival morning, particularly if it's cold and crisp and early, and seeing them all lined up waiting for their candles and dolls and little packets of holiday money, their innocent faces bright with the prospect of a whole five days' skiving off work, rubbishing the master, stuffing themselves until they're sick with rich food in the best dining room and generally behaving like a pig's backside with total impunity. Or at least technically: any slave stupid enough to go over the top by, say, pissing in the ornamental pool or trying it on with the mistress in the linen cupboard deserves all he gets – even if he can't be given it until after the party's over for another year. Rome might let her hair down on occasion, but you don't mess with her.

So there we were, in the lead-up to the

7

Winter Festival, tucked away in the Alban Hills, visiting our adopted daughter Marilla and her new husband Clarus at what had been, the year before, Perilla's Aunt Marcia's villa outside Castrimoenium. Me, I'm a city boy, myself, but Castrimoenium – or the villa, rather – is special. Courtesy aunt or not (she and Perilla weren't directly related), Marcia and her husband Fabius Maximus had been practically the only family she'd had, and when Maximus died just before the Ovid business that first brought me and the lady together, Marcia had sold up and moved out of Rome, to what until now had been a holiday property. Since we'd been married, Perilla and I had been coming through to stay pretty regularly, at least once or twice a year. For all she was a damn-your-eyes straight-down-the-line old-style blue-blooded aristocrat I'd had a lot of respect for old Marcia. Then Marilla had appeared and almost immediately moved in for keeps. It'd suited them both: Marcia had no family herself, at least none living, while Marilla with her penchant for collecting lame-duck animals – particularly the bloody-minded, eccentric or just plain weird ones – had never been happy in Rome. Besides, the city had painful memories. Then there was Clarus, the local doctor's son, and that was that. When Marcia had died she'd left them the villa – lock, stock and menagerie.

Mind you, it wasn't all sweetness and light. We were expecting Mother and her older-than-time-itself husband Priscus, the antiquarian's antiquarian, in a few days. Fortunately, she'd be leaving her serial-poisoner chef Phormio behind in Rome, just as we'd left Meton. Not Bathyllus, though: he'd always had a soft spot for Marilla, and I couldn't do that to the little guy, not at Winter Festival time. Meton, now ... well, Meton was different; being in Castrimoenium did something to his already-warped brain. After the business with Dassa the oenophilic sheep and his more recent celebrity chef scam, I wasn't risking letting that scheming bastard anywhere near the place.

It had been a quiet morning, for me, at least, which suited me fine. Perilla and Marilla were out with the hellhound Placida, terrorizing the local wild boar population plus any stray wolf silly enough to get in the way – or at least Placida was – while Clarus made his rounds: his father's eyesight had deteriorated badly these past few months, and Clarus was gradually taking over the practice. I was stretched out on one of the atrium couches, with half a jug of more-than-decent Alban on the side table, and was just giving myself a top-up when Lupercus came in. Lupercus was Clarus and Marilla's major-domo, the replacement for old Laertes who'd been given his freedom in

Marcia's will and had gone off to the flesh-pots of Baiae to live with his sister. Not a bad lad, Lupercus, albeit – in the arch-conservative Bathyllus's view, anyway – on the far-too-young and over-sassy side for the job. He and the little guy seemed to be getting along fine. Just about. If you could call pointedly ignoring each other's existence getting along. Still, there'd been no blood spilled so far, which by my reckoning was a definite plus.

Taking Bathyllus aside just before we'd left home and warning him that I'd shove his feather duster where the sun didn't shine if there were trouble might have helped, mind. Never discount the power of intimidation.

'Publius Silius Nerva to see you, sir,' Lupercus said.

I sat up. 'Who?'

'The senator, sir. From Bovillae. He said to mention a connection with Quintus Libanius?'

Oh. Right. Fuzz-face Libanius I knew, the only non-Greek I'd ever met with a beard you could hide a badger in, and First Speaker of the Castrimoenian Senate. The last time I'd seen him he'd been trying not to throw up over a corpse.

'So what's it about, pal?' I said.

He shrugged; something that, if Bathyllus had seen it, would've had the little guy tearing his hair. If he had any, that is, which he doesn't. 'I don't know, sir. But he says it's important.'

I sighed; there went the quiet morning. And I didn't like the mention of Libanius much, either.

'OK,' I said. 'Wheel him in.'

Lupercus did. Nerva was a little tubby guy impeccably dressed in a broad-striped mantle that looked like it'd come from one of the best shops in Rome. Which made sense, because the Silii are one of the top Roman families. Bovillan senator he might be, but I'd guess he was one of the honorary appointees, a local only by residence who'd been drafted in because he'd held office in Rome itself.

'Ah, Corvinus, glad you could see me,' he said. 'Enjoying your holiday?'

'Yeah.' Up to now I had been, anyway. 'Take a couch. You like a cup of wine?'

'It's a little early for me, thank you.' He lay down. 'Do carry on yourself, though. Quintus Libanius sends his regards.'

I took a sip of the Alban. I was sorely puzzled: something was definitely not right here. Oh, sure, Bovillae's only four or five miles away, the other side of the Appian Road, but you didn't get one of their senators dropping in on an out-of-the-way villa just to pass the time with a visiting stranger, particularly a top-notcher from the very crest of the social tree like Silius Nerva. 'So,' I said. 'What can

11

I do for you?'

He cleared his throat. 'It's, ah, a little embarrassing.'

'Yeah? In what way?'

'There is...' He hesitated and began again. 'Not to beat about the bush, my dear fellow, we in the Bovillan Senate are faced with what amounts to a rather unfortunate and sensitive problem at present. I happened to be, ah, discussing this over dinner with Libanius yesterday evening and he mentioned your name, plus the fact that you were currently visiting. He suggested that since you have a certain amount of experience in these matters it might be worth the senate's while to contact you.'

Uh-oh. I was getting a very bad feeling about this. Men of Nerva's standing and background are used to fixing you with their eye and telling you straight out what they want you to do for them. They don't expect any arguments or backchat, either. What they *don't* do is what Nerva was doing here: hum and haw and go round as many bloody houses as would make up a substantial city block in the process. Evidently a small nudge was called for or we wouldn't cut to the chase this side of the festival.

'Uh ... I don't want to hurry you, pal,' I said. 'But do you think you could be just a tad more explicit?' Before we all died of old age and boredom.

'I'm sorry, Corvinus. Quite right, quite right.' He cleared his throat again. 'To be brief, Libanius told me about that terrible business involving Lucius Hostilius last year here in Castrimoenium and how good you'd been in, ah, bringing things on behalf of the Castrimoenian Senate to a satisfactory conclusion. He thought you might be able to help us in a similar way.'

Gods! Well, one of us had to spell it out, and from the looks of things it wasn't going to be mealy-mouthed Nerva here.

'You mean there's been another murder,' I said.

He winced like a dowager confronted by a dirty picture. 'Ah ... not to put too fine a point on it,' he said. 'Yes. Yes, there has. That is indeed the case.'

Hell. Oh, I knew it had to be something like that – Libanius wouldn't have sent the guy to me if he'd only wanted a recommendation for a good wine to serve with duck – but just before the Winter Festival, for the gods' sake! Like he'd said, I was on holiday here. Perilla would definitely be unchuffed, for a start. The lady gets really, really serious about murders at holiday times.

Even so, I was still slightly puzzled. Murders aren't nice, but they can happen even in the most well-regulated families. It still really didn't account for the guy's embarrassment.

'OK,' I said. 'Who was the victim?'

13

'Our censor-elect. Quintus Caesius.'

Well, that explained the high-powered emissary, anyway. A single provincial censor is appointed every five years in place of the town's normal two chief magistrates, taking up office on the first of January. Like his Roman equivalent, his prime job is to revise the list of senators and citizens, cutting out the dead wood. But it doesn't stop there: he's also responsible for the settlement of the community's finances for the next five-year period, which means he has the power to choose new contractors to handle the sources of that finance, such as publicly owned land, commercial businesses and the like, and to terminate any existing contracts, as he sees fit. The operative phrase being that last one. Oh, sure, technically any decisions he makes are only recommendations and so subject to full senatorial approval, but human nature being what it is they usually go through on the nod. Plus, because for that particular year he's on his own at the top, with no equally empowered colleague to queer his pitch if he has a mind to, given that said senate has a hundred members who are generally more interested in getting through the day's agenda and home for a cup of wine and an early dinner than actually thinking of the implications of what they're voting for, so long as he's careful and a good talker he can do whatever he likes.

All of which means that a censor is a pretty big cheese. Ipso facto, he also has to be a pillar of honesty, morality, sobriety and rectitude, the best exponent the community can show of traditional provincial family values. At least, that's the theory. Don't laugh. It could technically happen, although the chances of these qualities coinciding with an interest in politics is well within the flying-pigs category.

'So how did he die?' I said.

Nerva cleared his throat yet again and swallowed before he answered. His expression had gone wooden. 'He was, ah, found with his head beaten in at the back entrance to the local brothel.'

I stared at him. The silence lengthened. Finally, I said: 'Ah.'

I could see now why he'd had difficulty getting down to the nitty-gritty: now the dreadful truth was out, the guy was literally glowing with embarrassment, so brightly you could've used his face to roast Winter Festival chestnuts.

'"Ah" is right!' he said. 'It's appalling!'

It had its funny side, too, mind, but Nerva wouldn't've seen that, so I kept my face straight.

'So was he actually on his way in or out when it happened?' I said.

He pursed his lips primly. 'I don't know.'

'Oh, come on, pal! You must know that, at

15

least!'

He gave me a look that would've curdled milk. 'I don't know, Corvinus,' he said slowly, 'because I haven't asked. Nor do I intend to. My task – with the full approval of the Bovillan Senate, naturally – is simply to put the matter completely into your capable hands, if you'll accept the charge. As an outsider...' He stopped.

Yeah, well, I could see where he was heading. If there was dirt to be dug – and there undoubtedly would be – then the solid citizens of Bovillae would rather not know the details; while if a visitor from Rome were to do the digging none of them need be personally, embarrassingly, involved in the investigation. Nevertheless, the guy wasn't getting off that easily.

'OK,' I said. 'Let's get some facts at least, things that you *do* know. First of all: when did this happen?'

'Two nights ago. At least, the body was found yesterday morning, as I said in the alleyway behind the brothel.'

'He couldn't've just been passing the door?'

'No. The alley is a dead end. And all the other buildings are shops and storehouses. They would have been – in fact, were – locked and shuttered for the night.'

'The brothel owner tell you anything useful? About exact timing, for example?' He just looked at me. Yeah. Right. Got it. 'OK, forget that. I can find it out for myself. Next. Who do you think might've done it?'

'How should I know?' he snapped. 'That's your job to find out, surely.'

I sighed. 'Come on, pal! I'm not asking you to make an accusation, but I need somewhere to start. What about a straightforward mugging? That's the most likely solution.'

Nerva shook his head. 'Unfortunately, it isn't – in fact it's most improbable. A mugging might well happen in Rome, yes, but not in Bovillae. We have our share of crime, certainly, but not that sort. Besides, his purse was still on his belt.'

'So it was deliberate. He was targeted.' No answer, but the guy was looking more and more uncomfortable. 'Fine. So what about enemies? Who did he know locally who might want him dead?'

Nerva bridled. 'Really, Corvinus! I already said Bovillae isn't Rome. Quintus Caesius was a highly respected and respectable member of the community, and a major public figure. He didn't mix with people of that stamp. And our prominent citizens do *not* go around committing murder!'

Jupiter. Not a flicker to show he was aware of a contradiction here. Still, that was par for the course where good old-fashioned Romans like Silius Nerva were concerned. I closed my eyes briefly. 'OK,' I said. 'No problem. I'll put it another way. Had he had any recent quarrels that you know about? Any violent disagreements?' He hesitated. 'Come on! You're not helping here!'

'There was the incident with Quintus Roscius, naturally. It was a disagreement, yes, if you care to use that word. But it wasn't violent.'

'Suppose you tell me about it.'

'It happened two days before the murder, in the main street. Roscius came up to Caesius and they ... had words.'

'About what? And who's this Roscius?'

'One of the local small farmers.' Nerva was looking embarrassed again. 'Caesius is – was – in property. Buying and selling. As I understand it he and Roscius had a business arrangement and there had been some disagreement over the interpretation of the terms.'

'More specifically?'

'I'm sorry, Corvinus, I can't help you there. You'd have to ask the fellow yourself. He's quite easy to find – in fact, you'd pass the end of the track up to his farm on the way into Bovillae from here, just before the town limits.'

Can't help you or *won't help you?* Me, I was inclined to the latter. I'd the distinct feeling that this case was showing all the signs of closing ranks and dragging feet. Caesius had been very much one of the local Great and

18

Good, and these guys have Principles, very much with the capital attached: they don't peach on their own, particularly where a bit of sharp practice or a slightly dubious business deal is concerned. You never knew when it might get reciprocated and you'd find yourself shopped down the river.

'OK,' I said. 'So tell me more about Caesius himself. Married? Family man?'

'He was married, until a few months ago when his wife died. There were no children.'

'So who inherits?'

Another hesitation, this time with a pursing of the lips. 'His younger brother, I suppose. Lucius. But you'd have to ask Publius Novius about that. Novius is—'

'The family lawyer.'

He looked surprised. 'You know him?'

'We've met.' Yeah, although maybe *collided* was a better word. I'd run into Novius a year or so back, in connection with the Lucius Hostilius business. He might not be an actual crook – the jury was still out on that one – but he certainly wasn't above a bit of legal skulduggery when he thought he could get away with it.

'Oh, excellent!' Nerva had brightened; this was the way things should go, with the Old Pals' network swinging into smooth operation and no embarrassing slugs in the salad of life. 'Then there should be no problem. He's a splendid fellow, isn't he, old Publius;

19

one of the best. Marvellous for his age, and very helpful.'

'Yeah. So I found.' I kept the dryness and sarcasm out of my voice. 'Anything else you can tell me?' In addition to the miserable pittance I've finally managed to screw out of you, you closed-mouthed bastard. Gods!

'No. No, I don't think so. Or nothing of much importance, anyway. You'll take the case for us?'

'Yeah. I'll come over to Bovillae and ask a few questions, if you like. Starting tomorrow.'

'Splendid!' He got to his feet, looking relieved. I half-expected him to wash his hands in the ornamental pool. 'Anything more I can do to help, just ask. I'm an easy man to find.'

'Actually, there's something now,' I said. 'I'll need Caesius's address, so I can have a word with his major-domo.' A good rule, when you're digging the dirt, is to talk early on to the bought help. Caesius's major-domo might not be too forthcoming in the event – there was such a thing as loyalty – but he would sure as hell know about his master's private concerns, if anyone did.

'Yes, of course,' Nerva said. 'It's in town, the big old house near the Arician Gate. Easy to find. The major-domo's name is Anthus. Not that he'll be able to tell you much.'

Par for the course, so far. Ah, well.

'Thanks, pal,' I said. 'I'll be in touch.'

We shook hands and he left quickly, oozing relief from every pore in his not-inconsiderable body.

Now I had to break the news to Perilla. The hard ones first.

She got back about an hour later, with Marilla and – unfortunately – Placida. The hellhound did her usual haven't-seen-you-for-years dash at me, put her paws on my chest and licked my face. I fended her off.

'Don't encourage her, Corvinus,' Marilla said. 'She's not really supposed to be in here before she's had a bath. She found something dead up by the Maecilius place and rolled in it before we could stop her.'

Aaargh! Mind you, in our brief bout of physical contact I'd sort of half-concluded that already. Plus from the smell of her breath she'd gone on to eat most of it after she'd finished. Ah, the joys of owning a dog. If, indeed, Placida qualified as such, which I doubted. Me, I'd put her in a category that included the Lernaean Hydra myself.

Perilla had grabbed her by the collar and hauled her back.

'Lupercus? If you would?' she said through gritted teeth, the major-domo having edged in behind them. 'Quickly, please!' The brute's claws scrabbled on the marble floor tiles and the panting and slavering grew more frantic.

'Certainly, madam.'

Placida was removed, and fresh air returned slowly to the world.

'So.' Perilla took a deep breath and gave me a brittle smile. 'How was your morning, dear? Did you have a nice time?'

'Uh, it was OK. Quiet.'

'But Lupercus said that you had a visitor.'

Bugger! How had the blabbermouth managed to squeeze that one in between opening the front door and hauling off our ballistic boarhound? 'Ah ... Yeah. Come to mention it, I did at that.'

'A senator from Bovillae, no less. What did he want?'

There was no escape, so I told her the basics while she sat down on the other couch and stared at me. Hard.

'Oh, Marcus!' she said when I'd finished. '*Not* just before the Winter Festival! We're on holiday! And you said you'd do it, I suppose? Look into things for them?'

'More or less. It was sort of difficult to refuse.'

'Why would you want to do that?' Marilla was perched on the third couch, grinning. 'I think it's fantastic. Clarus will, too. And of course if you need any help...'

'No,' I said firmly. 'I will *not* need any help. Besides, it happened over in Bovillae.'

22

'That's only four miles away. And Clarus knows people there. We could...'

'No. That's final.' Jupiter! Marriage hadn't cured the ghoulish streak in her, anyway. 'I can handle this perfectly well on my own, Princess. Just forget it, right?'

'We've got your mother and Priscus arriving, too,' Perilla said. 'Marcus, I do wish you'd think before you agree to things and upset all the arrangements. I mean, it's only a murder after all.'

Said without a blink. Sometimes I wonder about the lady's sense of priorities. 'Look, Perilla...'

Bathyllus shimmered in. This business of having two major-domos in the house simultaneously was going to be confusing, particularly since each of them ignored the other's existence. Still, I supposed Lupercus had his hands full at present with fumigating the hellhound, and we'd brought it on ourselves.

'Lunch is served,' he said.

'Good. I'm starving,' Marilla said. 'Any sign of Clarus, Bathyllus? He said he might be back.'

'No, madam. He sent word to say he'd be delayed and you were to start without him.'

Madam. We were getting the perfect butler act here. I suspected the little guy was making a point: where *savoir-faire* and a general awareness of what was Done and Not Done

23

went, some major-domos had what it took in spades, while others were only fit to sluice down the dog. I grinned at him and got a poached-egg-eyed stare back.

'Yes, sir?' he said. 'Did you wish to comment?'

'No, Bathyllus. Lunch it is.'

We went through to put on the nosebag. As to the murder, when push came to shove I wasn't particularly worried. The lady would come round, Festival or no: Perilla couldn't resist a case, any more than I could. The difference was that she would never admit it.

It was only a matter of time, really.

TWO

I rode over to Bovillae mid-morning the next day, wearing my heaviest cloak because it was raining cats and dogs, with a cutting wind from the north. Par for the course: the weather had been unsettled for days now, with rain being the default. *Not* my favourite Winter Festival weather, by a long chalk.

Nerva had said that Quintus Roscius, the guy who'd had the set-to with Caesius in the street a couple of days before he died, owned a farm on the Castrimoenian side of town. I passed quite a few tracks on the way – most of the rural properties in the Alban Hills are smallholdings, those that haven't been bought up by wealthy punters from Rome and converted into luxury homes-from-home, that is – but there was no indication as to which one was his. Besides, it was a case of first things first. Roscius and his spat with the dead man could wait until I'd had a talk with the brothel-keeper.

I reached Bovillae, left my horse – not my usual mare, who was back in Rome, but the quietest nag I could find in the villa's stable

– at the snazzy drinking trough on the edge of the market square, and got directions to the brothel from the first likely looking passer-by. It turned out to be quite close, in one of the side streets a bit further along the main drag, just past the burned-out shell of a large building with a weed-strewn court-yard and, from the carved-phallus plaque by the door and the graffiti on the surrounding masonry, easy to identify. I knocked – these places are open all hours, to catch the pass-ing trade – and was let in by the door slave.

'Boss around, pal?' I said. 'I'm not a customer. It's business.'

'I'll check, sir,' he said. 'If you'd like to wait here?'

'No problem.'

He padded away into the interior. I took off my sodden travelling cloak, hung it up to drip on one of the pegs behind the door, and cast an assessing eye over the lobby itself. The decoration was predictable stuff, at least the painting on the main wall was, a frieze of self-consciously bare-breasted dancing girls brandishing tambourines above their heads and wearing what looked like fringed bootlaces round their middles. Someone had scrawled a graffito in the corner recom-mending Phyllis. I hoped she wasn't the squint-eyed one immediately above the lettering, but if the frieze was intended to show who the establishment had on offer it was so old and worn that in any case the lady was probably a grandmother by now. Up-market here we definitely weren't. Still, Bovillae was only a provincial town with a limited clientele, so you couldn't expect too much.

The slave came padding back. He was at least as old as the frieze.

'The mistress says that'll be fine, sir,' he said. 'If you'd like to follow me I'll take you to her.'

We went down a corridor with doors on either side. One of them opened as we pass-ed, and a girl in the obligatory bootlace but without a tambourine looked out briefly, grunted, and shut it again. At the end of the corridor, before it took a turn to the left, the old guy stopped and opened the final door.

'Here we are,' he said. 'Just go in.'

After the lobby I hadn't been expecting anything fancy, but I was met with a com-fortable, well-lit sitting room hardly bigger than a cubbyhole, most of which was taken up by a couch with a woman lying on it reading a book. Not a bad looker, late thir-ties, well made up and wearing an impres-sively coiffured wig, with a Coan silk scarf wrapped round her neck.

The woman laid the book on the table. The scarf slipped down a little as she bent for-ward, and in the light from the lamps I caught a glimpse of the scar tissue it covered, the red, puckered flesh of a serious burn. It wasn't, from the look of it, all that old either.

'This'll be about the murder, will it?' she said.

Business-like and to the point. 'Yeah, that's right,' I said.

'I was expecting someone to drop round. Pull over that stool behind you, sit down and make yourself comfortable.' I did. 'Carillus, the customer in Number Five's time is up. Give him a knock in passing, please.'

'Yes, madam.' The old guy closed the door at my back. I could hear him shuffling off back down the corridor, then the sound of a double-knock.

The woman was giving me a long appraising look.

'You aren't local, are you?' she said finally.

'No,' I said. 'The name's Marcus Corvinus. I'm just visiting from Rome. Castrimoenium, not Bovillae.'

'Mm.' I had the feeling she was filing the information away carefully for future reference, and her eyes hadn't moved from my face. 'Pleased to meet you. I'm Andromeda. Opilia Andromeda.' A freedwoman; yeah, well, it made sense for a brothel-keeper, although I'd've thought she was pretty young not only to have her freedom but to be the owner of a business into the bargain. 'So why you, Marcus Corvinus?'

'How do you mean?'

'As someone to be looking into a Bovillan murder. Why a visitor?'

I shrugged. 'Because Silius Nerva of the local senate asked me to.'

I got the distinct impression that the answer hadn't satisfied her, which was fair enough because it didn't really say anything. Still, the really interesting thing was that she'd asked the question. I gestured at the book beside her.

'Anything interesting?' I said.

She frowned. 'Oh, just a bit of Alexandrian froth. I need to be here all day to keep an eye on things, and I have to pass the time somehow.'

Yeah, right. Only I'd caught a glimpse of the tag on the roller before she'd put the book down, and it'd looked more like a copy of Plato's *Gorgias* to me. In the original. Sure, it was none of my business how she spent her mornings, and she could read what she liked as far as I was concerned, but even so it was interesting that she'd taken the trouble to lie. I filed that one away on my own account.

'Well, then.' She raised herself on the couch and turned to face me fully. 'Back to the business of the old man's murder. What do you want to know?'

'Anything and everything you can tell me.'

'Such as what, to start with?'

'Was he a regular customer?'

29

'Over the past two or three months, yes, fairly regular. Before that, only occasionally.'

'The past two or three months? Why just then?'

'His wife died in September. That could have been the reason – it sometimes is, with a certain type of client – but I really can't say for definite.'

Delivered coldly and clinically. She could-have been a doctor giving a case history. 'He was, uh, quite active for his age, then?' I said. Nerva hadn't told me what that had been, but if he'd been elected censor he must've been touching sixty, at least, and she'd referred to him as an old man, so it seemed a logical deduction.

'Well, now, Corvinus.' Andromeda smiled and lowered her head. 'That isn't a question I can answer personally. You'd have to ask Lydia.'

'Who's Lydia?'

'His favourite partner. Oh, he'd go with one of the others willingly enough when she wasn't available, but he always asked for her.'

'Was she the girl he was with the evening he died?'

'Yes, that's right.'

'Could I talk to her now?'

'Certainly, if you want. She's occupied at present, but she shouldn't be long. When you've finished with me I'll fetch her for you.'

'Thanks. That'd be great.'

'So.' Her hand went to the silk scarf, and she tugged it back down until it covered her lower neck completely. 'What can I tell you myself?'

'Just the basic background details would be useful. Nerva didn't give me any of those.'

'Yes, well, he wouldn't, would he?' She smiled. 'All this is so dreadfully sordid and embarrassing for him and his cronies in the senate, is it not? A prominent man like Quintus Caesius being found dead outside a brothel.' I said nothing. 'Which details did you want exactly?'

'The time frame, for a start. When did he arrive and leave?'

'He arrived just after sunset and left about an hour later.'

'That his usual time for visiting?'

'Yes. Or perhaps slightly earlier than usual. He never came before sunset, when the shops in the alleyway were open and there would be people to see and recognize him. A very cautious man, Quintus Caesius. One of his most signal traits.' This time she didn't smile, but it was there in her eyes.

'And he always left through the back door?'

Andromeda laughed. 'But of course! Corvinus, he was a highly respected and very familiar public figure! Cloaked and hooded or not, there was always a chance that he'd be known. He came in that way, too, by arrangement. It's very private; if you'd carried on past this room and round the corner you would've seen that for yourself.'

'How so?'

'There are no bedrooms between it and here; Lydia's is the first, and that's immediately next door to us. In fact, I suspect that was why the girl *was* his favourite, and it was a matter of convenience and safety as much as personal preference.'

'The door isn't used otherwise? By the customers, I mean.'

'Oh, yes. On occasion, and for the same reason. Don't be naïve, Corvinus; Quintus Caesius wasn't – isn't – the only important man in Bovillae who makes use of our services, and as you can imagine the town's great and good are not very keen to bump into an ordinary client, or use the front entrance on the main street and run the risk of being seen. So we have a special arrangement for our special guests. I can easily hear a knock on the back door from here, and I open it myself; not even Carillus is involved, so it's all done very discreetly. Discretion is something that I pride myself on, and our more special clients know it, which is why they continue to *be* our clients.'

'Could you show me it?'

'Now? Certainly, if you like. I'll take you.' She got up – she was big, tall for a woman –

and led the way into the corridor. Nice figure, and walking immediately behind her I caught the scent of her perfume: seriously expensive stuff, if I was any judge.

Like she'd said, the door was no more than a few yards further on, at the corridor's end. She slid back the central bolt, opened it and stepped back.

'There you are.'

Winter sunlight flooded in: at least the rain had stopped for the time being. We were under an external flight of steps that led up to the building's first floor, at the dead end of a short alleyway with a couple of open-fronted shops in it, a general merchant's and a bootmaker's. At the open end of the alley I could see people passing the gap. A main street, obviously, or at least one busy enough to have regular pedestrians.

'He was lying on the ground over there.' Andromeda pointed to a spot a few yards from the door, then waved at the bootmaker, who was sitting outside his shop a few yards away, stitching the upper of a shoe to the sole. 'Good morning to you, Gratianus!' He waved back. 'Gratianus was the one who found the body, Corvinus. He'd be able to give you fuller details, so you may want to talk to him later.'

'Yeah. Yeah, I'll do that,' I said. 'Presumably no one went through this way – coming in or going out – after Caesius left?'

'No. That was the last time it was opened that evening.' She turned. 'So. You've seen enough for the present?'

'Sure.'

'We'll go back in, then. Lydia will probably be finishing off by now. Unless I can help you further, I'll send her to you. You're welcome to use my room. Hers will probably be a bit of a mess, and it's rather cramped.'

We went back inside, and she re-bolted the door.

'Did you let Caesius out yourself?' I said.

'No, I didn't. I never do, for any of our specials, because there's no need. I heard him go, naturally, when he passed my door, and the sound of this door being opened and closed, but there was no reason for me to see him out personally. I came out and locked up again, of course, a few minutes later.'

'You didn't hear anything else? Noises outside, maybe?'

'No, nothing. That would've been most unlikely, whatever they were. As you can see, the door is quite thick, and the door of my own room was closed.'

Fair enough. 'Ah ... one last question, lady. Not about the murder as such. Like you said, the guy was a public figure. All this hole-in-the-corner stuff, doesn't it get to you at all? I mean...'

She smiled. 'You mean, don't I think it's a bit hypocritical? On the part of the clients?'

'Yeah. That was it. More or less.'

'Corvinus, I have a business to run. I don't judge, at least not outside the privacy of my own head, which is my affair and no one else's. How long do you think I could stay open if I put Bovillae's most respected citizens' backs up by advertising the fact that they're just as human as the rest of the world? Besides, their money's as good as anyone's. Better, in fact, because they're willing to pay well over the odds for that discretion I mentioned. Now, if you've finished with me I'll tell Lydia you want to see her. Use my room to talk to her as if it was your own, and take as long as you please. When you've done, let yourself out the back. Did you have a cloak?'

'Yeah. Yeah, it's hanging in the lobby.'

'Then I'll have Carillus bring it to you. Remember, please do take as long as you like; you're not inconveniencing anyone.' We'd reached the door of her room. She opened it and stood aside. 'I'm delighted to have met you.'

Delivered with all the formal politeness of an elderly dowager. I went inside and closed the door behind me. The book was still lying on the table. I picked it up and partly unrolled it. Plato's *Gorgias* in Greek it was, and annotated in the margins in a neat, small hand that I'd guess was Andromeda's own. An interesting lady, right enough.

A couple of minutes later there was a soft knock on the door and a girl came in. Heavy-featured, suicide blonde, with a good half inch of black hair showing at the roots. She was wearing a thin dressing gown, and not much else, as far as I could see.

'Lydia?' I said.

'Yeah.' She closed the door behind her. 'Madam said you wanted to talk to me.'

Lydia, my foot: with that accent she couldn't've come from anywhere further east than Fidenae. And if she was Caesius's favourite for any other reason than the convenient placement of her room then he must've liked them large, heavy and sullen. I was sitting on the stool. I stood up and moved aside. 'You want to take the couch?' I said.

'Nah, I wouldn't dare. It's madam's. She'd have a fit.'

'Fair enough.' I sat down again. She leaned back against the door. 'So. You were with Caesius the evening he died.'

'Yeah, that's right.'

'For how long?'

She shrugged. The dressing-gown slipped off one shoulder, and she pulled it back with a casual twitch of her fingers. 'An hour. More or less. The usual time, anyway.'

'He was a regular of yours, so I'm told. How regular would that be?'

Another shrug. 'I don't keep score. Often enough.'

36

'He talk to you at all about anything? That time or ever?'

She snorted; it could've been a laugh, but it was mostly mucus. 'What do you think? He was a paying customer, and talking's not what they're here for, is it? Nah, we didn't talk.'

'And the last time you saw him. Was that any different from any of the others?' She just looked at me with complete, bovine incomprehension. Jupiter, this was heavy going! 'I mean, there was nothing unusual about it in any way?'

'Nah. He was just the same.'

'So there's nothing you can tell me?'

'Nah. Not really.' There was a knock on the door. She glanced over her shoulder and moved away. The door opened.

'Your cloak, sir.' It was Carillus.

'That's fine, pal.' I stood up. 'I'm just about finished here.' I looked at the girl. Not a flicker of reaction, or interest. 'Thanks for your help, Lydia.'

'You're welcome. See you.' She slid out. A moment or two later, I heard the door of the neighbouring room open and close.

Ah, well.

I draped the still-sodden cloak over my arm, made my thanks to Carillus, unbolted the back door and went out into the alley to talk to the bootmaker.

★ ★ ★

He was still working on the shoe, but he put it down when he saw me coming. I'd thought that the right-hand side of the alley, between the brothel and the guy's shop, was formed by a continuous, solid wall, but more or less halfway there was an opening that looked like it had originally contained a small shrine or a statue. If so, whichever it had been wasn't there any longer, and all that was left was an embrasure big enough to take a man standing.

'Gratianus, right?' I said.

'Yeah, that's me. And you are?'

'Marcus Corvinus. I'm looking into the murder two or three nights back on behalf of the senate.'

'That so, now?'

'You found the body?'

'Yeah. Just after first light, it was, when I came to take down the shutters.'

'You recognize the corpse?'

He grinned. He only had a couple of teeth in the front, and they looked like they were fighting a losing battle. 'You kidding? There isn't anyone in Bovillae wouldn't know Quintus Caesius when they saw him, even with the back of his head stove in.'

'You want to tell me about it?'

'Not much to tell. He was lying there–' the spot was just shy of the embrasure – 'covered with his cloak. I think he's just a drunk sleeping it off, so I go over to wake him up.

Only when I pull back the hood and see his face, plus the damage, that's that, isn't it? Goodnight sunshine, and the town's down one appointee censor. So I leave him where he's lying, go down to the town hall and call it in, then come back here with the undertaker's men who cart the poor bugger away. End of story.'

'Was there much blood? On the ground, I mean.'

'Nah. It was throwing it down, had been all night. The alley was like a river.'

Well, that seemed straightforward enough; certainly everything fitted. I was turning to go when I had another thought. 'You know Opilia Andromeda, the brothel-keeper, right?'

'Sure. Everyone does, round about here. She's OK, Andromeda, always says hello, like you saw. We pass the time of day sometimes, when trade's slack. Not that we have any contact professionally, so to speak. I'm a married man, myself, and if I did try anything on my wife'd kill me.'

'She been here long?'

'About a year. She's from Tibur, originally. Bought the business cheap from old Mama Tyche when she retired.'

'How did she manage that? I mean, cheap or not it must've cost a fair slice of cash.'

'Oh, well, now.' He sucked on a tooth. 'It's quite a story, that. No secret, mind, it was all over the neighbourhood five minutes after she arrived. You notice she wears a scarf?'

'Yeah. To cover a burn scar. A big one, from the looks of it.'

'Right. She got that in a house fire. She was in the business herself, just one of the girls. Slave, not free.'

I remembered the burned-out shell I'd passed on the same street as the brothel entrance. 'A fire? The one in the building further down the road near the main drag?'

'Nah, nothing to do with that. That only happened a few months ago, and the place was a warehouse. "House fire", I said. It was back in Tibur, before she came here. There was an accident with a lamp, some drunk or other in one of the rooms playing silly buggers, and the place went up like a torch. She pulled the madam – that was her owner, Opilia – out of the flames and got herself burned doing it. Opilia freed her and gave her her stake. Lucky chance, that was. She's no spring chicken, Andromeda, and no one wants to go with a girl that's damaged goods, even over in Tibur.'

Interesting. I'd've liked to know how a slave-prostitute had developed a taste for Plato, mind. I doubted that Lydia – free or slave – could get the length of reading even the graffiti on the brothel walls. Unusual lady was right.

40

I thanked the guy, and left. The next place I needed to go was the victim Caesius's own house, for a word with his major-domo.

THREE

I made my way back round to the main
street – what they call the Hinge in Bovillae
– and headed left towards the Arician Gate.
A big, old house, Nerva had told me. There
weren't many of these to start with, and
besides the biggest of the lot had cypress
branches hung up round the door, which
was, no pun intended, a dead giveaway: it
was Caesius's, for sure. I knocked, and the
door was opened by a young slave with the
front of his fringe shorn off close to the
scalp.

'Valerius Corvinus, pal,' I said. 'Silius
Nerva asked me to look into the death of
your master. Could I have a word with the
major-domo, do you think? Anthus, isn't it?'

'Yes, sir. Of course.' He stood aside. 'Just
go through to the atrium. I'll fetch him for
you.'

I did, and stopped short at the entrance.
What I hadn't been expecting was that Caesius himself would still be in residence, laid
out on a funeral couch in his magistrate's
mantle and with a pan of incense burning

beside him.

Under these circumstances you have to observe the niceties. I took the pair of shears from the small table at the couch's foot, snipped off a lock of my own hair, put it in the waiting basket at the corpse's feet, and added a pinch of incense to the pan.

Then I took a closer look at him.

Sixty was about right, maybe a bit over. He'd been a good-looking man, Caesius, with a strong face – it still had crumbs of dry plaster on the sideburns from when they'd taken the death-mask – and a full head of silvered hair. No sign of the wound that had killed him; that'd be on the back of the head, and the undertakers would've cleaned it up and made sure it wasn't immediately visible when they laid him out. The gold coins covering his eyes glinted at me in the sunlight filtering through the gap above the ornamental pool.

'A fine-looking man, wasn't he, sir?'

I turned. Anthus, obviously. Small and stooped, about the same age as his master.

'Yeah. Yeah, he must've been,' I said. 'When's the funeral?'

'This afternoon. The senate is giving it at public expense.' There was no mistaking the pride in the old guy's voice. 'That doesn't often happen, as you know. The master would've been very gratified, and appreciated the honour very deeply. You'll be attending yourself, sir, of course.'

I hadn't planned on it, but I couldn't well say no, not to the guy's face. I wasn't wearing a mourning mantle, sure, and there wasn't time to go back to Castrimoenium to change, but under the circumstances I didn't think that'd matter much if I stuck to the sidelines. No doubt it being a public funeral there'd be quite a crowd there just to watch.

A public funeral explained why the body was still here, too. These things take time to organize.

'Yeah,' I said. 'Yeah, I'll be going.'

'The ceremony begins an hour after noon. Processing from here, sir, naturally, but I should simply wait in the market square if I were you. That's where they'll be delivering the eulogy.' A glance at my mantle-less tunic and still-very-damp and far-from-new cloak; under normal circumstances the guy would probably have added a Bathyllus-type sniff, but as it was I got off easy. 'Now. Young Titus said that you were investigating the master's death on behalf of the senate. How can I be of assistance?'

'Just a few questions, pal, and a bit of background information.'

'Anything. Anything at all. Ask away, please, and I'll do the best I can.'

'Ah ... do you think we could go somewhere, uh...?' I gestured at the corpse, not sure how to finish the question. *Quieter* or *less public* didn't quite seem to fit the bill, somehow.

'More convenient.' He nodded. 'Yes, of course. The master's study, perhaps. If you'd like to follow me.'

I did. He led me through to the study, behind an ornately panelled wooden door.

'Here we are, sir,' he said. 'Do sit down on the couch. I'll stand, myself, if you don't mind.'

I'd expected the usual books, and there were a few of these, right enough, in a book-cubby beside the window, plus the other normal items of study furniture such as the expensive-looking rosewood desk and an iron strongbox, but most of the walls were lined with open cupboards whose shelves were almost full of artwork: pots, figurines, small bronzes. Old Greek, mostly, and pretty good stuff, from what I could tell. On the writing desk itself, there was a lovely marble group of the Abduction of Ganymede that must've set the guy back a good slice of his yearly income.

Anthus saw me looking.

'It was the master's hobby, sir,' he said. 'Almost his obsession. He was a keen collector, as you can see, for many years. Very knowledgeable, too. Now. What exactly did you want to know?'

'Nothing specific,' I said. 'Or at least, nothing more than anything else. Like I told you,

45

I'm just feeling my way, working on the background at present. Silius Nerva said your master was a widower. His wife died quite recently, and there were no children. That right?'

'Yes. The Lady Vatinia passed on just over two months ago. And no, they had no family, unfortunately.'

'There's a brother, I understand.'

Was that a flicker? 'That's correct. Master Lucius. He was – is – five years younger than the master.'

'Living in Bovillae?'

'Yes. Or so I believe.'

'So you *believe*?'

A hesitation. 'He and the master didn't get on, sir. Not for a great many years, since their father died, in fact.'

'Why would that be, now?'

'I really couldn't say.'

Flat statement, delivered with a poker face and with all the indications that that was all I'd be getting on the subject. Bugger; I recognized the signs. I'd hit the Faithful Retainer syndrome head on. *Couldn't say* summed it up: I'd bet a combination of the thumbscrew and wild horses wouldn't have dragged the words out of him. Not to a stranger, certainly.

Leave it. For the present, at least.

'Pity,' I said easily. 'So. Do you have any idea where I'd find him? Brother Lucius?'

46

'I'd imagine in one of the local wine shops.' That came out sharper than probably even he'd expected, because he visibly clammed up after he'd said it. Still, his loyalties would lie with the elder brother, not the younger one, so it didn't come as the shock that it might have.

'He, uh, likes a cup or two of wine, then?' No answer. 'Are you saying he's an actual drunk?' Again, silence, which was an answer in itself. 'Come on, pal! You're not breaking any major confidences here. Bovillae's a small town. Someone else'll tell me anyway, if you won't. Besides, it's no big deal. Lots of families have them.'

'Master Lucius does have a problem in that regard, sir, yes. A very long-standing one.'

'He'll be his brother's heir, though, won't he? If there aren't any children?'

'That I can't strictly say, sir.' Anthus was looking prim. 'Presumably. Although that's no concern of mine, because the master has given me my freedom. I know that already.'

So when Lucius the Lush moved in – if he moved in – Anthus would be gone, and from the looks of things not sorry to go, either. Well, fair enough. 'Congratulations,' I said. 'You have any plans made?'

A blush – or what, in this Bathyllus look-alike, passed for one. 'There is a certain widow-lady, sir. A baker with a shop near the

47

Circus. We've had an understanding for several years now, ever since her husband died. She's freeborn, so up to now that's been an impediment. But when I get my cap ... well, yes, I do have plans.'

'Good for you, pal. The best of luck.'

'Thank you.'

'So, uh, Brother Lucius is the only living relative, is he?'

Another hesitation. 'Well, sir, to be strictly accurate, no, he isn't. The master also had a nephew on his wife's side. A young gentleman by the name of Aulus Mettius.' There was just the smidgeon of an edge on the word 'gentleman'.

'Uh-huh. And he lives where, exactly?'

'Here in Bovillae. Or rather, the family villa is just outside town, beyond the Tiburtine Gate. He isn't married, and he lives there with his mother. She, as I said, was the late mistress's younger sister. She's been a widow now for many years.'

'And this Aulus Mettius and his uncle didn't get on either, I suppose, right?'

'No, sir. In fact, I don't think the master has had any contact whatsoever with him for the past ten years, at least. Not since he was relegated.'

'Relegated?' I said sharply. Relegation's the punishment for a crime, a minor form of exile where the convicted man is forbidden to come within, say, a hundred miles of his

48

home town for a fixed period; the difference being that he isn't permanently deprived of citizenship or stripped of his assets. 'For what?'

'Theft, sir. He was caught stealing money from his employer. A local lawyer. Master Aulus was relegated for ten years, and the period only expired recently.'

Uh-huh. 'The lawyer wouldn't be a guy called Publius Novius, would it, by any chance?'

He looked surprised. 'Yes, it would, as it happens. You know him?'

'Yeah. Slightly. He was your master's lawyer, too, wasn't he?'

'Of course. Naturally. Publius Novius is the only lawyer in Bovillae, sir, and has been these forty years and more. Master Aulus was his apprentice clerk. In fact, it was the master who got the young man his position, originally. He and Novius were long-standing friends. He felt very guilty over the affair, sir. Very guilty indeed.'

Yeah, well, no surprises there. As far as the original recommendation was concerned, it was normal procedure in any family, particularly a well-connected one: a close relative had a duty to help launch a young man just starting out on his career, if he could, and if he was part of the Old Boy network, as Caesius obviously was, then that was the way it was done. The guilt was understand-

49

able, too: as his nephew's patron and sponsor Caesius would've felt personally responsible when everything went pear-shaped.

'So that was the reason for the estrangement,' I said. 'The theft and his nephew's relegation, yes?'

Anthus shook his head. 'Oh, no, sir. Not at all,' he said. 'Although of course it did confirm the master in his opinion. The actual break itself had already taken place, a few years previously but subsequent to the young man's being taken on by the legal gentleman. His nephew was always a great disappointment to Master Quintus.'

'So what was the reason, then?'

The major-domo hesitated, and I thought he wasn't going to answer; Old Retainer Syndrome kicking in again. Finally, though, he cleared his throat and said, 'Master Aulus entered into an unsuitable romantic entanglement with a girl well beneath him socially, sir. He always was a very unconventional young man, and completely unrealistic in his outlook.'

Uh-huh. Reading between the lines, I could make a fair guess at what had happened, and given the guy's family circumstances why it had led to a breach. A casual sexual liaison between the son of the house and a girl from a lower class, sure, that wouldn't have mattered: it happened all the time, and no one gave it a second thought.

50

He might even set her up as a mistress without raising too many eyebrows, let alone hackles. But anything more serious – which was what Anthus was implying here – would cause major ructions. And I'd guess, from what I knew of him already, that Quintus Caesius hadn't been one to hold liberal views.

'So who was the lady?' I said. Silence. 'Come on, Anthus! Give!'

'I'm sorry, sir. That I can't tell you, and in any case it's old history now.'

Can't or *won't* again? Probably the second. Ah well, being ancient history it probably wasn't important, anyway. Mind you, I'd have to have a word pretty soon with this Aulus Mettius. 'OK,' I said. 'So let's talk about the murder itself. Anything there you can tell me about?'

'Such as what, sir?'

'Your master had, uh, made a habit of visiting the local brothel these past couple of months, so I understand.'

Anthus's lips formed a tight line. 'I'm afraid, Valerius Corvinus, that I really cannot help you there.'

'Oh, come on, pal! It can't be a sensitive subject, surely. That's where he was found, remember.'

He shook his head. 'No, sir,' he said firmly. 'I'm sorry. The master was a very private man, who kept himself to himself. His personal life was none of my concern, unless he chose to make it so. He did not, in that regard, and it was certainly not my place to pry. Nor, if you'll forgive me, to discuss the matter with strangers.'

Yeah, well; that was me told. And maybe I had been pushing things, to be fair. Besides, I'd already got all the information on the subject that I needed from Andromeda.

'Fine,' I said. 'OK. Moving on. What about the period immediately prior to his death? Anything significant there that you noticed?'

'No, sir. He behaved much as usual.'

'No mention of an enemy, or a quarrel, or even a recent disagreement with anyone?'

'There was an unpleasant incident in the main street with one of the local farmers. A Quintus Roscius, as I recall.'

'Yeah, I know about that. Something to do with business, wasn't it?'

'Yes, sir. I'm afraid I don't know the details. It was connected with the repayment of a loan, I think.'

'Caesius was in the loans business?'

'No, not as such. He dealt in property. Buying and selling. Particularly with clients in Rome who were interested in acquiring land in the area for building purposes. He travelled to Rome quite frequently, at least once a month.'

'So you can't think of anyone he was on bad terms with? Apart from this Roscius.'

'No, I'm afraid not. Certainly not recently. Oh, I'm not saying that he got on perfectly with everyone he had dealings with. The master was very much a man of business, and he would drive the best bargain he could. But he never acted in a way that anyone could honestly complain about.'

Well, I couldn't really expect more than that. Men like Caesius – and I knew plenty of them in Rome – were pretty tough nuts. They had to be, to pay the bills at the end of the month, and in the world of business softness and a readiness to allow the other guy the best of the deal weren't survival traits. Besides, I wasn't too dissatisfied: I'd got quite a lot from Anthus, all I could for the time being, anyway. Certainly the background was filling in as well as I could've hoped.

I stood up.

'OK, pal,' I said. 'Thanks. You've been very helpful.'

'Don't mention it, sir. If it helps to find the master's killer then it's my pleasure. I'll see you out.'

So. An estranged brother who'd inherit and a nephew with form who'd just moved back into the area, right?

Things were complicating nicely.

FOUR

After leaving Caesius's house I headed back along the Hinge towards the centre of town.

So. The funeral was at the seventh hour, was it? I glanced up at the sun. Just shy of noon: I'd just over an hour to kill. So who did I have to talk to? There was Novius, of course, the dodgy lawyer; where the matter of a will and so the question of *cui bono* went, he was the logical next interviewee, plus he might be able to point me in the direction of Caesius's brother Lucius. His office, if I remembered rightly from before, was in the top part of town near the baths, only a couple of blocks up from the market square where as far as I was concerned the ceremony would start from. Close enough, in other words, for a there-and-back where available time went. Chances were, though, that he wouldn't be there at present: as one of Bovillae's Great and Good, and a close friend and associate of the dead man's, he was probably at home changing into his mourning mantle for the funeral. Novius could wait for another day. Besides, when

54

you're digging the dirt on a local celebrity there ain't no better place to start than a bar, and I reckoned I'd earned a break.

When I came down to Bovillae I had a favourite one, where the owner knew his way around the Second Growth local wines and stocked the best his customers could afford. It was pretty close, too, down one of the streets directly across from the market square itself. So I made for that.

There was a small antiques shop a few yards before it that was either new or one that I hadn't noticed before: a chi-chi rarity that you're beginning to see more of these days in the towns of the Alban Hills, now the big money's arrived in the form of well-heeled second-home owners from Rome. I slowed as I passed; like I said, we were expecting Mother and Priscus to join us for the festival, and the old guy's birthday – which particular one it was exactly I wasn't absolutely certain, probably, by the look of him, his hundred and forty-seventh – was in four days' time. Oh, sure, Perilla had probably already bought him something – she was the shopper in the family – but it wouldn't hurt to take a look. And these places out in the sticks are still a lot cheaper than Rome. With some of the prices they charge in the Saepta, if you want something decent you have to pawn your grandmother.

I went in.

It was well-stocked; some pretty nice stuff, too. The shopkeeper, an old guy in a freedman's cap, was arthritically polishing up the bronze of a horseman that looked like it was way outside my price bracket.

'Can I help you, sir?' he said.

'No, that's OK, pal, you just carry on.' I closed the door behind me. 'I'll just browse, if you don't mind.'

'Certainly. Feel free.' He went back to his polishing. Good sign. Me, I'm no fan of pressure salesmanship, and in some places in Rome the guy behind the desk would have been up and starting his personal guided tour of the priciest items before you could say 'hustler'.

It was good stuff, right enough, and to be fair the prices weren't exorbitant. Which meant the numbers didn't completely fill the tags. Still, I kept to the shallow end of the range: miniatures, rings, clay figurines, that sort of thing. On one of the tables there was a collection of nice little ivory plaques, like you see inlaid in trinket boxes. I drifted over, picked one up, and examined it.

The plaque showed a philosopher, or a rhetoric-teacher, or something, finger raised and frozen in the act of making an abstruse point to a bored-looking student standing beside him. I grinned: the philosopher was the spitting image of Priscus sounding off about the optative mood in Ancient Sabine.

Perfect; absolutely perfect. The thing wasn't all that expensive, either: even if Perilla had got him something already, we could add it to the pot.

I took it over to the guy on the desk.

'I'll have this one, friend,' I said.

'Ah, yes.' He peered at it myopically. 'Syracusan. A good choice, sir.'

'How old is it, do you know?'

'A century and a half, it would be. Give or take a decade.'

Yeah, well, that'd fit with Priscus, then. Like I said, perfect.

'You've got some nice pieces here.' I took out my purse. 'How long have you had the shop?'

'Oh, it isn't mine, sir. I just run it for the owner. Quintus Baebius, that is. A very knowledgeable gentleman, and a keen collector himself.'

A collector, right? 'Like Quintus Caesius,' I said, handing over the money and putting the plaque into the purse for safe keeping. 'They, uh, friends or associates at all?'

'The magistrate?' The old man laughed. 'Oh, bless you, no, sir! He's got no time for Caesius, has the master.'

'Is that so, now?'

'He won't hear his name mentioned, not this long time. You're a friend of his yourself?'

I shot him a look, but there was nothing in

his rather simple expression other than polite curiosity. 'I, uh, met him recently, yeah,' I said. Well, I had, in a manner of speaking. 'You don't get out much, do you?'

'No, sir, I must confess I'm afraid that I don't, or as little as I can. I live over the shop, you see. And my legs aren't strong these days. Nor my eyesight. I go with the master to an auction sometimes, just out of interest, so long as it's close by and there's things worth seeing, but that's about all.'

I made a point of examining the bronze horseman that he'd set down on the desk. 'So what's Baebius got against Quintus Caesius, then?' I said casually. 'If you don't mind my asking?'

'Oh, no, sir, I don't mind at all. No secret there. They're real birds of a feather, Caesius and the master. Don't like to be beat, neither of them, and living practically cheek by jowl's made it worse. You should see them at the auctions; it's a tonic, especially when they're both after the same piece. Spitting cats isn't in it.'

'That happens often, does it?' I was pushing, sure, but the old guy didn't seem to notice. He chuckled and shook his head.

'Gods bless you! It happens all the time! Proper sideshow sometimes – you'd pay good money to see it.'

'Anything, uh, particularly recent?'

'Not particularly so, sir. The last was a

couple of months back, at a sale of effects belonging to old Plautius Silvanus. Did you know him at all, yourself? A Roman gentleman. He had the big villa down the Appian Road a few miles outside town.'

'Ah ... no. No, I didn't.' I'd given up the pretended examination of the horseman. No need for subterfuge here, evidently: if I wanted to shut the old guy up I might be able to do it with a right hook to the chin, but I reckoned that's what it would take.

'A real aristocrat, Plautius Silvanus – well, you can tell by the name, can't you – but not stuck-up for all that. Lovely man when he was alive, very courteous and soft-spoken. He'd been a governor out east somewhere, Asia or such, brought some pieces back with him. When he died the heir sold up, lock, stock and barrel. There was a bronze figurine of a runner, beautiful thing, over two and a half centuries old, and perfect as the day it was made. You should've seen the detail, sir, every fingernail and curl clear as clear. The master'd set his heart on it, so along we went.' He chuckled. 'Only when the auction came up it wasn't there, was it, because old Caesius'd slipped in early and bought it off the heir direct for cash money down.'

'Is that right, now?'

'He saved the man the auctioneer's fee, you see, and that wouldn't've been nothing, so he wasn't crying. The master was livid, sir, simply livid. Cursed Caesius root and branch all the way home, and threatened he'd do I don't know what to him.' He was still chuckling and shaking his head. 'I laughed about it for days. Not in the master's presence, mind, that wouldn't've been right, and I didn't mean anything by it. Present, was it, sir?'

I blinked. 'What? Oh, the plaque. Yeah. For my stepfather. A birthday present.'

'I hope he likes it, then. And if he's in the neighbourhood perhaps you'll suggest he steps in and has a look round for himself. No obligation to buy, none at all. We're always open, I don't see many people as a rule, and I enjoy a bit of a chat.'

So much was obvious, given that the chat all went the one way; still, I wasn't complaining, because it had added another name to my list. 'Yeah. Yeah, I'll do that,' I said. 'Thanks, pal. See you around.'

'Give Quintus Caesius my regards, sir, when next you talk to him. I've got every respect for the gentleman, professionally, whatever the master may think of him. It's nothing personal, on my side.'

'I'll do that, too,' I said. 'If I see him again.'

I left.

The wine shop was quietly busy. I nodded to the other barflies, parked myself on a stool at the counter, and ordered a cup of Alban. Just a cup: if you're going to a funeral, even as a bystander, it's not quite the done thing to turn up smashed. Still, because the owner knew his wine, we at least had quality here: the Alban was pretty good – not the best stuff, of course, from one of the top vineyards; that all goes to well-heeled buyers in Rome, and it'd be far too pricey even in small amounts for the local punters – but a decent-enough *deuxième cru* which some of my more weak-chinned acquaintances would say amused by its brash pushiness.

'You want anything to go with it, sir?' Scaptius, the barman-owner, asked. 'A bit of garlic sausage and pickle, maybe?'

'Yeah, OK.' I took out my purse.

He put the plate, plus the filled cup, in front of me. 'Down here from Rome again, then, are you?'

Like I say, this was my local on the rare occasions I came through to Bovillae while we were at the villa. I couldn't be called a regular, mind – as I would be at Pontius's in Castrimoenium – but you don't see many Roman purple-stripers in a provincial wine shop, and they tend to get noticed. Besides, I took it for the conversational opener that it was.

'Well, obviously,' I said.

Scaptius grinned. 'Going to the big funeral?'

'That's the idea.' I sipped my wine.

'I hear the senate's asked you to look into the death. That true?'

'Did you, now?' Well, I shouldn't've been surprised, really. Gossip in a wine shop goes both ways, and in a small town like Bovillae most secrets don't stay secret for long. Not that there was anything to hide in this instance. And it made asking straight questions easier. 'Yeah, it's true enough. Popular man, was he, old Caesius?'

'He was OK. For a politician. Straighter than some.'

'Straighter than fucking Manlius, for a start,' said one of the other punters further along the counter to my left. 'Him and his mate the fucking quaestor, they're a right pair of chancers.'

Par for the course: slagging off the local politicians over a jug of wine is the national pastime wherever you go. It's done on principle. Me, I don't pay much attention, normally: if the guys weren't crooked in some way, or at least on the make, then they wouldn't be in politics in the first place. Ipso facto.

Why state the obvious?

There were a few chuckles, and I noticed one or two heads nodding. Scaptius grunted.

'Manlius?' I said to him. 'Who's he?'

'One of the aediles,' he said. 'Quaestor's Sextus Canidius.' The aediles were the two top magistrates in a normal year; the quaestor was the guy in charge of the town's finances. 'Manlius ran against Caesius for censor. He's big in the wool business.'

'Big in the wool *burning* business,' the guy along the row said. Chuckles again, and a 'Too bloody right, mate' from someone else in the line.

'Well now, Battus, my boy,' Scaptius said equably, turning round to face him, 'we'll never know the truth of that, will we?'

'Yeah, that's for fucking sure.'

'Indeed it is. So just shut it, please. And watch the language.'

I took a bit of the garlic sausage. Strong stuff – more garlic than sausage by the taste of it. I'd be pretty unpopular when I got back home. Maybe I'd stick with the pickles.

'Wool burning?' I said.

Scaptius turned back to me and shrugged. 'The town farms out the right to broker the sale of wool from the public herds every season to a private dealer,' he said. 'This year the guy's business folded just after the contract was signed, and Canidius got the senate to transfer it over to Manlius. The bales were stored in a warehouse that caught fire and burned down—'

'*Mysteriously and unaccountably* caught fire and burned down.'

Scaptius sighed, but this time he didn't turn. 'Sod off, Battus,' he said. 'I'm telling this, right? Anyway, it burned down, June,

63

that'd be, just after the shearing, with a year's worth of wool in it, and—'

'What Manlius *claimed* was a year's worth of fucking wool.'

Scaptius's hand slammed down on the counter and he glared along the line. 'Battus, you bastard,' he said, 'one more word – just one – and you're barred until the festival, right? And I've already told you: less of the sodding language, OK?'

'Yeah, yeah.'

He turned back to me. 'Anyway, when Caesius ran for censor he promised that if he won there'd be a full investigation. That's not going to happen now, is it? Not with Manlius himself practically dead cert to replace him.'

I tried a pickle and spat it out. Jupiter! The gods knew where Scaptius bought them from, but I was surprised they hadn't burned a hole in the jar. When he was crossing the Alps, Hannibal was supposed to have broken up the boulders from avalanches by heating them and pouring on vinegar. This must've been the stuff. Come to that, it could've done the job on its own. 'There'll be a new election, surely,' I said when I'd stopped coughing. 'From scratch.'

'Oh, sure, but the chances are that no one else'll run. With Caesius gone Manlius has the senate in his pocket. Or he and Canidius have between them. Their two families have been the top ones in Bovillae for the past

64

three hundred years. Caesius, sure, he was old-Bovillae too, but his family's only notched up one magistracy to every ten of theirs. And they're rich as Croesus into the bargain. If Caesius hadn't been so highly thought of, Manlius could've bought his way into the censorship easily. When he lost it really put his nose out of joint.'

'He can buy my vote any time,' a punter – not Battus this time – growled. 'And he gives decent games; you have to say that for him.'

'Come on, now, Thermus,' Scaptius said wearily. 'You're the sort of materialistic bastard that keeps these sods in office!'

'Yeah, that's me. Materialist to the core. Wouldn't be anything else. Proud of it.'

I pushed the plate of suspect nibbles away to where it wouldn't do any more damage and took a throat-clearing swallow of wine. 'So,' I said. 'This fire. No one knows how it started?'

'Sure they do,' Scaptius said. 'That was just Battus sounding off. The night watchman was drunk; he tipped over a lamp and set some straw alight. Or that's the official version, anyway.'

'Fucking right it's the official version.' Battus again. 'And it's a lie from start to finish, because old Garganius never touched a drop in his life when he was on duty. If you want to hear the true story you talk to him, pal. Sextus Garganius. Lives over by the fucking meat market.'

'Battus, I warned you! Out!'

'Yeah, yeah.' The punter set his cup down. 'It's OK. Keep your hair on, Scaptius, I was just going anyway. See you later, guys. Enjoy the festival.' There was a chorus of grunts, whistles and cat-calls. He lurched towards the door, and – finally – through it.

'Prat!' Scaptius muttered and reached for a cloth to wipe the counter.

'Just out of interest,' I said to him, 'do you happen to know where I can find Caesius's brother?'

'Lucius?' He gave me a sharp look and put the cloth down. 'What do you want with him?'

'I just need a quick word, that's all. For the sake of completeness.'

'To do with the death?' I said nothing. 'Well, it's no business of mine, sir, and no skin off my nose. Sure I know. Far as I re-member, he rents a room in the first street to the right of the square, above Cammius's bakery.' He turned to the other punters. 'That so, lads?' There were a few affirmative grunts. 'You might see him at the funeral, but I wouldn't count on it. He and his broth-er weren't exactly on friendly terms.'

'So I'm told,' I said. *Rents a room*, right? So the guy was obviously seriously strapped for cash. Something that was probably just going to change, and pretty drastically, from

66

what I'd seen of the Caesius *ménage*; if he was the dead man's only heir, he'd be worth quite a bit, shortly. I sank the remaining wine in my cup and stood up. 'Thanks,' I said. 'Catch you later.'

'Have a good festival if we don't see you before,' Scaptius said.

'You too, pal.'

Right. Back to the job in hand. Or at least to the victim's funeral.

FIVE

The market square was beginning to fill up, with crowds starting to form in the porticoes which surrounded it. They'd erected a temporary dais in the centre, wreathed along its edges with cypress, and there were a few curule stools on top for the dignitaries and the actors that'd be playing the dead man's magistrate ancestors. I found a place with a good view, next to a pillar, and leaned my back against it to wait.

'Down from Rome, are you, sir?' the guy beside me said. He was chewing on a sausage.

'Yeah. Just through for the festival.'

'That's it,' he said smugly. 'I could tell straight away from the haircut. Me, I'm a barber by trade. That's a Big City haircut you've got there, right?'

'Yeah,' I said. 'It is.'

'Thought so. Easy to spot, when you know the trick of it.' He nodded in the direction of the dais and took another bite of his take-away lunch. 'They're giving him a good send-off, at any rate, the randy old devil.

Visiting brothels at his time of life, eh? Who would've thought it, a respectable man like Caesius, too. You live and learn, don't you, sir?'

'Yeah. You certainly do.'

'Still, good on him, whatever anyone else says. Showed he was human after all, with a bit of red blood in his veins. That's what a lot of these cold bastards need, a bit of good red blood. Too much thinking – well, it isn't good for you, is it?'

I grunted vague agreement and looked away. The facts of the case had got around fast enough, that was for sure. Not that it was surprising, mind: Bovillae's a small place, and nothing spreads quicker than scandal. Plus the guy was a barber, after all. Gossip – particularly salacious gossip – is part of a barber's stock in trade. Forget the Daily Register: if you want to keep up with the breaking news anywhere in the empire the way to do it is to go down to the local market square every morning for a shave and trim.

We were about ready for the off: I could hear the wailing of flutes and the clashing of cymbals from the direction of the Arician Gate, and a couple of minutes later the funeral procession itself appeared. They were giving him a good send-off, right enough; the Bovillan Senate, bless their little cotton socks, had pulled out all the stops. The

69

musicians and professional mourners came first, then the bier with the dead man on it. Behind were his magistrate 'ancestors' in mourning mantles, the actors wearing the original death-masks. Scaptius the barman had been right; there were only half a dozen of them, quite a poor showing. Finally, the senate themselves, the town's greatest and best, led by the two current aediles with their attendant rod men. Among the follow-ons, I recognized Nerva and the fugitive from an Egyptian tomb that was old Publius Novius, Bovillae's sharp-as-a-knife lawyer.

The procession filled the centre of the square. The death-couch was set down, and the 'ancestors' plus the chief magistrates and top town officials took their places on the dais. One of the aediles raised his hand for silence. The music stopped. He took a scroll out of his mantle-pouch and unrolled it. So. They hadn't asked Brother Lucius as next-of-kin to read the eulogy, which would've been the normal way of doing things. Or – and I guessed it was the more likely explanation – he hadn't offered. Interesting.

'Who's giving the speech?' I said to my barber pal.

He spat a piece of gristle from the sausage into his palm and threw it away. 'Marcus Manlius,' he said.

The guy involved in the wool-store scam. If it was a scam. Yeah, Scaptius had said he was one of the aediles. I took a more careful look. A bit younger than Caesius had been, mid-fifties, maybe, with that sleek, plump, self-satisfied look you often get with rich political types: the fat-cat who's swallowed the canary and then gone on to lick up whatever cream's going before complaining that they've been short-changed, and besides, who had been responsible for providing the cream in the first place?

Manlius was definitely someone else I had to talk to.

'How about Canidius?' I said to the informative barber. 'He here?'

'The quaestor?' He pointed. 'That's him, behind Manlius's shoulder. The long drink of water.'

I followed the pointing finger with my eye, and grinned: 'long drink of water' summed the guy up perfectly. Tall, thin as a rake, early- to mid-forties, pasty-faced, looked like his nose had a permanent drip, and that there was something nasty under it. A prime candidate, obviously, for a pint or two of my barber pal's good red blood.

Manlius was getting into his stride. As eulogies went, it was standard, off-the-peg, ten-sesterces-the-yard stuff, delivered in the po-faced, self-consciously pious manner common to politicians and priests every-where: pillar of the community, honest, reliable, honourable, life devoted to the service of the people of Bovillae, tragic loss, never see his like again. Pick-and-mix, like I say, all pretty general, but with the noticeable omission of the usual bits concerning sterling moral rectitude and the closeness of the dead man's family ties. Either Manlius – if he'd written the speech himself, which was possible, judging by its banality – wasn't a total hypocrite, or more likely he just wasn't risking catcalls from the less respectful members of the crowd. That sort you always get, at politicos' funerals, and if their comments aren't always exactly PC at least they inject a bit of honesty into the proceedings.

Which reminded me ... I turned to my chatty neighbour.

'Any sign of the dead man's brother here, pal?' I said. 'Lucius Caesius? Or his nephew Mettius? You know either of them by sight?'

'Sure.' The barber scanned the crowd, taking his time and chewing on the last of his sausage. 'I can't see the brother,' he said finally. 'Although that's not surprising. The two couldn't stand each other, no secret about it. But there' – he pointed again, over to the far left – 'that's your Mettius. Standing over there by the shrine of the Goddess Rome, next to the fat woman with the chickens.'

I looked. There was only one possible candidate, a middle-aged guy in a sharp tunic and hairstyle years too young for him.

His back was against the shrine, his arms were folded, and he was smiling with the relaxed air of someone just out to enjoy the show.

Which was just about over. Manlius had delivered his last pompous phrase and was rolling up the text of his speech and nodding to the slaves carrying the death-couch; at least, most of them were slaves, but I noticed that one of them was Anthus, in his new freedman's cap. So they'd let him carry his master on his last journey. I was pleased about that.

The flute and cymbal players struck up again and the cortège moved off, followed by the dignitaries and whoever was going on to attend the final burning outside the town limits. Quite a few of these last, it seemed, and a fair number of them were ordinary punters: despite the circumstances, Caesius must still be popular. There again, in these small country towns you have to take what amusement you can get, and maybe even a funeral wasn't to be sneezed at. I said goodbye and thanks to my barber pal and tagged along, glancing over my shoulder to see who else was coming.

Surprisingly – at least, it was a surprise to me – it included the nephew, who'd slipped in at the tail-end of the crowd. An even bigger surprise was that walking beside him was the brothel owner, Opilia Andromeda.

Interesting.

We went through the town, back the way the procession had come, past Caesius's house and out of the Arician Gate, where the tombs started. A few hundred yards on, there was a big funeral pyre covered again with branches of pine and cypress, next to what was presumably the family pile. The bearers manoeuvred the death-couch on to the top of the pyre and stepped back while one of the undertakers' men handed Manlius, as chief mourner, the lighted torch. He pushed it into the oil-soaked wood, the flames leapt up and smoke billowed, caught by a freshening breeze and shrouding the corpse.

Once the fire had properly taken hold a fairly large chunk of the crowd began to drift off back in the direction of town, leaving a hard core mostly consisting of mantle-wearers. Me, I stuck around too: this is the point in the proceedings for socialising, while the corpse is burned and the chief mourners plus the undertakers' men wait for the fire to die down so that they can cool the ashes with wine and collect the bones for burial. I looked for the lawyer, Publius Novius – after all, I'd have to talk to him before too long – but I couldn't see him. That was understandable, sure: the day was turning cold, no weather for an old man to be out for long in, and he'd probably have packed it in as soon as it was decent. Nevertheless, most of the senators were still around, chatting in groups; I got a nod from Silius Nerva, although he didn't come over. Also hanging on for the final rites – surprisingly, I thought, all things considered – was the nephew Mettius. Not Andromeda, though, who I'd noticed slipping away practically as soon as the pyre was lit – out of tact, probably, since the odds were that the high-profile mourners included some of her regular customers. But there again, maybe I was doing her an injustice. She'd come to the burning, after all, and she was a busy lady with a business to run.

Mettius was standing on his own, looking at the flames and obviously lost in his own thoughts. I drifted across to him, and he glanced up when he saw me coming. He did a double-take, and his eyes widened slightly.

I might've been wrong, but I had the distinct impression that the guy was steeling himself.

'Hi,' I said. 'I'm—'

'Marcus Corvinus,' he said. 'Yes, I know who you are. You're down here from Rome, and you're investigating the old man's death, right?'

Old man. Not *my uncle.* Well, it made sense, I suppose, given the background and the fact that they'd had no contact for over ten years. 'Yeah,' I said. 'Although there's no actual connection between the two. So how did you

75

know, exactly?'

He shrugged; an elegant lifting of the shoulders. Ageing lad-about-town was right: the guy might dress and be barbered like a twenty-year-old dandy, but he was at least thirty-five, probably closer to forty, and he looked ten years older; it's not the mileage that gets you, sometimes, it's the booze, and I reckoned Mettius had sunk his fair share over the years. Not that I'm one to talk, of course.

'Andromeda told me,' he said.

'Right. Right.' I nodded. 'I noticed you were together. You, uh, know her well?'

'That all depends on what you mean. We're on familiar terms, yes, of course we are, as no doubt you'll've guessed from the fact that we came out here in one another's company.' His eyes were challenging. 'Knowing her *well*, however – in the sense in which I suspect you used the word – is something else entirely. I'm not married, Corvinus, but like a lot of other men in this town, married and single, I enjoy sex for its own sake and am willing to pay for it, so I'm a customer of hers. The big difference between me and a large number of her other regular clients is that I'm not ashamed to admit it.'

'Fair enough,' I said easily. 'I've no problem with that.' I glanced round at the pyre, still blazing away: the undertakers' men were pouring on perfume and adding dried, sweet herbs, to mask the smell of cooking meat: Caesius would be almost gone now. 'You didn't get on with your uncle, so I'm told.'

'You were told right.' His mouth twisted. 'But that's putting it far too mildly. I hated the bastard's guts.' I blinked; not something you expect to hear, under these circumstances, with the man himself turning to ash just a few feet away. 'So. Surprised that I'm here, are you?'

'A bit, yeah.'

'Don't be. The reason's quite simple. I wanted to see him burn.'

There was no anger in the tone, and that made the words more chilling. 'And why would that be, now?' I said neutrally.

'It's no secret. And if you don't know already, which I doubt, some public-spirited citizen'll be delighted to tell you eventually, so I'm getting in first. You know I was relegated? For theft?'

'Yeah. I knew that.'

'Caesius fixed that. Him and his lawyer friend Novius. They set me up.'

'Set you up? Why would they want to do that?'

He gave me a long, appraising look, then smiled and shook his head. 'Oh, no, Corvinus,' he said. 'No, that's my business, and the details don't matter. All I'm telling you is that I was innocent, just so you know. Ten fucking years!' He glanced around at the

77

chatting groups. 'Mind you, missing out on the company of this po-faced crowd was no hardship, so maybe I shouldn't complain too much. Bloody holier-than-thou hypocrites, the lot of them.' He hadn't lowered his voice, and I noticed a few sharply turned heads and disapproving frowns. Mettius had noticed them, too; he grinned, carefully raised his middle finger in the direction of the nearest ones, and held it there.

'Screw you,' he said sweetly, loudly and distinctly. The heads swung back. 'So.' He turned to face me again, still grinning. 'I wish you luck. You carry on digging, with my full blessing. The more dirt you find, the better. And believe me, dirt there will be. Well...' He glanced at the pyre; the centre had collapsed now, and there was no sign of the corpse. 'Fun's over, and I'd best be getting on. Things to do, places to go. I'm pleased to have met you, Corvinus. Look after yourself, and a happy Winter Festival when it comes. I'll see you around, OK?'

And with that he walked off towards the main drag, leaving me staring. I was still looking at his disappearing back when Silius Nerva came over: he'd been, I'd noticed, one of the punters Mettius had given the finger to.

'I'm sorry about that, Corvinus,' he said. 'Really sorry. The man's a complete disgrace, and foul-mouthed into the bargain.

From a good, respectable family, too; his father would've been ashamed. Why he came back to Bovillae after his period of relegation expired I simply don't know. Never mind.' He clapped me on the shoulder. 'Thank you for coming today; it's appreciated. Now. Come and meet our aedile, Marcus Manlius. I was just telling him about you, that you're looking after things for us, and he'd like to thank you personally.'

He led me across to where Manlius was standing with my barber pal's long drink of water, Canidius. They turned and smiled at me.

'Marcus Valerius Corvinus, Marcus Manlius and Sextus Canidius,' he said.

'Pleased to meet you, Corvinus,' Manlius said. Canidius gave me a benign nod. 'We're very grateful – I speak for the senate as a whole, of course – that you're helping us over this business. Most embarrassing, most embarrassing! And I noticed that that woman from the brothel had the nerve to turn up. Very poor taste, that.'

'You recognized her, then?' I said.

He coloured. 'I've ... seen her, yes. Around and about in town.'

Uh-huh. There was a short, embarrassed silence that I wasn't going to be the one to break. I just smiled and kept on smiling.

'So,' Canidius said finally. From close up he looked a bit like a fastidious ostrich getting ready to produce an egg. 'How *is* the investigation going, exactly?'

'Give the man a chance, Sextus!' Nerva laughed. 'He's only just started!'

'Not that we want to know too many of the sordid details, mind you,' Manlius chuckled. 'Leave poor old Quintus some shreds of his reputation intact, eh?'

I felt my teeth grit; between Mettius and these solid Bovillan citizens I'd take the foul-mouthed one any time. 'As it happens,' I said to Canidius, 'the investigation's going not too badly.'

'Really?' He beamed at me. 'That *is* encouraging! Well done, you!'

'Yeah. In fact, I've got a few promising leads already. This business with the burned-down wool store, for example.' I was still smiling. 'I understand you and Manlius here were directly concerned. I mean with the original contract, of course, not the burning itself. You like to fill me in on the background to that, while I'm here?'

I could feel the temperature plummet like the slate from a tenement roof. The smiles vanished, and the looks I got from Bovillae's two serving magistrates would've skewered a rhino.

'That has nothing whatsoever to do with Caesius's death!' Canidius snapped. 'It was a complete accident, and it happened six months ago!'

I'd kept my own smile going. 'Even so,' I said, 'and correct me if I'm wrong – when he took up office as censor in January he was going to set up an enquiry, wasn't he? And that won't be happening now. Or will it?'

I was still getting the glares, but they were silent ones.

'That has yet to be decided, Corvinus,' Nerva said. 'By the senate as a body.'

'Not by the new censor? I was sort of assuming there'd be a new election.'

'Of course, naturally there will be, but...'

'And from what I'm told, Manlius here is likely to be the lucky replacement, right?'

The aedile's glare went up a notch. 'Only if the citizens of Bovillae elect me as such,' he said stiffly. 'Which would be the outcome of due democratic process.'

'Yeah. Right,' I said. 'Naturally, so it would, at that. I'm sorry. And of course there'll be other candidates, won't there?'

'*That* is up to any interested parties to decide for themselves!'

I nodded. 'Sure. Sure. My apologies again. Well, we'll just have to wait and see what happens, won't we?'

'*You* will not, Corvinus,' Canidius said sharply. 'You're not a citizen of Bovillae, only a visitor. You'll be long gone.'

'Assuming I've cleared up this little problem for you by then.'

'Oh, I'm convinced you'll've done that, my

dear fellow!' Nerva beamed at me, after shooting Canidius a sideways look. 'Don't be so modest. Quintus Libanius over in Castrimoenium tells me he has every confidence in your abilities.'

'Well, I'll certainly do my very best in that direction, sir. We'll get there eventually, don't you worry. Wherever *there* happens to be.' I gave him a corresponding beam of my own. 'Now if you'll excuse me, I must be getting back home. Delighted to have met you, gentlemen. A real honour.'

I turned and walked away, feeling their eyes boring into my shoulder blades. I'd enjoyed that little exchange. Like I said, I'd take Mettius over those two smarmy buggers any day of the month.

The flames were dying down, and the undertakers' men were beginning to move in, pulling the pyre apart at its edges with hooked poles so that it collapsed completely in a flurry of burning wood and sparks. Enough for today; I reckoned I'd done pretty well, all told. At least it was a start. And I could consider Manlius's and Canidius's cages well and truly rattled.

Home.

SIX

I got back just a smidgeon late for dinner, which with Clarus and Marilla's chef Euclidus running things as opposed to the ultra-picky Meton was no big deal for a change. Euclidus might not be anything like Meton's class, but at least you didn't get the five-star tantrum and the three-day sulk if you weren't exactly on time for a meal. As it was, the slaves had just ferried in the plates and the range of starters, so we hadn't missed anything important. I lay down on the couch next to Perilla, filled my wine cup, and helped myself to a selection.

'So how did you get on, dear?' she said when I was firmly ensconced. 'Successful first day?'

'It was OK,' I said, reaching for the snails in oil and oregano. 'In fact, pretty good, all told.' While we worked our way through the nibbles, I gave the three of them – Clarus and Marilla were sharing one of the other two couches – the basic run-down of events. 'It's a lot too early for any definite theories yet, sure, but at least the leads and the list of possible perps are firming up nicely. Pillar of the community and solid citizen the guy might have been, but he was obviously a lot less than popular in some quarters. And getting himself murdered less than a month before he was due to take up office when he'd promised to look into a fire in the town's wool store is a tad too coincidental for comfort.'

Clarus was helping himself to the haricot bean purée. 'I'd heard about that,' he said. 'It was a real scandal at the time. Rumour was that Manlius had shifted a lot of the bales elsewhere beforehand, sold them off privately, and started the fire himself to cover things up.'

'Yeah,' I said. 'That much I got at the wine shop. Mind you, that's par for the course. A warehouse fire's a conspiracy-theory godsend to your wine-shop punter, particularly when a public figure's involved. Me, I'd've been surprised if there hadn't been rumours.'

'Wouldn't something like that be noticed?' Perilla said.

'Oh, no.' Marilla shelled a quail's egg and dipped it in the fish sauce. 'Or at least it probably wouldn't. Once the shearing was over there'd be no need for anyone to go into the place, would there? Not until the fleeces were sold, anyway. And scams like that go on all the time.'

84

'How interesting. Do they really, dear?' Perilla said quietly. She had her prim look on. 'And how would you know, now?'

Uh-oh.

'Corvinus?' Marilla grinned at me. 'I am right, aren't I? They do.'

Uh-oh was right: straight in with both feet. A lovely girl in many ways, our adopted daughter, but sometimes she was as sensitive to the nuances as a brick. I glanced sideways at Perilla. Her lips were set in a disapproving line: it was OK for me to play the sleuth, but the lady had her standards where Marilla was concerned. We might be in for a few squalls here. Time for a bit of tact. 'Yeah, well, Princess,' I said. 'Maybe so. But so far it's just that – no more than a rumour. Oh, sure, Manlius and his pal Canidius might well be as bent as a couple of tin sesterces, in which case it may be relevant, but I'm suspending judgement at present.'

'I'd take the whole thing with a pinch of salt myself, Corvinus,' Clarus said. 'From what I've heard, those two may have an eye out for the main chance, but they're no worse than your average local politician, and even if they were it doesn't make them potential murderers, does it? Besides—'

There was a loud crash just outside the dining-room door.

'What the fuck?' I said.

'*Marcus!*' Perilla snapped.

'Yeah, well...'

Bathyllus came in holding a silver tray; just the tray itself, with nothing on it. He was closely followed by Lupercus, and neither of them, to use a gross understatement, looked a happy bunny. No eye contact between them, for a start.

Bugger. This did *not* look good. The family dinner was turning into a major disaster.

'I'm sorry, sir,' Lupercus said stiffly to Clarus. 'There's been an accident with the wine. No real damage done though, and I'll see that the mess is cleared up immediately.'

'Yes, OK, Lupercus,' Clarus said. 'No problem. These things happen. Go ahead.'

'Thank you, sir.' He turned.

Accident, nothing: I hadn't seen our respective major-domos put in a simultaneous appearance since we'd got here. And going by the body language blood was within an ace of being spilled on both sides.

'Hang on a minute, Lupercus,' I said. 'OK, Bathyllus, your turn. Let's have your version of the story. In detail, and unexpurgated this time, please.'

'I don't know what you mean, sir.' Innocence radiating from every pore, combined with overtones of politely understated outrage: a chief Vestal nailed for shoplifting couldn't've done it better. Still, I wasn't having any of that, not even from Bathyllus. When someone says *I don't know what you*

mean, the chances are that they know damn-
ed well, and the business smells as high as an
eight-day-old sprat.

'Think about it, sunshine,' I said. 'Weigh
up all the semantic possibilities. Meanwhile,
I'll count to five, and if you still haven't given
me a straight answer you'll be mucking out
the latrines with a very small sponge. Clear?
One.'

'Lupercus has already told you, sir. It was
a simple accident.'

'Two.'

'He was carrying the tray of wine cups and
the jug and he tripped.'

'Three, four, five.'

'Sir, that is not fair! You cheated!'

'Bugger that. Just take a deep breath, think
of the latrines and tell me the truth. Now.
Last chance.'

Bathyllus fizzed for a bit. Finally, he held
up the tray he was carrying.

'There's a thumbprint on this, sir,' he said.
'A *greasy* thumbprint.'

'*What?*'

'It's perfectly distinct. Look for yourself.'
He thrust the tray under my nose. 'I've told
him several times about washing his hands
before he touches the silver, but he just
won't listen. It's appalling! Besides, serving
the wine is my job. It has to be done properly.'

I stared at him. He was almost gabbling,

which was about as likely from Bathyllus as seeing him do a tap dance round the dining room wearing a tutu and clogs.

'Is that all?' I said. 'This is all about a fucking *thumbprint*?'

'But, sir!'

Jupiter in bloody spangles! 'Right, little guy,' I said. 'A word, please. Outside. Now.'

He gave me a look, then tucked the tray under his arm and marched out into the corridor. I got up and followed.

'Now,' I said quietly when I'd got him alone. 'You remember what I said when we arrived? About give and take while we're here?'

'Yes, sir, I remember very well.'

'So quote me. Verbatim.'

'You said, "We are not at home to Mr Refuse to Compromise", sir.' A sniff. 'Whatever that meant.'

'Correct. And never mind the qualification; you get the general gist, don't you?' He didn't answer. 'Listen, pal, we've all got to learn to share, OK? It'll be the Winter Festival in a few days, and that's no time for throwing tantrums, is it?' Still silence. 'Now you go back in there and apologise to Lupercus, or you go straight home on the next available cart. Got it?'

'But...'

'Ah-ah. I mean it. No buts. Just do as you're told. Repeat after me: "Lupercus, I

88

am very sorry..."'

'Sir!'

'Come on, Bathyllus. You can do it if you try. "Lupercus, I am very sorry..."'

He clenched his teeth. 'Lupercus'm'ver'-sorry...'

'"For the way I behaved..."'

'F'r'way I b'haved.'

'"And it won't happen again."'

''N' it won't h'ppn 'gain.'

I patted him on the shoulder. 'Good. Well done. That wasn't so difficult, was it? Now in you come.'

I went back in, with Bathyllus trailing behind.

'Bathyllus has something to say to you, Lupercus,' I said, lying down again. 'Go ahead, sunshine. In your own time.'

Bathyllus drew himself up to his full five feet four. 'Lupercus,' he said, 'I apologise for having tried to take the wine tray from you before you brought it in, even if its filthy condition was totally obvious to anyone not completely devoid of—'

'Bathyllus!'

'Yes, sir,' he said stiffly. 'I am doing what you asked. Apologising.' He turned back to Lupercus. 'Please accept my assurances that the incident will not be repeated. Always, that is, given that in future you—'

Gods! 'Bathyllus! Just cut it out, OK?'

'Yes, sir. Of course. That is all I have to say

at present, Lupercus. Now if you'll excuse me, sir, madam.' He left, with huge dignity.

Bugger.

'You can go too, Lupercus,' Clarus said. 'Tidy up the mess, please, and bring us some more wine.'

'Certainly, sir.' Lupercus left. There was a long silence.

'Oh dear,' Perilla said faintly. 'Oh dear, oh dear, oh dear.'

Marilla giggled.

The lady put down the stuffed olive she'd been holding. 'It's not funny, Marilla,' she said. 'Not really. Bathyllus takes himself and his position very seriously. And he has very high standards.'

'Yeah, well,' I said. 'Like I told him outside, he's got to learn to share. This isn't his house; he's a guest, even if he is one below stairs. Lupercus is the major-domo here, and there's an end of it. He'll just have to accept that.'

'Do you think he will?' Perilla said.

'Maybe not. But that's his problem, unless he wants to be shipped back to Rome and spend the festival there. I told him that, too.'

'You ever happen to notice the interesting thing about thumbprints, Corvinus?' Clarus said. 'Any fingerprints, really.'

'What?' I looked at him blankly. Shit, you expected non sequiturs like that from airheads like Priscus, but Clarus was the solid,

90

no-nonsense, sensible type.

'They've got sort of whorls, and every one's just that little bit different.'

'Yeah?' I said. 'So?'

'So if someone picked something up, like a silver tray, like Lupercus did, and left a fingerprint on it, you'd be able to tell who'd done it. Picked up the tray, I mean.' He was looking at the expression on my face. 'Because if you got him to leave another fingerprint on something else and compared the two it'd prove that ... I mean, you'd know...' We were all staring at him now. He tailed off and cleared his throat in embarrassment. 'Or there again maybe you wouldn't. Forget it. It was just an idea.'

Gods! And I'd thought Priscus was bad! 'You been talking to Alexis, pal?' I said. Our clever-clever gardener had this theory that you could breed better peas by using a small brush to smear the pollen from one plant inside the flower of another one. The philosophy of it seemed fairly run-of-the-mill conventional, no problems there – something about each grain of pollen containing the element of bigness or hardiness or whatever embodied in the whole plant – but it wasn't a comfortable thing to watch, especially when he explained it in terms of male and female.

Clarus shrugged. 'Yes, well,' he said. 'Like I said, it was only an idea. Never mind. It doesn't matter. So. Back to the case. What comes next, Corvinus?'

'Bread-and-butter procedural stuff,' I said. 'Just doing the rounds of the names on the list. I've got to see the guy who had the argument with Caesius a couple of days before he was killed. Quintus Roscius. Then there's the elusive brother, the town drunk or whatever, and Publius Novius, our old pal the dodgy lawyer. Also, I'd like to know more about why exactly the nephew had his knife in. Like I say, there're plenty of leads, and Caesius seems to have put a lot of people's backs up.'

'As long as you remember, dear, that we are on holiday,' Perilla said. 'And Priscus and your mother will expect to see something of you when they arrive. You can't be away in Bovillae all day from breakfast to dinner. It isn't polite. Particularly since it's Priscus's birthday while they're here.'

'Gods, Perilla, they only live up the hill from us in Rome! It's not as if we don't see them at other times.'

'Not very often. Only for the occasional meal.'

'That's out of self-preservation, lady. It's not so bad when they come to us. But when you go round to their place to eat you take your life in your hands.'

'Nonsense, Marcus! Phormio's an excellent chef.' She paused. Perilla can be pretty dogmatic, sure, but at root she's fair and honest. 'In his way. By his own lights. Within certain parameters. It's simply that he can be rather too ... inventive at times.'

Inventive. Well, that was one word for the bastard. It wouldn't be the one that I'd choose, mind. Still, there was no point in starting an argument I knew I couldn't win. 'Oh, incidentally,' I said, 'I picked up something for the birthday boy when I was in town.' I reached for my purse, took out the ivory plaque, and handed it over.

'But that's lovely!' Perilla said, examining it. 'Where did you get it?'

'A little antiques shop near the market square. Owned by a guy named Baebius. Coincidentally, he was at daggers drawn with Caesius as well.'

'We'll give him that, then. I'd got him a copy of Varro's *Antiquities*, but that'll do for a Festival present. An antiques shop, you say? That's quite unusual for a country town like Bovillae, isn't it? Of course, there are a lot of incomers buying up the old estates, so I suppose there's more of a market for luxuries these days.'

'You know the Satellius one's just been sold?' Clarus said. 'Trebbius was telling me.' Trebbius was one of Clarus's regular patients, a card-carrying hypochondriac and prime source of up-to-the-minute local gossip. 'Some bigwig in the Roman civil service. At a pretty good price, too. Trebbius didn't know the man's name, but he's converting the old farmhouse into a top-class villa. Three dining rooms, landscaped garden, the lot. The Satellius family's been a fixture around here for generations, but the offer was just too tempting.'

'I think it's a shame,' Marilla said. 'All the little working farms are going. We'll soon be just a holiday-home suburb of Rome.'

'Well, that's progress,' I said. 'You can't...'

Lupercus and Bathyllus came in together, both carrying loaded wine trays.

'Uh ... what's going on, pal?' I said to Bathyllus. 'Serving the wine needs two of you?'

He sniffed. 'According to your instructions, sir, and in the interests of peace and harmony we have reached an amicable compromise. I will serve you and the mistress, while the ... local staff will attend to the rest of the household. I trust that is acceptable?'

Oh, gods, *acceptable*? It just sounded plain bloody childish and silly to me. Nevertheless...

I looked at Clarus. He nodded wearily.

'Yeah, OK, little guy,' I said. 'So long as it works, do it however you like. But just be careful, because you're skating on very thin ice here. Lupercus, you all right with this?'

'Yes, sir.' I noticed that he didn't look at Bathyllus. Still no love lost there, then. Well, we couldn't have everything. And I'd settle for peace and harmony, even if it did mean getting childish and silly into the bargain.

'Fine. Marvellous.' I sighed. 'We'll give it a try, for what it's worth. Now wheel in the main course, will you, before we starve to death. And no demarcation disputes over who pushes the bloody trolley.'

Bugger. Life between now and the end of the festival, when we could decently go home and get back to normal, was going to be fun, fun, fun. Not only that, but we'd still got the joys of Mother and Priscus to look forward to.

Thank goodness I'd got a case to work on. Say what you liked about a murder investigation: at least it was clean and straight-forward. It'd get me out and about, anyway.

SEVEN

I went back into Bovillae the next day after breakfast.

First on the list of things to do was talk to Quintus Roscius. Nerva had told me his farm was on the Castrimoenium side of town, so once Bovillae was in view I stopped to ask a guy clearing out the drainage ditch at the edge of a field next to the road for directions.

The farmhouse turned out to be an old building a few hundred yards up a dirt track; quite a sizeable property for the extent of the holding, although most of it, of course, would be storage sheds plus roofed-over areas for the grape press and threshing floor. Roscius evidently kept it in good condition, despite its age; there were new tiles on the roof, the walls were whitewashed, and the yard in front was tidy and swept, with two or three plump chickens strutting about pecking for grain.

I dismounted and knocked at the door. It was opened by a good-looking woman in her mid-twenties with a toddler clinging to the

96

hem of her tunic and staring at me, thumb in mouth.

'Sorry to disturb you, lady,' I said. 'Is this the Roscius place?'

'It is.' She frowned and brushed a strand of hair from her eyes. 'Was it my husband you wanted?'

'If he's around.'

'He's muck-spreading the top field. Just carry on as far as you can go.'

I thanked her, remounted the horse and walked it up the track, past a dozen rows of vine-stocks, ditto of what were probably fruit trees, and a field that was bare at present but showed signs of having been tilled and got ready for the first season's planting: small enough for a farm, sure, but altogether, like the farmhouse itself, well-managed and in pretty good shape – or so it looked to my townie's eye, anyway. Certainly a lot of hard work had gone in there. Whatever else Roscius was, he was no slacker.

As far as you can go, his wife had said. Sure enough, two or three hundred yards further along the track ended in a field where a guy with a fork was spreading manure from the back of an ox wagon.

I tied the horse's rein to one of the hurdles at the field's edge and went on over. 'Quintus Roscius?' I said.

He stopped, glanced up, frowned, and grounded the fork.

'That's me.' The frown had settled into a scowl.

'Marcus Corvinus. I'm—'

'I know who you are.' He was a big guy, easily six feet, and built like an ox himself, heavily muscled, dark-browed and broad as a barn door. He hawked and spat to one side. 'Or I can make a good guess. I've been expecting you.'

He didn't sound or look too friendly, but that was natural under the circumstances. 'Fine,' I said easily. 'No problem. That'll save a bit of trouble. You got time for a chat?'

'No. But go ahead anyway. Get it over with.'

'Fair enough.' I paused. 'You, uh, had a run-in with Caesius in town, so I'm told, a couple of days before he died. Care to tell me about it?'

The scowl deepened. '"Run-in" isn't what I'd call it,' he said. 'We had words, sure, him and me, mostly on my side. But it was no more than that. Just words. And I'll tell you now, straight out, I'd nothing to do with his death.'

'I'm not accusing you, pal,' I said. 'I'm just getting my facts straight, that's all. So what were these words about? Something to do with a loan, wasn't it?'

'Yeah.'

'You like to elaborate, maybe?'

'It's simple enough. We do OK here, generally, but the profit margin is pretty small, and the past couple of years I'd been going through a bad patch. Three poor harvests in a row, stock dying, spoiled seed. One thing after another, and they just mounted up. Finally, I went to Caesius – his family and mine have links that go way back – and he loaned me a few thousand with the farm as collateral. No hurry to pay him back, he said; just as soon as I could manage. He was only too pleased to help me out. Only then, seven days ago, he sends round his bailiff saying he wants the debt settled by the end of the year or he'll foreclose.'

'You didn't have a contract? Something in writing?'

'Sure I had. For what it was worth. Only I'm no great reader, me, and nor is the wife. Letters, straightforward stuff, sure, no problem, but a legal document's different. I haven't got the head for that. I signed what he gave me and took him at his word about the *no hurry* business. It turned out that his lawyer pal had put in a clause about settlement being due on the first day of the new year or the property was forfeit, so he had me over a barrel.'

'"Lawyer pal"? That'd be Publius Novius, would it?'

'Yeah, that's the one. There's another bastard. They're all hand-in-glove, these nobs. Anyway, there was no way I could get the money together, not in hard cash, not a quarter of it. I went over to Caesius's house right away to explain, ask for a bit of extra time, but he sent out word he was too busy to see me. So then when I saw him in the street the next day I went up to him and asked him to his face. When he tried to give me the bum's rush again I lost my temper and told him straight what I thought of him, right there in the open where everyone could hear.' He shrugged. 'That's all that happened, the long and short of it. The farm's worth ten times the loan, easy, and Caesius knew it. What would you have done?'

Yeah; fair enough. Me, I'd probably have punched the bugger's lights out into the bargain and got into even worse trouble. 'So what happens now?' I said.

'If we can't pay, then like I said come next month we're out. But my family's been here for five generations, and I won't go easy. Maybe now Caesius is dead I can cut a deal with his brother. We'll just have to see. Meanwhile, whatever happens' – he indicated the manure – 'the jobs've got to be done, so I do them.'

'A deal with Lucius?'

'Sure, with Lucius. Who else? He's bound to be the heir, isn't he? Caesius didn't have any other family.'

'You know him?'

'Well enough to speak to, anyway. Most

people do. Old Lucius Caesius isn't a bad lad, for all he's got a drink problem, and he's been up against it himself these last thirty, forty years since his father threw him out. When things're settled he'll have more money than he needs to last him for the rest of his days without bothering about taking my farm from me.' He reached for the manure fork. 'Anyway, that's what I'm hoping.'

'Yeah. Yeah, right.' I hesitated. 'You, uh, go into town often of an evening?'

'Sometimes.' The hand on the fork paused, and his tone was guarded. 'For a cup or two of wine and a chat with friends, like anyone else.'

'How about the night Caesius was killed?'

'No. I was at home. You can ask my wife. She'll tell you.'

'Fair enough.' Well, he seemed pretty genuine, and I'd no cause from what had gone before to think any different. There wasn't anything else I could do here at present. 'Thanks for your time, pal. Sorry to disturb you. I'll leave you to it.'

'That's all?' The frown finally lifted, and he looked relieved.

'Sure. Why not? I told you, I'm just getting my facts straight. I'll see you around.'

I collected my horse, rode back down the track, and carried on into town.

OK, now for my old friend Publius Novius.

His office, I remembered from the last time I'd talked to him a year and a half previously, was this side of the town centre, near the baths: a pretty up-market affair for a provincial law business, heavy on the marble – or marble facing, anyway – and obviously meant to impress on his clients that here was a guy at the top of his professional tree.

Just inside the Tiburtine Gate – which was the one the road from Castrimoenium passed through – was a horse trough with two or three nags already in residence. This time of day, the town would be at its busiest, and if I was going to be using the back streets – which I was, to get to the baths – I'd do better on foot. I left my horse for later collection moored to a vacant iron ring and happily fraternising with the mare parked next to him and headed off in the direction of Novius's.

It wasn't difficult to find: exactly where I remembered it, in the street that started opposite the baths and carried on down to the market square. I mounted the carefully scrubbed and polished steps, flanked by their marble-faced pillars, and went inside.

'Hi, pal,' I said to the young clerk on the lobby desk. 'Novius in and free at present?'

'Did you have an appointment, sir?' The clerk reached for the wax tablet beside him.

'No. But the name's Marcus Corvinus. He'll know who I am. Silius Nerva of the senate asked me to look into the death of Quintus Caesius. I understand he was a friend and client.'

'Indeed he was, sir. And you're not un-expected.' The guy got up. 'Novius *is* in and alone, but I'll just check to see if he's free. If you'd care to wait a moment.'

'Sure. No problem.'

He crossed to the communicating door, knocked, opened it and went in. I listened to the murmur of voices while I inspected the mural on the wall behind the desk: Hermes, Greek god of eloquence, whispering in the ear of what was evidently a lawyer in a court-room presenting his case. Slick-smart ad-vocate though Novius undoubtedly was, I reckoned he was purblind when it came to irony: silver-tongued Hermes is also the god of thieves, tricksters, shysters and liars. Of course, it was possible that I might be doing the guy an injustice and he'd fully realized the double implication when he commis-sioned the thing, but from what I recalled of Novius, self-parody wasn't his bag.

The clerk came back out. 'He'll see you, if you'd like to go in.'

I did, and he closed the door behind me. Novius was sitting behind his desk, the same little wrinkled prune of a man in a sharp mantle I'd talked to eighteen months before.

'Valerius Corvinus,' he said. 'I heard that you were in town. And indeed why. Such a pleasure to see you again, even under these melancholy circumstances. Do have a seat.'

Well, maybe I'd been wrong about the irony. Whatever he was feeling about seeing me, it certainly wasn't pleasure, not after the last conversation we'd had in this room. Still, if that was how he wanted to play it then it was fine with me. I pulled up the visitors' stool and sat down.

'So how's your pal Castor?' I said.

He didn't blink. 'Well enough, as far as I know, and living now in Pisa. I understand he married a rich widow up there.'

'Bully for him,' I said drily. 'He meet her before or after her husband died?'

Again, not a flicker; I got a look as blind as a marble bust of Homer's. 'That I really can't tell you, Corvinus,' he said. 'I have no knowledge of the matter beyond the bare facts that I've just given you. Or indeed interest in it.' He moved the stylus on his desktop a few inches to the right. 'Now. How can I be of service?'

'No hassle. You being Caesius's lawyer I just need some basic background information. At present, anyway.' Still no blink; the sharp eyes were watching me benignly, like I was a performing dog. Which probably, as far as Novius was concerned, summed up his view of me pretty well. 'First off: the heir. That would be his brother, wouldn't it?'

'Lucius, yes.'

'The town drunk.'

He moved the stylus back again carefully to its original position and looked me straight in the eye before answering.

'Corvinus,' he said. 'Let us be clear about this. The law is only interested in relationships, not character flaws, unless these are criminal ones. Lucius Caesius does, indeed, have a problem in that direction, but as the executor of his brother's estate it is no concern of mine. Nor, forgive me, should it be one of yours.'

Yeah, well, fair enough; maybe I had been out of order, at that. I let it go.

'Caesius named him as heir in his will?' I said.

'No, as it happens he died intestate. Or rather, in his only existing will, made shortly after his marriage thirty-five years ago, he left everything, barring some small personal bequests, to his wife Vatinia, and should she predecease him to any children of the union. In the event, of course, there was no family, and his wife died two months ago. I'd advised him very strongly after her death – and naturally several times on previous occasions over the years – to draft a new will, but as far as I'm aware he had not yet done so.'

'Yeah? Why would that be, now?'

Novius shrugged. 'Quintus, I'm afraid, was the lawyer's nightmare, the chronic procrastinator. The situation was made even more

105

complex by the fact that he genuinely could think of no alternative principal heir, and so put things off *sine die*. As a result – and I agree that the result is an unfortunate one, which Quintus himself would have deplored – under the circumstances the estate reverts to the nearest male relative, who is his younger brother.'

'And Lucius Caesius knew this?'

'That I'm afraid I can't tell you. You would have to ask him.'

There was something puzzling me. 'His major-domo, Anthus. He said his master had freed him.'

'Indeed he did. But the freeing was done not in accordance with a will but as the result of a Declaration of Intent.'

'Which is?'

'Exactly what it says. Fortunately for Anthus, it happens that several years ago Quintus promised him, in my personal hearing and in the presence of other witnesses, that when the time came he would have his freedom. I was delighted to be able to confirm this and so make it legally binding, as no doubt Quintus would have wanted.'

'The two brothers had nothing to do with each other, as I understand. And it went a long way back. In fact, the estrangement was originally between Lucius and his father.'

'Who told you that?' Novius said sharply. I said nothing. 'Well, it's true enough, as it happens, and no secret. Lucius was always a wastrel. Old Caesius – Marcus Caesius, that was, the father – was extremely patient with him for many years after he'd put on his adult mantle, but finally he gave him up. Oh, he didn't actually go as far as disinheriting him, or not at that stage, but he did make it clear that he wanted no further contact. The feeling, I should say, was quite mutual, and from the time Lucius was about twenty-five until his father's death they had no connection barring the financial one.'

'Financial?'

'Yes. I acted as the intermediary myself, as it happens. Marcus Caesius made his son a small allowance, payable each month. After he died, Quintus continued it.'

'Hang on, pal,' I said. 'I'm no lawyer, sure, but even I can see an inconsistency there. If the father didn't disinherit Lucius then why was it necessary? Why didn't Lucius get half the property in his own right when the old man died?'

'I did say "at that stage", Corvinus. Old Caesius disinherited Lucius in his will. The whole property went to Quintus.'

I sat back. *'What?'*

Novius shrugged again. 'It was perfectly legal. And Lucius had no right to expect anything else, after all that time. He and his father – and, of course, his brother – had been virtual strangers for most of their lives.

Also, Lucius had got quite enough out of him already over the years.'

'When did the father die?'

'Comparatively recently. Only eleven years ago, in fact. He was a very old man, well into his eighties.'

'Just before Aulus Mettius was relegated, in other words.'

This time Novius did blink. 'I beg your pardon?'

'Mettius. Caesius's nephew.' I'd rattled him, which was the hope and intention. 'He was working for you at the time, I think.'

'I'm afraid I don't see the connection.'

I gave him my sunniest smile. 'I didn't say there was one. Is there?'

'Certainly not! Why should there be?'

'No reason. But he was the other thing I wanted to ask you about. Theft, wasn't it? And you were the injured party?'

Rattled was right: the old guy's mottled face was almost purple.

'Corvinus, this has nothing whatsoever to do with Quintus Caesius's death!' he snapped.

'Maybe it hasn't. I don't know. But like I said I'm just getting an idea of the background here, so indulge me. Unless it's a secret, naturally.'

'Of course it isn't! The circumstances are a matter of public record!'

'Then there's no problem, is there?' I

carried on smiling, and waited.

Novius frowned and cleared his throat. 'Very well, Corvinus,' he said. 'But this is under protest, and only to prevent you from thinking that I'm concealing something from you. I should point out, however – and Silius Nerva would agree with me here – that you are greatly exceeding your mandate.'

'Fine,' I said equably. 'I can go with that.'

'Theft, then, is not quite the correct term for Aulus Mettius's crime. What he was guilty of was embezzlement. He had been with me as clerk-apprentice for just under five years, initially on Quintus's recommendation. I discovered that he was, and had been for much of that time, helping himself from the clients' fees, of which he had administrative charge. Under the circumstances, prosecution was my only option.'

'You didn't think that maybe just a smack over the knuckles and a warning would be enough? Considering that he was your friend Caesius's nephew?'

'No. The man was a crook. And Quintus agreed with me. He'd already washed his hands of him.' He picked up the stylus. 'And now, unless you have any other questions more germane to the issue, I'm an extremely busy man. No doubt there are already clients waiting outside. I'll bid you good day.'

I stood up. 'Yeah, right,' I said. 'Thanks for your time, pal. If I do have any more germane questions – which I probably will, when things get going – I know where to find you.'

I left him glaring after me.

EIGHT

So, onwards and upwards. Time to talk to the brother and – as far as the *cui bono* aspect of things went – prime contender for wishing Caesius dead and burned. *If* I could get a hold of him...

My barman friend Scaptius had said that Lucius rented a room in the street to the right of the market square, above a bakery. That should be easy to find, although at this time of day he probably wouldn't be at home, unless he was sleeping things off. Which, I supposed, was possible.

I came back down the steps. Before turning left and heading towards the centre of town, I happened to glance the other way, up the road in the direction of the baths at the end of it. And I noticed something odd.

It was a quiet street, virtually a backwater. When I'd first arrived, there'd been only one other punter in evidence, on the far side of the road but walking parallel at the same pace: a big guy in a freedman's cap. When I'd gone into Novius's office he'd kept on going, presumably bound for the baths. But now there he was again, leaning against the wall and communing with nature a few yards up from me.

Uh-huh.

I set off slowly down the road, gave it a couple of minutes, then turned round as casually as I could manage. Chummie was tagging along, a few dozen yards behind, moving at the same unnaturally slow speed. So. Unless my paranoia was getting worse in my old age the bugger was tailing me sure enough. The big questions, of course, were why and who for?

OK. The first thing was to rule paranoia and coincidence out of the equation. I crossed the next street, stopped on the far side and turned round. Chummie, a dozen yards behind, slowed almost to a halt and became very interested in the sandals on display outside the shop just shy of the corner itself. I ignored him, but instead of retracing my steps, or carrying on past the street, I turned down it: by my reckoning, it would run parallel to the top end of the square, so it'd bring me out more or less where I wanted to go in any case.

It was much busier than the street I'd been on. A couple of dozen yards further along it was a guy selling poppy-seed bread rings from a hand cart. I stopped and bought one, glancing behind me as I took the copper coin from my belt pouch. There was no sign of the freedman. OK; so maybe it had been straightforward paranoia, after all. Or maybe – which was just as likely, if not more so – the bastard had realized he'd been sussed and decided to cut his losses for the present. Whatever the reason, I'd lost him.

The strange thing was that, when I'd turned round at the corner and got a proper look, something about him had rung a bell. Not his face, which I'd seen clearly; I'd be ready to swear that to my knowledge I'd never clapped eyes on the guy before in my life. It was just the way he moved and held himself...

Memory tugged.

Ah, bugger. Leave it. No doubt if I wasn't actually on the brink of wearing my underpants on my head and he had been tailing me for some reason it wouldn't be the last time he did it. Next time, I'd be ready.

I carried on along the street and took a right at the corner. Yeah, this was the street the barman had meant, all right: I could see the bakery a few yards down. On the other hand, there was a wine shop a bit further along, on the opposite side, just after the entrance to an alleyway. Maybe a better place to try, at least in the first instance: the chances were that one so close to home would be Lucius's local. I crossed the road and walked towards it, glancing down the alleyway as I passed.

It was a cul-de-sac, with two small shops in it: a general merchant's and a bootmaker's. Check. Yeah, I'd thought there was something familiar about the street I was on. I'd come down it, or the bottom half of it, rather, the day before, heading for the main drag and Caesius's house, after I'd left the brothel by its back door. The alley was the same one, the one behind the brothel, seen from the other direction.

I carried on to the wine shop, pushed open the door and went in.

The place was pretty basic, cheap and not particularly cheerful, not much more than a stone counter beside which stood two or three barflies who looked like they'd come as a package with the furniture and fittings. There wasn't a lot of choice on the board, either. Still, I wasn't there for the wine list or the ambience. I waited until the barman had served the punter on my immediate left with his cup of wine and then caught his eye.

'What can I get you, sir?' he said.

'Actually, I was looking for a Lucius Caesius,' I said. 'He come in here at all?'

The guy grinned. 'He does. In fact...' He turned towards the punter at the end of the row to my right and raised his voice. 'Hey, Lucius. You've got company.'

The punter was half-slumped over the counter on his forearms, a jug and a cup in front of him. He raised his head. I recognized the resemblance straight off, but where Quintus Caesius's silvery hair had been carefully trimmed his brother's grey equivalent looked like he'd cut it himself. Sawn at it, rather, and with a blunt knife at that. Younger brother or not, he wouldn't've passed for seventy, let alone ten years short of it. His tunic hadn't seen the inside of a fuller's for quite some time, either, and from its condition probably wouldn't survive the experience if it did.

The phrase 'human wreckage' came to mind. Well-preserved, bursting with self-respect and in good shape for his age he was not.

'Who wants me?' he said.

I made another quick inspection of the wines on offer; none of them looked very promising this time round, either. 'Make it a half jug of your best, pal,' I said to the barman. 'Whichever that is.'

'That'd be the Arician, then.'

'Arician it is.' I moved over to join what was left of Lucius Caesius and pulled up the stool next to him. 'Hi,' I said. 'The name's Marcus Corvinus.'

'Corvinus?' He gave me an uncomprehending poached-egg-eyes stare. 'Is that so?' Then he nodded. 'Oh. Right. I've got you now. You're the Roman those bastards in the senate have got to look into my brother's death. Doing the rounds of the suspects, are you?'

'More or less,' I said easily. The barman came over and set the jug and cup down beside me. I paid and poured, then held the jug poised. 'You want some of this?'

'If it's going spare, sure. Mine's dead.'

I filled his cup. 'Health,' I said, and sipped from my own. Actually, maybe I'd misjudged the place, because it wasn't bad stuff, certainly a lot better than I'd been expecting. Mind you, if you can't get a decent house wine in the Alban Hills then where else can you get it? And Aricia wasn't far away; the landlord probably had family connections with the vineyard.

Lucius took a good long swallow and wiped his mouth with the back of his hand.

'Mind if we talk?' I said.

'Suit yourself. You're buying, and I'm not doing anything special.'

I glanced behind me. There was one small table with a couple of stools, squeezed away in a corner. 'Over there?' I said. 'It's more private.'

'I'll be saying nothing that I'd be ashamed gets overheard,' he said. But he picked up his cup, levered himself off the stool and walked carefully to the table. I followed and sat down opposite him. 'Now. Talk away.'

'You weren't at the funeral,' I said.

His face with its three-day-old stubble split into something between a grin and a snarl.

He wasn't doing so well in the teeth department, either. I reckoned four or five, all told, but I might've been over-generous. 'Bugger that,' he said. 'I'd no truck with my brother when he was alive and I'll have none with him now he's dead.' He drained his cup at a gulp and edged it over in my direction. Wordlessly, I refilled it. 'Shock you, that, does it? Offend your nice Roman-patrician sensibilities? Well, disapprove all you like. I'm no hypocrite, and I don't do platitudes.' He must've noticed my expression, because he said, 'Also, I'm a drunk by choice and inclination. That doesn't mean I'm a monosyllabic oaf. So don't patronize me either, right?'

Jupiter! Talk about having a chip on your shoulder! The one this guy was carrying around was so big you could use it as a doorstop.

'I wasn't going to, pal,' I said. 'And no, it doesn't shock me at all. Still, you're his heir, aren't you?'

'Indeed I am, seemingly.' He half-emptied his newly refilled cup and smacked his lips. '*The* Caesius now. The only living representative of the family. No surprises there, then.'

'How do you mean?'

'"Concerning the dead, nothing except good." That how the old tag goes? Well, since I can't in all honesty manage the qualification without gagging I'll settle for the first option and say nothing. I can afford to, after all; I reckon I'm worth a good million-plus now, thanks to dear brother Quintus, what with his own money and my late sister-in-law's dowry, and if that means drawing a line under his sacred memory then so be it.' He belched. 'Pardon. He had his head beaten in, they tell me, coming out of our local knocking shop. That right?'

'Yeah. More or less.'

'Couldn't've happened to a better person. And that fact in itself is a glittering wonder and marvel to all who knew and loved him. Or didn't, as the case might be.' He chuckled to himself and took another swallow of wine. I said nothing. 'So. Rest his bones, whatever the truth of it. *Concerning the dead* and so on; I've no quarrel with him now. How's your investigation going? If I'm allowed to ask?'

I shrugged. 'As well as can be expected. I've just started. As you say, I'm just doing the rounds of the suspects at present.'

'That's nice. I'll tell you what.' He struggled to his feet, swaying. 'Put the interrogation on hold for a minute, will you, while I take a leak round the back. The old bladder's not what it was. I promise I won't run.'

'Sure. No problem,' I said.

'You'll excuse me, then?'

I waited while he staggered out of the door and closed it behind him. Then I got up and

118

went over to the bar.

'Yes, sir,' the barman said. 'You want the other half?'

'No. Just the answer to a quick question, pal, if you will. Four nights ago. Was Lucius in here at all, do you remember?'

He shot me a look. 'The night of his brother's murder?'

'Yeah, that's right.'

'Sure. Same as he always is, from the time we open right up until closing time. He was where you're sitting now, talking to Roscius.'

I stared at him. '*Roscius*? You mean Quintus Roscius?'

'Yeah. Farms just outside town on the Castrimoenium road.'

Shit! 'He a regular?'

'He comes in now and again.'

'Pally with Lucius?'

'Not especially, but it was a quiet night, what with the weather being so bad. They were the only two in the place.'

'Until closing time, you said. Sunset, would that be?'

'About an hour after.'

'That late?'

'I wasn't in any hurry. Lucius is a good customer, and I didn't have the heart to throw him out. My brother has an olive farm, and he lets me have the oil cheap. It's not the best stuff, third pressing standard if that, but it's good enough for the punters I get from around here. And keeping open the extra hour sometimes is good for business. These days, you have to make use of every edge you can get.'

'They leave together?'

'Yeah. When I closed up.'

'Thanks, pal.' I went back to my seat. Bugger! There went straight-as-a-die Roscius's alibi! When the bastard had told me he'd been at home the evening of the murder he'd been lying through his teeth!

Lucius came back in and sat down with a sigh. 'That's better,' he said. He topped up his cup from my jug. 'Now where were we? Oh, right. Your investigation. You've just started, you say.'

'Yeah.' No harm in putting out a few feelers and seeing if they produced any result. 'I was round at Publius Novius's earlier. The lawyer.'

'I know who Novius is. Scumbag.'

'He tells me that you were disinherited in your father's will, ten or so years back. That so?'

Lucius scowled. 'My father never made that will, Corvinus. Oh, sure, we'd had nothing to do with each other for twenty-odd years before that, but he wasn't the bastard that Quintus was. He wouldn't've done that to me, disinherited his own son.'

'Hang on,' I said carefully. 'You're saying the will was a fake?'

120

'Of course it was. It must've been. I'm telling you, my father would never have cut me off without a penny. Quintus and that slimy lawyer pal of his cooked the will up between them. Did Novius tell you I challenged it?'

'What?'

'No, he wouldn't, the canny bastard. Certainly I did. In open court. For all the good it did me.' He emptied his cup again; at this rate I'd have to get the other half jug after all, but at least it didn't seem to be having much effect. If anything, the old guy seemed to be sobering. Mind you, it was only halfway through the morning, and he was used to it. 'Novius and Quintus and their like lead the senate by the nose. They *are* the senate. And the senate provide the aediles, and the aediles do the judging. Two solid citizens and a jury stacked with their pals against a drunk with a grudge? What do you think the verdict'd be?'

Yeah, well, that was true enough, whatever the ins and outs of the rest of it: you couldn't buck the Old Boy network, whether it was in Bovillae or Rome, once they'd made their minds up about something. I took a sip of my own wine. 'Still,' I said, 'your brother carried on paying your allowance.'

'Novius told you about that as well, did he?' Lucius said sardonically. 'Talkative little shit, isn't he? Oh, yes, I got that regularly

121

enough every month, for what it was worth. Then, at least. But did he mention that Quintus had stopped it recently?'

'No. No, he didn't.'

'Fact. A couple of months ago, it was, just after Vatinia died. You know who Vatinia was?'

'Your brother's wife. Sure.'

'My brother's, as you say, *wife*.' He gave the half-grin, half-snarl and sank another mouthful of wine. 'Yes. She was OK, Vatinia. A real lady, patient and tolerant as hell. She had to be, mind, the bugger didn't deserve her. Well-off, too, in her own right. She'd money of her own, quite a bit of it, a lot more than he had, originally. When he married her, Quintus got by far the best of the deal, and not just financially. Anyway, the allowance came from her, or from the income from her own holdings. She was the one who insisted that he pay it. When she died, Quintus decided that wasn't necessary any more, so when I went to see Novius as usual on the next kalends to pick up my month's cash I got the straight finger. Still' – after pouring me a token splash, he topped up his cup with the rest of the wine in the jug – 'all's well that ends well, isn't it? Novius'll just have to grit his teeth and cough up the whole boiling. I'm all right now.'

'Yeah. You are.' He was, at that – by his own estimate, about a million sesterces all right. I picked up the cup, drained it, and got to my feet. 'Thanks for the chat. I'll see you around.'

'You leaving?' he said. Surprised, evidently, but that was his business.

'Yeah. No more questions. Interrogation done and dusted.' There was the business of his hobnobbing with Roscius the night of the murder to go into, sure, but I wanted to think that one over before I faced him with it. Roscius, too, for that matter. Besides, I'd had about enough of Brother Lucius as I could stomach for one day. Personally, my sympathies were with the dead Caesius; brother or not, the guy was a useless git, and a prime sponger. The fact that he was obviously intelligent only made things worse. 'Things to do, places to go.'

'Yeah? Where would that be, then?'

I hadn't really thought about it, but if I had I wouldn't have told him. Out of there and away from Lucius bloody Caesius was enough for me, for the time being.

So where was I going? There was still a fair slice of the day left, but I'd no one else to see, not at present, anyway, barring the rival collector (Baebius, wasn't it?) that the old guy in the antiques shop had said had gone home furious with Caesius for stealing a march on him over the purchase of a Greek figurine. I could easily go back to the shop and get his address, sure, but I reckoned that could wait; Baebius hadn't exactly sounded the type likely to hang around the back of a brothel after sunset waiting to zero his co-auction-goer in a fit of pique. Mind you, it wasn't beyond the bounds of possibility: some of these antiquities nuts were, well, nuts. Look at Priscus. No, Baebius would keep; I'd got enough to think about at present. Maybe I should just go back home, talk with Perilla and start putting things together.

Only there was one other place I could go to follow up an angle I knew about already. It probably wouldn't take long, and since I was in Bovillae in any case with time on my hands I might as well do it now. When we'd been talking about the wool store fire in the wine shop the argumentative punter (what was his name? Battus, right?) had mentioned a night watchman who lived over by the meat market. Garganius. Sextus Garganius. I might as well look him up, see what I could get.

One good thing about a small town like Bovillae, as opposed to Rome, is that everywhere's practically within spitting distance of the centre. The meat market was only a few hundred yards further along the Hinge from market square, in the direction of the Roman Gate. I cut back through the square and turned right.

124

This time of day, the market was crowded with the local wives and bought help shopping for the evening's dinner. The guy running the third stall I asked at pointed me towards a side street closer to the gate, and an old biddy trudging along the pavement lugging a string-net bag full of assorted root vegetables and chitterlings narrowed the search to the last house along, next to an oil shop on the corner. I knocked on the door and it was opened by a youngish woman holding a baby on her hip.

'Sextus Garganius live here?' I said.

'Yes.' She hefted the baby. 'Who wants him?'

'He doesn't know me,' I said. 'I just wanted a quick word, if that's OK.'

She frowned, but opened the door wider and stepped aside. 'You'd best come in, then,' she said, then shouted, 'Dad! Someone to see you!' She turned back to me. 'Go ahead. He's in the kitchen, round to the right. Excuse me, I was just going to change Quintus here.'

Yeah, I could smell that that was pretty urgent. She took the kid off to some inner fastness to repair the spreading damage while I followed her directions.

Garganius was standing next to the kitchen brazier, stirring a pot of bean stew: a little old guy with grizzled hair and a wall eye. He looked round.

'Yeah?' he said. 'Who're you?'

I gave him my name. 'It's about the fire a few months back. In the town's wool store. I understand you were the night watchman.'

His single good eye looked me over suspiciously. 'I was,' he said. 'So what?'

'I was hoping you'd tell me what happened.'

'What's to tell? The place caught fire and burned down. That's all there was to it, and you could've got that much from anyone.'

'I was talking to a guy named Battus.' No point in complicating the issue. 'He said it wasn't an accident.'

The suspicious look toned down a tad. 'I know Battus, sure. He send you here?'

'More or less. He told me where to find you, anyway. I'm looking into the death of Quintus Caesius. The censor-elect. Seemingly he was planning to open an investigation.'

That got me a grunt. 'Maybe he was,' Garganius said. 'But that isn't going to happen now, is it?'

I shrugged. 'It might. It all depends.'

'Depends on what?'

'Maybe on what you tell me.'

He went back to stirring the pot. A minute passed in silence. Then without looking at me, he said, 'You down here from Rome?'

'Sure.'

126

'Official?'

'More or less, again. Where Caesius is concerned, certainly.'

'Fine.' He nodded, like he'd made a decision. 'OK. They're saying I knocked over a lamp when I was drunk. That's a lie. I wasn't, and I didn't. Truth is, I'd nothing to do with starting the fire.'

'Who did, then?'

'Search me, pal. All I know is that I was in my cubby just inside the door as usual. Oh, I may've been dozing, sure – what do you expect at that time of night – but I was stone-cold sober. I woke up and found the place full of smoke, so I got the hell out and raised the alarm. For all the good it did. By that time the rafters'd caught and the roof was coming down.'

'This wouldn't be the burned-out warehouse just off the main drag the other side of the market square, would it? In the same street as the brothel?'

'That's right. It was lucky the place was free-standing, or the whole middle of town could've gone up. Specially at that time of year. Everything was dry as a bone.'

'Could someone have got in? To start the fire, I mean?'

'Sure. No problem, it would've been easy enough. I told you, I was inside, wasn't I? You think I locked the door behind me? And after all, who's going to steal a warehouse worth of fucking wool bales?'

'Unless they'd been stolen already.'

He gave me a long, considering look, tasted the bean stew and put the spoon back in, all without a word.

'Of course,' I went on, 'that would've been pretty difficult to cover for, during daylight hours, considering the number of bales that must've been involved.' No response. 'I mean, something on that scale would tend to get noticed, wouldn't it, during the day? A night operation, now, small loads, a bit at a time spread over a month or two, single-cart stuff, early hours of the morning, well, that'd be different.' Still silence. 'Come on, pal! If that was how it was done then you must've known all about it from start to finish. And if so you're up the proverbial creek without a paddle. Now, I don't want to make trouble, especially for the little guy who probably had his arm twisted and only got a handful of silver pieces out of it. I'm not even a fucking Bovillan citizen, for the gods' sake. Arson's not my business; I couldn't care less about a little thing like that. What is my business, however, is murder. All I want is to get the facts straight so I can get on with my job. Clear?'

He took a deep breath. 'OK, fair enough,' he said. 'Let's say – just for argument's sake – that most of the wool was already gone and what was in nine tenths of the bales was rags;

that I may've suspected it, but I didn't know for certain because I made damn sure that I didn't; that I had nothing to do with the switch; and that you forget you were here talking to me. No names, no pointing fingers, and no comeback, right? I'm just a dumb watchman who doesn't know zilch. That do you?'

'Yeah,' I said. 'I'll settle for that.'

'Good. We have a deal.' He went back to stirring the pot. 'Mind you, putting me in the frame wasn't nice. I don't like that. The guy who had the wool contract. Name begins with "M". You know who I'm talking about?'

'Yeah. Yeah, I know.'

'Well, he might be able to help with a few facts, too. I'm not saying he will, you understand, just that he might. Only a suggestion. Fair enough?'

'Fair enough,' I said. 'Thanks, pal.' I turned to go.

'Not a word, right? And it stops here?'

'Sure,' I said. 'Cross my heart. Thanks again.'

Well, I reckoned I'd got enough to be going on with. Back to the water trough by the Tiburtine Gate where I'd moored my horse, and then home for a think.

On my way along the main drag, I thought I spotted my pal the lounging freedman walking parallel to me on the opposite pavement. But he was only one face in a crowd, and I could've been wrong.

There again, there weren't any flying pigs.

NINE

Bathyllus was waiting for me with a cup of wine when I got back. No sign of Lupercus. Oh, yeah; the demarcation arrangements. Silly, like I said, but there you went, that was the bought help for you; these guys aren't on the same wavelength. Anything for a quiet life.

'Truce still holding, pal?' I said, taking the cup and handing him my wet cloak in exchange.

'Yes, sir, thank you.'

'See that it does, OK?'

'Yes, sir. The family are having lunch in the dining room.'

I took the cup through.

'You're home early, dear,' Perilla said when I'd kissed her.

'Yeah.' I settled down on the couch beside her. 'No problems, I just thought I'd done enough for the day. And, like you said, we're on holiday, so there's no point in overdoing things, is there?'

Smarm, smarm.

'So how are things going?' Clarus asked.

I helped myself to cold pork, bread, olives and cheese (Euclidus didn't take his cheffing duties as seriously as Meton did, at least where lunch was concerned, so as usual we were getting yesterday's dinner leftovers padded out with sundries from the store cupboard) and gave them the usual run-down of the morning's events.

'There you are, Clarus,' Marilla said with huge satisfaction. 'I told you the fire was a scam.'

Clarus shrugged.

'It looks like it, sure,' I said, reaching for my wine cup. 'But that's not to say it's connected with the murder. Whether or not Manlius – or his pal Canidius, or both of them together – would go to the lengths of killing Caesius just to stop an investigation and avoid a theft and arson charge is a moot point.'

'I don't agree at all, Marcus,' Perilla said. 'Not if they thought the investigation was a certainty and that the outcome was a foregone conclusion. The punishment for arson and theft on that scale would be relegation, or at least a crippling fine.' She spooned a reheated chicken dumpling on to her plate. 'In any case, you're forgetting the social side of things. You know how people's minds work in these small towns. If they were convicted, the disgrace would destroy them in Bovillae, socially and politically, and for men of their standing that would be far worse. No, dear, I'd say the motive was quite sufficient.'

'Yeah. Maybe so.' I took a swallow of the Alban; after the Arician I'd had in the wine shop it went past the tonsils like velvet. 'Still, there're plenty of other candidates with motives just as good or better.'

'You're getting very cautious in your old age.'

I nudged her in the ribs with my elbow. 'Less of the old age, lady!' Perilla's got a clear eighteen months on me. 'And I'm not being cautious, I'm being realistic. We haven't touched opportunity. What Manlius and Canidius were doing at the time of the murder we don't know yet, but at present where having the chance to belt Caesius as he was coming out of the brothel's concerned, his brother and Quintus Roscius are the front runners, no doubt. Me, I'd put my money on Roscius. Losing his farm would hit him hard, and he's a lot more physically capable of doing the murder than Lucius is.'

'So how would it've worked in practice?' Marilla was carefully putting together what was at least her third pork-and-pickle sandwich: the girl likes her food, always has done. 'The murder itself, I mean.'

'Marilla, dear,' Perilla said. 'I really don't think you should get too much involved in all this. It isn't proper.' She turned to me.

'And Marcus, you shouldn't be encouraging her.'

Marilla paused in the sandwich-construction process long enough to stick out her tongue before reaching for a third slice of pork to add to the pile. I grinned: *proper* wasn't exactly a word I'd ever have used in connection with our adopted daughter. We might not be related by blood, but there was a lot of me in the kid, and given her head she was a natural-born sleuth. As, indeed, was Perilla, if she'd only knuckle down and admit it.

Apropos of which...

'Come on, lady!' I said. 'Give the girl a break!'

'Very well, if you insist.' Perilla sniffed. 'Have it your own way, dear, as usual. But understand it's under protest.'

'Protest noted. For what it's worth.' I drained my cup and refilled it from the jug on the table. 'OK. So, to the actual murder. No problems there, the scenario's obvious. No premeditation, just sheer luck. Roscius comes out of the wine shop and sets off for home. He glances down the alleyway as he passes, sees Caesius coming out of the brothel at the far end, and decides to take the chance he's offered. He hustles the guy back in and brains him.' I took a swallow of wine. 'Job done.'

'What with?' Clarus said absently, looking

up from the olive he was dissecting.

I put the cup down. 'How do you mean, *what with*, pal?'

'Look.' Clarus sighed. 'He'd have had to use a weapon of some kind, yes?'

'Yeah, well, naturally. So?'

'So where did he get it from? Or do you think he was carrying a club on the off-chance?'

Bugger. There spoke the nit-picking wannabe forensics expert. 'How the hell should I know?' I said. 'Maybe there was an iron bar or a loose tile or something lying around. Me, I can't see that it matters all that much.'

'Was there? And if so could he see it in the dark? There wasn't much of a moon that night, and it was raining hard. Did he take it away with him, and if so why? And while we're on the subject, given the general lighting and weather conditions, how did he know it was Caesius? Especially since it's likely the man had his hood up.'

Jupiter bloody Best and Greatest, I didn't believe this! And I'd thought Perilla was bad where splitting hairs was concerned! 'Now look here...' I said.

'Actually, Clarus, he could've done it with his bare hands,' Marilla said. 'Oh, the recognition bit, you're right, dear, that is a difficulty. But if he were a big man ... is he, Corvinus?'

'Uh, yeah.' I frowned; things were slipping

135

away from me rapidly here. 'Pretty big.'

'Fine. Then he could've picked Caesius up and smashed his head against the wall.' She was still looking at Clarus. 'That would've had the same result, wouldn't it?'

Clarus nodded. 'Yes, it would. It'd take a lot of strength, mind, and I'd've had to see the wound to be sure one way or the other, but yes, it's theoretically possible.'

'It might even have been an accident. At least, the actual braining aspect of things.'

'True. True.'

Perilla had been looking at them, from one to the other, in growing disbelief, and I could just sense the ice crystals forming in the air and the spiders frantically legging it for cover. She opened her mouth to say something, but I got in first.

'Fine,' I said. 'OK. So let's leave Roscius and move on to Brother Lucius, yes? Same scenario and provisos apply, right?'

'Wrong,' Clarus said.

'*What?* Why?'

'Corvinus, Lucius is an old man. Oh, yes, he could've killed Caesius, given a weapon, but not in the way Marilla describes. At least, I don't think so. So in his case we're back to the weapon problem.'

'It could've been both of them, of course,' Marilla said, ruminatively taking another bite of her sandwich. 'After all, they left the wine shop together, didn't they?'

'Yeah, they did,' I said. It was a fair point, and it'd make sense, too: both would've had to walk past the alleyway to get where they were headed, Lucius to his room above the bakery and Roscius because it was in the direction of the Tiburtine Gate, so the chances were that if they'd left the wine shop in company when they got to the alley they'd still be together. And if they'd just spent the evening slagging off their mutual bugbear Caesius, which seemed the most likely topic of conversation between the pair of them, then the bond of solidarity would already have been forged...

Uh-huh. I'd go for that, certainly as a working theory. I turned to Perilla. 'What do you think, lady? Possible?'

She reached for her cup of fruit juice.

'It might be,' she said frostily. 'I'm not going to speculate, dear. The three of you seem to be managing quite well enough already on that score without me becoming involved.'

I shrugged. 'OK, suit yourself, sourpuss. But as a scenario, it's valid. Lucius certainly has motive and to spare in his own right. Double motive, in fact: with Vatinia's death he's now his brother's only heir, and he's just been told by Novius that Caesius is cutting him loose altogether, money-wise. I'd say by the looks of the guy when I talked to him he was living right on the edge already, and without his monthly allowance he'd be up the financial creek good and proper.' I frowned. 'That's an angle worth looking into, by the way. From what he said – or hinted at, anyway – most of the family's income as such was his sister-in-law's rather than Caesius's. Campaigning for censor – particularly against a seriously well-off guy like Manlius, desperate for the job – won't have been cheap. Me, I'd like to know for completeness' sake exactly how the woman died.'

Perilla set her cup down. 'Marcus, that is sheer nonsense!' she snapped. 'You have absolutely no grounds whatsoever for even *thinking* that Caesius might have killed Vatinia! Nothing we know about the man suggests that he'd be capable of anything like that; they'd been married for over thirty years, happily, or reasonably so, as far as we know or can assume, and he was a long-term politician. Of course she'd support him financially in running for office! As his wife, what else would she do?'

I smothered a smile. Got you! I knew she couldn't keep it up. Which was partly why I'd let loose that particular lame hare in the first place. Mind you, lame or not the theory was something worth checking, just on the off-chance. I've always been suspicious of so-called 'ordinary' deaths that happen too close to murders. Also, more important now

I came to think of it, Caesius as the perp wasn't the only possibility. If Lucius had planned to kill his brother in pursuit of his inheritance, to get where he was going he would've had to take Vatinia out of the picture as a first stage...

'Fine,' I said. 'Point taken, lady. Maybe it was a bit over the top, at that.'

'Well, then!'

'If we're working through the suspects, what about the nephew?' Marilla said. 'Mettius, wasn't it?'

'Yeah.' I picked up my wine cup and took a contemplative swallow. 'He's a distinct possible, too. If he's on the level about his uncle and Caesius's dodgy legal pal Novius cooking up the charge between them that got him relegated, then he's got good reason to bear a grudge. Plus, of course, he's only recently come back to the town, so the timing fits.'

'That's a bit odd in itself, isn't it?' Marilla said. 'I mean, if it was me Bovillae would be the last place I'd choose to live, even when I could go back. He isn't exactly popular locally, is he?'

I nodded. 'Right. Oh, sure, from what I know his mother's still there, but there'd be nothing else to bring him. Quite the reverse. So why take the trouble to come where he's not wanted, unless he reckons he's got unfinished business?'

'Maybe he wanted to make his peace,' Clarus said. 'Bury the hatchet.'

'From the impression I got, pal, the only place he'd want to do that was in his uncle's head. With Novius for seconds. Which may well be what he did, more or less. The guy's fully capable of it, if I'm any judge.'

'But why should Caesius and Novius want to fabricate a charge against him in the first place?' Marilla again.

I turned to Perilla. 'You like to answer that one?' I said easily.

She frowned. 'Well, it's obvious, isn't it? At least, the simple explanation is. Lucius claimed his father's will disinheriting him was a forgery. It was. Mettius was working for Novius at the time. He found out and tried to blackmail the guilty parties, so they got rid of him. And we all know, don't we, from past experience, that Novius has been involved before in dubious practices concerning a will. Not directly, admittedly, and it was suppression rather than actual forgery, but still.'

I smiled to myself. It worked every time: give Perilla a chance to show how smart she is and she can't resist it. Oh, it had taken a while on this occasion, sure, and it had been touch-and-go in places, but the lady had cracked in the end. It looked as if we had her with us on the team after all.

She was all right, Perilla, at base. Besides,

140

I'd known that she knew the answer as well as I did.

'Yeah,' I said. 'That's more or less how I saw things. Proving it, mind, is another story, and Mettius himself isn't saying. Which is fair enough if the blackmail side holds good.'

'But why should he do it?' Clarus said. 'Novius, I mean. Surely he'd be taking a terrible risk? If the truth got out then he'd be facing criminal charges himself. Caesius, too. As with Manlius and Canidius, socially at least as far as Bovillae was concerned they'd both be finished.'

'Sure they would,' I said. 'No arguments there, let alone explanations. Still, it's a lead to be followed.' I reached for the wine jug and poured myself more of the Alban. 'Getting back to Mettius himself, though, there's one more thing that makes him a prime contender.'

'Which is?'

'He's the only one on the list, as far as we know, at least, definitely to patronize the brothel. That gives him opportunity in spades, even more so than Roscius and Lucius had. If Mettius was the killer, then it clears the ground of a lot of dead wood. He could've been there, on the inside, the night his uncle was killed and seen him leave. He could even have planned the murder in advance, if he knew Caesius would be a visitor.'

'But surely that would mean the likelihood

that the brothel owner was involved.' Perilla was twisting her lock of hair. 'Andromeda, wasn't it? And if so then why should she be?'

'Pass, lady,' I said. 'Another lead to follow. They're friendly, sure – they were together at the funeral – but whether enough to warrant her helping out with a murder is as much your guess as mine. Also, it wouldn't have been strictly necessary. Oh, sure, on her part there's the professional confidentiality angle, but you can get round that, easy. She couldn't be responsible for her staff, and if the girl I talked to was anything to go by they're not the sharpest knives in the drawer. A word in the wrong place from one of them would've been enough. Still, it's early days yet. There's a lot of digging to do before we're done.' I looked round; Bathyllus and Lupercus had just come in. 'Hi, little guy.'

'We were just wondering if we could clear away, sir,' Bathyllus said. 'If you're finished, that is.'

'Sure. Go ahead.' We waited while they loaded the dishes on to trays, studiously – I noticed – ignoring each other. Bathyllus removed my plate and Perilla's; Lupercus did the same with Clarus's and Marilla's. The serving ones were carefully shared, turn about. I sighed: truce it might be, but it was an uneasy one, and well on the childish side at that. Fun, fun, fun.

'There's one person you haven't mentioned, Marcus,' Perilla said when they'd gone. 'The antiques collector.'

'Oh, yeah. Baebius,' I said. 'That's because I still don't know anything about him, barring what his freedman in the shop told me. I was planning to get his address tomorrow, pay him a visit, see how much in the running he actually is. Mind you, I'm not hopeful. The guy sounds like another Priscus. Can you imagine Priscus stalking a rival collector and beating his skull in? Because I can't. Mother, now, sure.'

'That's not fair, dear. Vipsania's a perfectly charming woman, even though she can be a little ... overpowering at times.' *Overpowering!* Me, I'd back Mother against a German berserker swinging a battle-axe any day. She would probably insist he go back outside and wipe his feet. Get her way, too. 'And you may be surprised. Not all collectors are as harmless as Priscus.'

Yeah, true. We'd just have to wait and see what tomorrow brought. In the meantime, I thought I deserved a quiet afternoon, maybe involving a stroll into town and a gossip with the punters at Pontius's wine shop.

I was on holiday, after all. Sleuthing isn't everything.

TEN

I had a leisurely breakfast the next morning before heading into Bovillae as usual. It wasn't far, sure, but I don't ride by choice, and covering the eight or so miles there and back was becoming a pretty tiresome routine.

I parked the horse by the market square water trough and set off gratefully on my own two feet. First things first: Baebius's address. I called in at the antiques shop, renewed my acquaintance with the old freedman who ran it, and came away with directions: Baebius, it seemed, lived up at the top of town, near the Alban Lake Gate.

Before talking to the possibly homicidal antiquities collector, though, I wanted another word with Caesius's major-domo, Anthus, regarding the death of his ex-mistress. Oh, the probability was that everything was above board – I'd only made the suggestion that it might not be to rattle Perilla's cage, and the dead woman must've been getting on a bit – but it was worth making sure. Also, there was the question of the will

144

to pursue.

So it was the Caesius place again first, further along the Hinge. The door slave showed me through to the atrium – the ordinary couches had been put back, now the funeral was over – and Anthus came in a couple of minutes later, wearing his squeaky-clean new freedman's cap.

'Good morning, sir,' he said. 'A pleasure to see you again. Presumably I can help you in some way?'

'Yeah,' I said. 'I'm sorry to bother you again so soon, pal, but I needed some more information from you, if you can give it to me.'

'Certainly. Although I'm afraid as far as the master's death goes I can't think what else I can tell you.'

'Actually, it was your late mistress I was interested in. Vatinia, wasn't it?'

He looked nonplussed. 'The mistress, sir? Why on earth would you be asking about her?'

'As I said, I'm just getting as many background details as I can. Indulge me, will you?'

'If you insist. But...'

'She was younger than your master, was she?'

'By a few years, yes, but not many. Four or five, I think.'

'And they were married for, what, thirty-five years, wasn't it?'

'That's correct, sir.'

'So she must've been well into her twenties at the time? Isn't that a bit late for a marriage?'

'The lady had been married previously, but her first husband had died. A summer fever. That marriage was childless, too.'

'So she was a wealthy widow, right?'

'Moderately wealthy.' He was beginning to give me funny looks, and I wondered how far I could push this without him clamming up on me. 'She was from a good family in Aricia, and her former husband owned quite a bit of property in Rome which of course she inherited at his death. He and the master had known each other through their shared business interests for some considerable time, so naturally their relationship was a long-standing one.'

'Fine.' I paused; this next bit was the really tricky part. 'Her, uh, death three months ago come as a surprise, at all?'

He frowned, but answered readily enough. 'No, except that it was so long delayed. The mistress was never a well lady, even when she was first married. Her heart was weak, and in the last ten years or so she was a chronic invalid. The doctor said it was a marvel she lasted as long as she did.'

Hell. That scotched that idea, then, at least as anything but an outside bet: thirty-five years was thirty-five years, and if Caesius had married her with an eye to her money knowing she was a bit tottery on her perch and not been averse to giving her a shove he'd taken his time in doing it. And if the death was a natural one it put the mockers on any involvement on Lucius's part, too. Still, it made for one oddity. 'I understand from your master's lawyer, Publius Novius, that he hadn't made a will to replace the original one of thirty-odd years back, naming her as his heir,' I said. 'Is that right?'

'Yes. To the best of my knowledge.'

'You don't find that a little unusual? After all, the chances were that he'd outlive her.'

Anthus was still frowning. 'It's not my place to say, sir. Or within my competence.'

'Maybe not. But you're the best person to ask. And it might be important.'

'Very well. If it will help, then certainly.' He hesitated, as if he was choosing his words carefully. 'He ... the master was a deeply private man, with very few friends. I don't mean that in a derogatory way, not at all; it's a simple fact. Oh, he was certainly no recluse; he had a great number of acquaintances, and he and the mistress when she was alive and able had a very busy social life. But none of them, even the closest, were really intimate, if you understand me.' I nodded. 'They were most of them very much part of his public rather than his private life.

And to the master, sir, as you must always remember, his public life was everything. As far as family went, apart from the mistress there was no one at all close. Quite the opposite, as you know yourself.'

'Meaning his brother and his nephew.'

'Exactly.' He ducked his head. 'I'm sorry. I'm being long-winded and possibly unclear, but what I'm saying really does answer your question. The result of all this was that, although he may have recognized that not to make another will was short-sighted at best, there was no one – family member or close friend – whom he could conscientiously name as heir.'

Yeah; that was more or less what Novius had told me. Even so...

'Even so,' I said aloud, 'the result's been that his brother inherits the property. Which, naturally, would now include your mistress's estate as well.'

'Indeed.'

'He must've known that would happen, and the two of them had no time for each other. Your master, so Lucius tells me, had even cancelled his allowance recently. Yet he deliberately let things slide, meaning his brother gets the whole boiling after all, both his money and his late wife's. I'm sorry, pal, but to me that doesn't make any sort of sense.'

Anthus hesitated again. 'May I speak freely? Far more freely than I have a right to do?'

'Sure. Go ahead.'

'It's only an idea that I have. I've nothing to base it on, and certainly nothing the master ever said to me, or in my presence, confirms it. Quite the opposite. But I did serve him all my working life, and I knew him as well as it was possible for any man. I truly think that Quintus Caesius wanted his brother to inherit. Certainly should the mistress predecease him, which as I said was more than likely.'

He'd fazed me. 'Uh ... come again, pal?' I said.

'It may be difficult to believe, sir. But personally I'm convinced it's the absolute truth. The master put off making a will deliberately so that if he died first then everything would go to Lucius.'

'Anthus, that makes no sense either! If he'd wanted the guy to be his heir beyond any legal doubt he'd have written a will to that effect. It'd be simple enough.'

The major-domo shook his head. 'No, sir. Quintus Caesius would never, ever have done that, not under any circumstances. You misunderstand.' He smiled. 'Frankly, I'm not sure I understand myself, and it's difficult even to put into words. You didn't know the master, so of course what I'm saying wouldn't make sense to you, but trust me it does. Despite what he said to anyone, me

149

and the mistress included, I'm convinced that he felt responsible for his brother.'

'Responsible?'

'For how he'd turned out, how he led his life. I hesitate to use the words "guilt" and "atonement", but I must. Although please keep in mind that he had – and knew he had – absolutely nothing concrete to feel guilty about or atone for. That's just the point.'

'I'm sorry,' I said. 'You've lost me completely.'

'Perhaps it's the difference between active and passive action, sir, if there is such a term. Believe me: the master disliked and despised his brother, completely and utterly. There's absolutely no doubt about that. He was also, in many ways, a hard-minded man, and as such had no desire to make things easy for him while he himself was alive. Quite the contrary, as his decision to terminate the allowance shows. On the other hand, if he could make amends simply by doing *nothing*, taking no action whatsoever, and leaving things to fate, then that was a different thing. Or perhaps he considered it as such.' He paused. 'I'm sorry, sir, I know I'm not expressing myself clearly, but it's the best I can do. Perhaps it's nonsense after all.'

'No,' I said slowly. 'Cock-eyed, sure, but not nonsense.' *Leaving things to fate*. Yeah, that was one way of putting it. Me, given what was at stake, I'd rather go for *tempting fate* where Brother Lucius was concerned. 'His father's will. The one that disinherited Lucius. You know about that?'

'Of course.'

'It was, uh, on the level, then?'

He frowned. 'I'm afraid I don't know what you mean.'

'The old guy – Marcus Caesius, senior – he actually made it?'

'Naturally, he did.'

'You're sure?'

'I never saw the actual document, sir, but the old master certainly intended to disinherit his son when he was in the process of writing it. I heard him say so myself. And it was formally witnessed.'

Damn. 'Who by? Can you remember?'

'Two of his business associates. Gaius Tucca and Lucius Ampudius.'

'They still around?'

'Tucca, no, sir. He died some five years ago. But Ampudius is still alive.'

'Where would I find him?'

'His house is up by the Alban Lake Gate, on the public baths side.'

Well, that was handy, at least. I could fit him in along with Baebius. 'Fine. Thanks, pal. I think that's about all for the moment.' I turned to go. 'No, it isn't. You know a guy called Quintus Baebius?'

'Oh, yes. But by name only. He's never set foot in the house, nor had the master in his, although he often talked about him. Not in complimentary terms. They were rival collectors – I think I told you about the master's hobby? I'm afraid I know no more about him than that.'

'I was told they had a head-to-head over buying a figurine two months back, and that Baebius lost out. That right?'

Anthus nodded. 'Perfectly correct, sir. A very fine Hellenistic bronze of a runner removing a thorn from his foot.'

'You think I could see it?'

'Of course. It's in the study. If you'd like to come through?'

I followed him. He opened the door and went over to one of the display shelves, then stopped.

'Something wrong?' I said.

He was looking blank. 'Now that is very curious. Very curious indeed. It isn't there.'

'*What?*'

He pointed to an empty space on the shelf. 'That's where it was, sir. But it's gone.'

'When did you last see it?'

'The day of the master's death. In the morning, when I did the dusting. I haven't been in here since, except when we had our talk. And then I can't say whether it was here or not.'

'Would someone have taken it since?'

'Not to my knowledge, sir. The room has not been entered. It's a mystery, I'm afraid.'

Yeah, I'd agree with him there. 'OK, pal,' I said. 'Leave it for now. Thanks again for your help. I'll see myself out.' I paused. 'Oh, incidentally. Brother Lucius. When does he move in?'

'The day after tomorrow, sir, or so I understand. I'll be staying on until then, but one of the other members of the household staff will be taking on my duties. Temporarily, at least.'

'You going to stay with your baker girlfriend?'

'That's right. We're being married straight away.'

'Good luck, then. Oh' – I took out my purse and removed a gold piece – 'maybe you can buy yourself a wedding present.'

'That's very generous of you, Valerius Corvinus. And good luck to you. I'll sleep easier when my master's killer is found. He was a decent man, at heart.'

Yeah, well, I'd heard worse obituaries. And coming from a guy like Anthus, short as it was, it had weight, more so than Manlius's public eulogy.

I left.

ELEVEN

So, to Quintus Baebius. And with the new development regarding the missing statuette I now had something definite to ask him about. The business with Caesius Senior's will had been a facer, though. I'd been convinced – as Perilla had – that there was something screwy about it, and where it left us vis-à-vis Mettius as a suspect I couldn't think. Still, I had the name and address of one of the witnesses, so at least I could make a confirmatory check.

I made my way up towards the Alban Lake Gate. Baebius, it transpired, lived in a very tidy property on the street that ran along the inside of the town wall, one of several similar tidy properties in what was obviously a prime residential district. There was a young slave outside, polishing the brass door knocker, so I gave him my name and waited in the atrium while he went to enquire whether the master was receiving.

Caesius's collecting rival wasn't strapped for cash, that was for sure: if the house's setting hadn't shown me that already, there was a very nice mural of the Judgement of Paris on the wall that from the quality of the artwork must've cost a packet, and three or four life-size bronzes which were either originals or first-rate copies. I was examining the one which had been given pride of place in front of the peristyle opening – a young Bacchus, holding up a bunch of grapes to Eros on his shoulder – when the man himself came in.

'Valerius Corvinus,' he said. 'I'm very pleased to meet you. Do sit down and make yourself comfortable. A cup of wine, perhaps? It's not too early for you?'

'Not at all,' I said. 'That'd be great.'

Cultured voice, mid to late forties, fit-looking despite the small paunch evident under the cover of his lounging tunic. Totally at ease, and very sure of himself. Antiquities nut Baebius might well prove to be, but one along the lines of Priscus he wasn't: Perilla had it right there. This was a guy in the prime of life who was socially confident and kept himself in good physical shape. I sat down on the nearest couch. That was impressive, too; one of a matching set of three that could've come over with Lucius Mummius two hundred years back, after he'd sacked Corinth for us.

The young slave I'd met at the door and who'd gone to fetch his master had come in at his heels. Baebius turned to him.

'Clitus? Wine, please, if you'd be so good,' he said. 'And some of those Alexandrian dates.' Well, that probably explained the paunch. Still, he had to have some weaknesses. The slave bowed and left. 'You're from Rome, Corvinus, I understand?'

'Yeah, that's right. Staying over with family in Castrimoenium for the festival.'

'I visit there quite often. Rome, I mean.'

'Business or pleasure?'

'Both, generally.' He smiled. 'Oh, nothing very demanding or wearying where the first's concerned. Quite the reverse. I've business interests in the city, yes, but I'm in the fortunate position of being largely a man of leisure and independent means. I'm ashamed to admit that what few business interests I have are really only an excuse for the frequency of the visits. A pleasant excuse, mind, because they do have a close connection with my private hobby.'

'Buying and selling antiques?'

His eyes widened. 'You know, then? Or was it an educated guess? But of course it wasn't; that's why you're here. You were talking to Nausiphanes the other day, I understand, and he gave you my name.'

'If he's the old freedman who manages the shop you own near market square, then yeah, that's right. I was in there buying a present for my stepfather, Helvius Priscus. You know him?'

'Priscus? No, not really, although we have met. An expert on the Etruscan period, isn't he?'

'Yeah, that's him.'

'It's not an area I'm particularly interested in as a collector, although if you like that sort of thing it produced some very fine pieces. I hope Nausiphanes gave you a good price. What did you buy?'

'Nothing too expensive. An ivory plaque.'

'Ah. One of the Sicilian ones, I suppose. Yes, they are rather nice, aren't they?' The slave came back with a loaded tray. Baebius smiled at him. 'Thank you, my boy. Just pour for us and leave us to it, if you will. The wine's Greek, I'm afraid, Corvinus. Pramnian. I prefer Greek wines, myself. A little idiosyncratic, perhaps even downright blasphemous, considering where we are, but the Alban ones are a little too forthright for my taste. See what you think.'

The slave gave me the cup, and I sipped. Too much on the perfumed side for me, but I couldn't complain about the quality, which was top-of-the-range. Only to be expected, I supposed: I was beginning to realize that Quintus Baebius didn't do second-rate. 'Very nice,' I said.

The slave handed Baebius his own cup, put the tray with the wine flask – antique Corinthian again, and solid silver – within reach, together with the tray of stuffed dates, bowed and went back out.

'Now,' Baebius said. 'To business. How can I help you? It's about that fellow Caesius's death, obviously, I know that, but beyond the simple fact I'm at a bit of a loss. Nausiphanes will have told you that we weren't on friendly terms, certainly, which is no doubt why you're here talking to me, but I'm afraid there's no more to it than that.'

'You had a disagreement a couple of months ago,' I said. 'Over a figurine?'

'Ah.' He laughed. 'Nausiphanes told you about the Runner, then, did he? My, what an old gossip he is! Well, it's true enough. A small bronze, yes, a beautiful little piece, made in Pergamum in the time of the first Attalus, probably by Epigonus or one of his better pupils. It was part of the estate of old Plautius Silvanus, who died in the summer, and Caesius had the good fortune to acquire it.'

'Before the auction.'

'Yes. Hardly ethical on his part, and very annoying, but there you are.'

'Nausiphanes said you were ... the word he used was "livid".'

Baebius took a careful sip of his wine before replying. 'He exaggerates,' he said. 'I wasn't pleased, certainly, in fact I was quite upset at the time – as I say, that is *not* how things are done in the antiques business – but "livid" is putting it far too strongly.'

158

I let that one go. 'And you'd be surprised to know that the thing's disappeared, would you?'

He gave me a sharp look. 'I certainly would. When did this happen?'

'According to Caesius's major-domo, sometime between the day of the murder and now. He can't explain it.'

'And nor can I, Valerius Corvinus, if that's what you're implying. I've never been inside Quintus Caesius's house in all the years I've known him, nor he in mine.'

'Yeah, so the major-domo said. It's a puzzle, right enough. Still, who else would be interested in it apart from you?'

'Oh, now, hold on a moment.' He'd set down his wine cup, and there was more than a touch of steel in his voice underlying the polite, civilized tone. 'You think I stole it? Or acquired it illegally by some means? Because if you do—'

'Look,' I said easily. 'All I'm interested in are the circumstances of Caesius's death, right? If the missing figurine has no connection with that, then fine, but I need to know one way or the other. Or to find out. Which, believe me, I will, eventually.'

'Now you look.' Baebius stood up; the steel was in his eyes, now, and the politeness was gone. 'I'm not used to being called a thief, let alone being accused by implication of murder. Certainly not in my own house by a guest who has invited himself in here. Nevertheless, I give you my word – and I'll swear to it, if you like – that it is not now and never has been in my possession. Now I'd be grateful if you'd leave, please. Good day to you.'

'Fair enough.' I set my own wine cup down carefully on the table beside me and got to my feet. 'That's that, then. Thanks for your time.'

I walked off towards the lobby. I'd reached the entrance to it and was heading through towards the front door when he called out: 'Corvinus!'

I looked round. 'Yeah?'

'Just a moment.'

I came back into the atrium. He was still standing there, frowning.

'I can't let you go like this,' he said. 'And perhaps I was rude in my turn, or at least a little abrupt. If so then I'm sorry. You have your job to do, and I should have taken that into consideration. Sit down, please.' I did; he did the same, and took a deep breath. 'Caesius sent me a note, the day he died. In it he said he was willing to let me have the Runner in exchange for a piece which I own – of the same date and quality, and by the same artist, a small bronze of a fisherman – plus a sum in cash; he'd bid against me for it a year or so ago, and on that occasion I was the one who'd been successful. Sheer opportunistic profiteering on his part, of course, since the pieces were of equal merit and value, and the sum of money he demanded was not small. If I agreed, he said, we could meet on neutral ground that evening and make the trade.'

'Isn't that a bit odd?' I said. 'Why not arrange to meet here, or at his place?'

'I told you, we've never been inside each other's houses. A point of pride. Call it childishness, if you like.' I did. 'Besides, the offer was in no way an overture for reconciliation, or made in friendship: it was purely a business deal, and not a fair one, at that.'

'But you agreed?'

'Yes. And sent him a reply to that effect. He had, he said, another appointment that evening – in retrospect, of course, I now know where and what that was – and that he'd make the exchange at sunset at the old wool store. That's the warehouse which burned down, behind the main street. You know it?' I nodded. 'In the event, he never turned up, and I came straight back home. That, Corvinus, is the truth. All of it.'

Yeah, well, it sounded plausible enough, allowing for the silly cloak-and-dagger business, and even that I could see happening. Just. Whether it was the truth or not, mind, was another thing entirely.

'OK,' I said, getting up again. 'Thanks for your help. And your candour.'

'You're very welcome. My apologies again for my bad manners, although I hope you can see the reason for them.' He stood. 'I'll see you out.'

'No, that's fine. I can manage. Thanks again. Oh ... just out of interest. The missing figurine. How much would it have been worth?'

'Caesius paid fifteen thousand for it, and it was worth at least a third more again. As I said, a beautiful piece. Not unique, but certainly very rare.'

I whistled: twenty thousand was a lot of gravy in anyone's book.

I went through the lobby and opened the front door. Clitus had gone back to polishing the knocker. He stepped back as I came out and smiled, and I paused before moving past him.

'Just a couple of questions before I go, pal,' I said quietly. 'You remember a note sent to your master six days back, from the censor-elect Quintus Caesius?' The smile faded, and he looked wary, which was understandable; if the guy knew nothing of the murder and when it had happened by this time, he was the only person in Bovillae who didn't. 'No hassle, no comeback. I'm just confirming what your master's just told me, that's all.'

The smile returned, with a look of relief. 'Then, yes, sir, of course I do,' he said. 'Early afternoon, it was. One of his slaves

162

brought it, and I took it to the master myself.'

'And delivered the reply?'

'Yes, sir. Half an hour or so later, to the
gentleman's house near the Arician Gate.'

'You happen to know what the contents
were? Of either note?'

'No, sir. Of course not. That was none of
my business, and naturally they were sealed.'

Fair enough. Still, it'd been worth asking.
'OK.' Second point. 'Your master also told
me he went out that evening. Just before
sunset.'

'That's right. He did.' The wariness was
back now.

'He say where he was going at all?'

'No, sir,' he said, stiffly. 'Again, it was not
my place to ask. But he came back an hour
later. Perhaps a little less.'

And Caesius had been in the brothel busy
with his 'other appointment' until a good
hour after sunset. Baebius – if he was the
murderer – wouldn't've had either the
opportunity or the time to kill the guy and
get all the way back up here to the Alban
Lake Gate, not even if Clitus's estimation
was well short of the reality. Damn! There
went a prime suspect, right at the start!

I'd give a lot to know why Caesius hadn't
showed, mind. And to know what had happened to the figurine, because the odds were
that when he left home he'd had it with him.

163

'Thanks, friend,' I said. 'Oh ... by the way. You wouldn't happen to know where Lucius Ampudius lives, would you?'

'Certainly, sir.' He pointed along the street. 'That way, past the crossroads and before the baths.'

'Thanks again.'

So. One suspect down, but there were still plenty in the bag, and after my conversation with Anthus, Brother Lucius – with or without his drinking crony Roscius's help – was a prime contender. Plus there was the question of possible skulduggery on our dodgy lawyer's part to consider.

I went to talk to the witness of old Marcus Caesius's will.

Ampudius must've been about the same age as Novius, or even older, which practically put him in the Priscus league. Even so, there was nothing frail or decrepit about the guy. Bald as a coot, sure, seriously lacking in teeth and wizened as a six-month-old apple, but the eyes that were giving me a considering look from where he lay on the atrium couch were bright and sharp as needles.

'Marcus Caesius, hey?' he said when I'd told him why I was there. 'Now there's a name from the past! Yes, I witnessed his will, me and Gaius Tucca, gods rest him. About fifteen years back, that would've been.'

'Did you read it?' I said.

'Of course I did! You fooling me, boy? Marcus insisted on it, said he didn't want anyone querying the thing when he was dead and burned, meaning that no-use second son of his. Quite rightly so, as it turned out, for all the good it did him.' He chuckled. 'He was a canny bugger in his time, was old Marcus, one of the best. You didn't get much past Marcus Caesius.'

'So he definitely disinherited Lucius? You're sure about that, sir?'

'Nothing wrong with my memory, son. I was in the banking business for sixty years, good at it, too, never mislaid a copper piece and practically carried the ledgers around in my head. When I start forgetting things as important as the content of wills you can shovel me into an urn and put the lid on.' He raised his voice. 'Is that not right, Desmus?' The old major-domo – he was at least as old as his master – nodded and carried on with his dusting. Ampudius turned back to me. 'That was the whole point of the thing, where Marcus was concerned. Ditch the useless bastard. He'd had his chance years before, several chances for that matter, and blown the lot. Marcus never did believe in throwing good money after bad, and letting that shiftless scrounger get his hands on half his property when he was gone would've been tantamount to dropping it down the nearest latrine.'

Damn. So Lucius Caesius's insistence that the will had been forged was complete wishful-thinking moonshine. Well, it made sense, and it certainly fitted in with everything else. Lucius had been pretty convincing at the time, sure, but maybe he couldn't admit the truth even to himself.

'He tried to get it overturned, of course,' Ampudius was saying. 'Lucius, I mean. You know about that?'

'Yeah,' I said. 'Not in any detail, though.'

'The bastard claimed undue influence by his brother while the balance of Marcus's mind was disturbed. That's how the fancy lawyer he drafted in from Rome put it.' He chuckled again. 'Means the old man was gaga when he came to make the will and Quintus virtually told him what to write. Rot, complete rot, then at least. I told the judge straight when I was called – that was Publius Avianus, he had the chair that year, fine old buffer, he's long dead himself now from a bad oyster, bless his socks – that Marcus was as sane as any of us at the time. And even if he'd been right about the influence, what did it matter? It was all for the best. Quintus Caesius was worth ten of that soak where a head for business was concerned. If he hadn't been practically running things single-handed in his father's last few years the family would've been paupers before you could spit.'

'Hold on, sir,' I said. 'You said Marcus Caesius was sane at the time he made the will. You mean things changed?'

'Certainly they did. The poor old bugger went downhill pretty quickly latterly, didn't he? Mentally as well as physically, body and mind a complete wreck. The full catastrophe. Could hardly do a blessed thing for himself at the end, no more than can a baby, and he'd nothing left in the attic, couldn't remember his own name, let alone anyone else's. Just a living shell. I was sorry as hell for old Marcus, because like I said he was a canny man of business in his day and sharp as a knife, but his son was quite right to have him declared incapable.'

'Quintus Caesius had his father certified?'

'Of course. About a year before the old man died, when things started to become obvious. Only thing he could've done, and choice didn't enter into it. Can't have a man who sits down to dinner in his underpants and dribbles in the soup making deals and signing important business documents, can you? If it was me, mind, I'd rather someone knocked me on the head and be done with it, but there you are.' He raised his voice again. 'Hey, Desmus? You hear what I'm saying? You'd do that for me, would you?'

The duster paused. 'Yes, master. It'd be a pleasure.'

Ampudius grinned toothlessly. 'Bugger off,

167

Desmus. Well, he was a good son, Quintus. He knew where his duty lay, however unpleasant it was, public or private.'

Shit. 'And he used his friend Publius Novius to get it done? The certifying?'

'Who else would he use, boy? He was the family lawyer, and it had to go through legal process. Besides, he's a smart man, Publius. There'd be no querying anything he drafted.'

My brain was buzzing. I stood up. 'Thanks for your help, sir. You've been very informative.'

'Don't mention it. My pleasure. I don't have many visitors these days, and I don't get out much myself. I was sorry to miss young Quintus's funeral. A good man, that, and a good citizen of Bovillae. It isn't often you get them both together, and the town's a lot poorer without him.'

'Yeah,' I said. 'Yeah, so I imagine.'

'You nail the bastard who killed him. You won't find us ungrateful, boy.'

'I'll try,' I said, and left.

TWELVE

Where to now?

Well, you win some, you lose some: that conversation had blown out of the water the theory that the will was a fake engineered first to last by Novius and Caesius together. Old, Ampudius might be, but he'd certainly got all his faculties intact, there was nothing wrong with his memory, and he'd convinced me absolutely on that score. So scrap the idea that Aulus Mettius had been blackmailing Caesius and his employer, got himself framed and relegated as a result, and stiffed his uncle in revenge as soon as the opportunity presented itself. Which didn't, of course, let him off the hook altogether: even if his reasons for hating Caesius hadn't been as clear cut as a trumped-up charge and a ten-year relegation would've made them, the hatred he'd shown at the funeral had been there in spades, whatever the cause of it had been, and the timing still fitted. So Nephew Mettius was still firmly in the frame.

There again, there was still the question of Quintus Caesius's power of attorney – or whatever the legal phrase was – to consider. Even if his father's will itself had been genuine, the business of the old man having been certified towards the end of his life was something I'd known nothing about, and it might well be a key point where relations between the two brothers were concerned; Ampudius had been pretty definite that Caesius Senior had been in sound mind when he disinherited Lucius, sure, no arguments, but he'd also said that the guy had known he was failing during his latter years and had relied increasingly on his elder son's judgement. Influence – possibly undue influence, based on personal motives – was a grey area, and if it'd been a factor in the disinheritance then it might be relevant, both where Lucius himself – and possibly even Mettius, if he'd come to know about it in some way – was concerned.

So another chat with Anthus was in order. Plus, following my interview with Baebius, he might be able to provide an update on the missing figurine; my gut feeling was telling me that that fitted in somewhere or other along the line, and I'd bet we hadn't heard the last of it. Also, since it was cropping up too frequently to be ignored, I thought I might give the burned-out wool store a quick look-over, if only for completeness' sake.

Even so, we were halfway through a busy

morning here. Like I'd said to Perilla, I was officially on holiday, and after dutifully talking to Baebius and Ampudius I reckoned I deserved a break and a cup of wine. So back towards the centre of town and my usual wine shop.

On the way – what made me do it, I don't know; call it instinct, if you like – I happened to glance over my shoulder. I hadn't been looking out for my pal the lounging freedman recently, but there he was, large as life, a dozen or so yards behind and keeping pace. Uh-huh. Coincidence, nothing, not this time: Bovillae wasn't all that small. Maybe it was time we had a word. I turned.

The guy had almost reached a corner. He slowed noticeably, then abruptly took a left.

Bugger this for a game of soldiers. I was getting too old for running suspicious tails down, particularly where it would involve pushing my way through the pack of Bovillae's usual morning crowd of strollers and shoppers. Chummie could wait until I had a better chance at him. That would come, I was sure.

At least now I knew that it hadn't been my imagination. The guy had questions to answer.

I found the street with the brothel and carried on down it. The ruined warehouse was on the same side, a few dozen yards past the door, its roof gone but with the burned timber and tiles cleared away, so that it was no more than a shell formed by the original stone walls reaching up to their original height. Like the watchman Garganius had said, the locals had been lucky the place was separate from the surrounding buildings: it'd been a fairly big place, and if its frontage had been flush with the rest of the street, with properties attached either side, fires in town being what they are, when it went up it would probably have taken a good chunk of the centre with it. As it was, what was left was surrounded by an open courtyard.

There was nothing much to see, really, but I reckoned that having made the effort I might as well do things properly. I'd just stepped off the pavement when I felt a hand grip the back of my tunic, hard.

My pal the wandering freedman. I turned round, fist raised to punch the guy's lights out—

And stopped. It wasn't the freedman; it was a little guy dressed in what had probably once been a sack, with a bulbous head far too big for his body that wobbled on his scrawny neck, a hunched back, a mouth that was mostly drool, and eyes that were looking everywhere but straight at me. He stank, too.

Gods. I lowered my fist. Some things I just can't take, and madness comes top of the list every time. From the looks of him, chummie here evidently wasn't just a couple of tiles short of a roof, he was missing the whole thing, and the rafters as well.

'Uh ... Hi, pal,' I said. 'You wanted something?'

He stepped back. When I'd turned, he'd shifted his grip to my tunic's front, and he was still holding on tight. My blood went cold and I had to fight the urge to pull myself free.

'You're the Roman, aren't you?' he said. At least, that's what it would've been, if the words hadn't been slurred and drooled half to hell. 'From Rome.'

'Yeah,' I said carefully. 'That's me. Roman from Rome. Well done, sunshine, you've got it in one. What can I do for you?'

'I didn't kill him. The old man.'

The hairs were beginning to crawl on the back of my neck, and I had to stop myself from shivering.

'I know that,' I said. 'No one's claiming that you did.' Jupiter! 'You, uh, like to let me go, maybe?'

'You got to believe me. I never touched him. Never. I wouldn't. It was someone else.'

'Right. Right.'

'You believe me?'

'Yeah, no worries. I believe you.'

'Thass good. Because it wasn't me that done it, it was someone else. Not me. Someone else.' The head twitched, scattering spit...

And he'd suddenly let go of me, turned, and was shambling off up the street, back the way I'd come. I watched him go. I was shaking like a leaf.

Gods, that had *not* been pleasant! Maybe I'd forget the tour of inspection and head straight for the wine shop. Sleuthing could wait; right now, what I could really do with was a cup of wine. In fact I could do with the whole jug.

I took a deep breath, pulled myself back together again, and carried on towards the main drag, turning right when I reached it in the direction of the market square. I'd got about halfway to the wine-shop street when I heard my name shouted. I turned; it was Aulus Mettius.

'Yeah?' I said when he'd caught me up. I wasn't at my best, currently, and impromptu interviews with suspects I could do without. 'What is it?'

'I was hoping to bump into you,' he said. 'How're things going?'

'OK,' I said cautiously.

'Turned up any more dirt?' I just looked at him. 'I hear you're interested in the wool store business. Our local arson scandal, although it's best not to call it that too openly.'

'Who told you that?' I said sharply.

'Word gets around. And it'd be natural enough. But if you are then I might have a tip for you.'

'Is that so, now?' I kept every smidgeon of encouragement out of my voice. Unsolicited information tends to make me suspicious at the best of times, and this Mother's Little Helper pose from someone who was himself definitely in the frame was just a bit too much to be credible.

'If I were you I would have a talk with a man called Ulpius. Marcus Ulpius. He runs a small carter's business near the circus, theatre side, and he owes me a favour. Just tell him I sent you. Or wait, that might not be enough.' He took a copper coin from his belt pouch, then followed it up with his penknife, and scratched a letter 'M' on the face. 'Show him this. That ought to do it.'

I pocketed the coin. 'One question. What's in it for you?'

'Suspicious?' He grinned. 'Well, you need-n't be; I'm no murderer. There's nothing in it for me, I promise you. Just personal satis-faction.'

'In terms of what?'

'I told you when we met at the funeral. I don't like hypocrites, particularly when they paint themselves whiter than white and are crooked bastards underneath. The more paint gets scraped off, the better, and if I can lend a helping hand in that direction then I'm more than happy to do so. Talk to Ulpius. I'll see you around.'

He turned to go.

'Hang on, pal,' I said.

'Yeah?'

'You happen to know a crazy guy, looks like something out of an Atellan farce, stinks like a dead cat in a heatwave?'

'Dossenus. Sure.' He frowned.

Dossenus. Well, I'd been spot-on with the Atellan farce bit: Dossenus is one of the stock figures in the plays, the hunchback. 'That his name?'

'Not his real one. But if he ever had another nobody uses it any more. I doubt if he even knows it himself. Sure, I know Dossenus, everyone does. He's a local character, been around for years. A tramp, crazy, like you say. Sleeps rough, lives on garbage and whatever he can scrounge. You run into him?'

'Yeah, a few minutes back. Or he ran into me, rather, at the old wool store.'

'What did he want with you?'

'To tell me he wasn't the murderer I was looking for.'

Mettius laughed. 'That's Dossenus, all right,' he said. 'He gets these ideas into his head, largely because they haven't got much competition. You don't need to worry about him, Corvinus, he's harmless for all his looks. Give you a start, did he?'

'A bit of one, sure.'

'Yes.' He was examining me closely. 'Yes, I can see that he did. Anyway, you get on over to Ulpius's. You'll find what he has to say interesting.'

And he was gone.

I carried on to the wine shop. This time of day, it was pretty busy with punters on their early lunch break, but I still wasn't up to company and conversation. I took my second cup of wine – I'd sunk the first as soon as it was poured, and it hadn't touched the sides – to an empty corner table and sat down.

Two more cups along the road, I was feeling more myself again. I set out in the direction of the circus.

It's in the lower quadrant of the town, between the centre and the Arician Gate, with the theatre close beside it; not a bit of Bovillae I know very well. However, I found Ulpius's yard easily enough – it was the only carter's business in the area – and went in through the open gate. There was a big guy with his back to me, chewing on a hunk of bread and watching a couple of slaves grease the wheels of a cart. I went up to him.

'You Marcus Ulpius?' I said.

He turned round. 'Who wants to know?'

'Name's Corvinus.'

That got me a suspicious look. 'The Roman? Looking into the death of the censor?'

Like Mettius had said, word gets around. Evidently, it had even got this far. 'Yeah,' I

177

said. 'That's me.'

'So what do you want here?'

Instead of answering, I took out the marked coin. 'Aulus Mettius said to show you this.'

He took it, looked at it and slipped it into his belt-pouch. 'And?' he said.

'Search me, pal. That's all there is to it. Only the implication was you knew something about the burning down of the wool store six months ago.'

He looked wary. Then he nodded abruptly and tossed the rest of the bread away. 'OK,' he said. 'We'll go inside.'

I followed him into the big shed in the corner of the yard where the hay and straw for the horses were kept. He sat down on one of the bales, and I sat opposite.

'Now,' he said. 'Let's get something clear before we start. This is a favour, right? I owe Mettius one, never mind for what, and for some reason he's calling it in. The favour's to him, and you're not involved. No comeback, no follow-up, no extras. It ends here, and when you leave I don't know you from fucking Romulus and I never saw you before in my life. Agreed?'

'Sure,' I said.

'So. You have the ball. Ask away.'

'You transported the missing wool for Marcus Manlius, right?' I said.

He scowled, then grinned. 'You're not as

green as you're cabbage-looking, are you, Roman? Yeah, I did. And brought in the bales of rags that replaced it. Took me quite a while, I can tell you.'

'You start the fire as well?'

'Nah, wasn't my job. And I was taking enough risks for what that bastard was paying me already. He got one of his own men to do that.'

'So where did it go? The wool, I mean?'

'To a wholesale merchant in Aricia, name of Gnaeus Pompeius.' He sniggered. 'Yeah, like the old general. No relation, though, and no "Magnus" tacked on the end. Would've been a joke if there had been, because he was a little runt of a guy I could've snapped in half with one hand. Big man locally, mind. He'd an empty warehouse on the edge of the town, and I just dropped the loads off there. What happened to it after that I don't know, but no doubt Manlius and him were doing nicely out of the deal. Now. That's all I can tell you.'

'What's Mettius got against Marcus Manlius? Specifically, I mean.' Yeah, sure, he'd told me he was giving me Ulpius's name out of pure altruism, but like I said I've never trusted suspect characters who provide unsolicited information *gratis*. The chances were that he had an axe to grind somewhere or other, and it'd be interesting to know what it was.

179

Ulpius shrugged. 'You'd have to ask him that yourself, although I'd be surprised if you got a straight answer. Oh, sure, Manlius's father was the aedile on the bench when he was relegated ten years back, and maybe that's enough. It would be for me. But Mettius is a strange cove. Me, I'm in it for the money, pure and simple, I'm not ashamed to admit the fact. I've got a wife and kids to keep, and the carting business doesn't bring in much. Mettius, well, he comes from a good family, so money's not a problem and never has been. He's crooked as they come and can lie to beat the band, sure, but if you ask me he does it out of pure devilment, just for the fun of it. He's always been wild. And he can't stand these pricks in the senate. Not that I blame him there. They're all a pack of chancers.' He stood up. 'Right. That's your lot. All there is, all you get. You tell Mettius when you see him the debt's paid.'

'I'll do that,' I said. 'Thanks a lot.'

I left the yard and started up towards the centre. I hadn't gone far when the old instinct kicked in again and I turned round.

Shit. The persistent freedman. Only this time he wasn't trying to hide, or to avoid me. He kept on coming.

Well, I was safe enough: we were still in Bovillae, after all, on a public street, and there were plenty of people around. I waited for him to catch up.

'OK, pal,' I said when he had. 'What's this all about?'

'I'm taking you to see the boss,' he said.

I didn't have to ask who the boss was, not any more, because now he was close up I'd placed him. He'd been at Caesius's funeral, in the market square, carrying a bundle of rods. Manlius's rod man, or one of them.

'Is that so, now?' I said. 'Care to tell me why?'

Instead of answering, his hand gripped my arm. I shook it off, grabbed it with both of mine, and bent the thumb back as far as it would go. He grunted and froze, his eyes wide.

'OK,' I said quietly. 'Public place, right? Not somewhere to cause any trouble, is it? Now you be nice and in return I won't break your fucking thumb. Deal?'

'Deal,' he said, through gritted teeth.

'Fine. That's better.' I let go.

'Look.' He was rubbing his hand. 'I was only to tail you, right? See where you went.'

'OK. You were doing that. So what's changed the rules?' He said nothing. 'Suit yourself, friend, I'll answer for you. I've been sniffing around the old wool store, I talked to Sextus Garganius, and I've just been to Marcus Ulpius's place. Tick three boxes. That's at least one too many for your boss's peace of mind. So now you've decided that Manlius will want to have an urgent word with me about the wool store business in person, yes?' Still nothing. 'Come on, you bastard! You know damn well what's going on! If Manlius used one of his own men to set the fire – which he did – then it isn't hard to guess who picked the lucky number.' He gawped at me, and I sighed; rod men as a profession don't need to be too bright, sure, but this one couldn't even manage a glimmer. And most of the size wasn't muscle but flab. Heaven help the empire. 'Fair enough, forget it, sunshine. I'd've been calling on Manlius soon in any case. Off we go.'

It wasn't far: on the main drag again, and only a couple of hundred yards centre-side of Caesius's place. My none-too-friendly rod man nodded to the door slave sitting outside, who opened the door for us, and we went in. The major-domo met us in the atrium.

'Boss around, Flavus?' Rod said.

The major-domo was looking at me with obvious curiosity. 'Yes, he is,' he said. 'In the study, with Sextus Canidius.'

'You want to tell him I've got Valerius Corvinus here? He'll know what it's about.'

The major-domo gave me another curious look and went out.

'You don't need to stay, pal, if you've got

other things to do,' I said. 'I can take it from here. I'm a big boy now. I don't need nanny-ing.'

'The boss'll want me to deliver you personally, so I'm delivering you personally.'

Well, you couldn't argue with that; stark in its simplicity, and offering no room for interpretation. We waited in silence until the major-domo came back.

'This way, sir, please,' he said to me.

I followed him through to the study, with Rod tagging along behind. Manlius and Canidius were sitting on stools at a small table neatly stacked with various items of paperwork and wax tablets. They looked up as I came in, their faces expressionless.

'He's just been talking to Ulpius, sir,' Rod said to Manlius. 'I thought you might want a word.'

'All right, Decimus. Well done, you can go.' Manlius waited until the door had shut behind him. 'Good afternoon, Valerius Corvinus.'

There was another stool by the desk. I pulled it up and sat down.

'Interrupting something, am I?' I said.

'Just some everyday administrative matters. They'll keep.' He was watching me carefully.

'OK,' I said. 'Do you want to do the talking or shall I?' Silence. I crossed my legs. 'Fine. The wool store business was a scam from the start. Canidius here, as quaestor, made sure you got the contract when it fell unexpectedly vacant. Technically that should've been illegal, since you were and are a serving aedile, but you've got the senate in your pocket and it went through on the nod. You squared the night watchman Sextus Garganius and had a crooked carter by the name of Marcus Ulpius switch most of the bales for rags and take the wool over to Aricia where it was sold on by a guy called Gnaeus Pompeius, presumably splitting the proceeds between you. Then, to cover the theft, you staged a fire set by the tame gorilla who brought me here. Decimus, wasn't it?' I paused for a response that didn't come. 'How am I doing?'

Manlius was looking green. Canidius was just ... looking.

'Corvinus,' Manlius said, 'I swear—'

Canidius put a hand on his arm. He hadn't taken his eyes off me. 'So how much do you want?' he said.

'Wrong question, pal. Wrong attitude.'

'No one was hurt in the fire. There wasn't even any other property damage. We made sure of that.'

'True. And that makes it OK, does it?' I uncrossed my legs. 'Look. I'll level with you here. My mandate's just to find out who killed Quintus Caesius. That still stands, and to be honest the fact that the guy had promised an investigation when he took up office puts you two well and truly in the frame.' Manlius started to say something, but another touch on the arm from his pal made him clam up. 'Now it could be that you're just another couple of crooked politicians on the make, so where the actual scam's concerned I'm willing to cut you a bit of slack. Option one: I take what I know to, say, an outsider member of the senate such as Silius Nerva and let him deal with it as he sees fit.' Manlius blanched, but said nothing. 'Option two: well, you must've turned a pretty substantial profit out of all this, while the town's out a season's wool plus one of the communal buildings. Maybe it'd be a nice gesture if two of their solid citizens made it up to them. Say by offering to pay out of their own pockets for a snazzy new public meeting-hall with all the trimmings on the empty site. Plus rebuilding the warehouse elsewhere, of course.'

'That would cost a small fortune!' Canidius snapped. 'Far more than double what we...' He caught himself, and his lips formed a tight line. 'This is sheer blackmail!'

'Suit yourself, pal,' I said. 'Like I told you, it's only one of the options on offer. Choose the other one if you prefer.'

He and Manlius exchanged a look.

'We'll consider it,' Canidius said, through gritted teeth.

'The offer's limited as far as time goes, so don't take too long, will you? Let's say until the festival, max?' I smiled. 'Fine. That's got that out of the way. Now. Alibis.'

'*What?*' Manlius goggled.

'For the night Caesius was killed. I told you, you're both in the frame for the murder, together and separately.'

'Corvinus, this is an insult,' Canidius said softly. 'We had nothing to do with Quintus Caesius's death.'

'OK,' I said. 'Prove it.'

Again, the exchanged glance. 'As it happens,' Canidius said, 'we were together, here. We'd been discussing some town business until late in the afternoon and hadn't finished. Marcus invited me to stay to a working dinner. As a result, I didn't leave until almost midnight.'

'That's right.' Manlius nodded violently.

'Uh-huh,' I said, and stood up. 'Convenient. Well, thank you, gentlemen, it's been very instructive. I'll see you around.'

I could feel their eyes on me all the way to the door.

Rod had gone, but the major-domo was still in the atrium filling the lamps.

'Uh ... Flavus, wasn't it?' I said.

'Yes, sir.'

'Just a question, pal. Silly, but still. When Sextus Canidius had dinner here six days ago what did you serve for the main course?

186

You remember that, by any chance?'

He frowned. 'But Master Canidius didn't stay for dinner that evening, sir,' he said. 'He left about an hour before sunset.'

'Ah. Right. My mistake. No problem, it doesn't matter.'

'I'll see you out, sir.'

I glanced up at the sun. Still a fair bit of the day left, and the weather wasn't looking too bad. I'd time for that chat with Anthus about old Marcus Caesius. It shouldn't take long – Caesius's house was only a couple of hundred yards down the road towards the gate – and I could still be back home well before dinner.

Things were shaping up nicely.

THIRTEEN

'Back again, Valerius Corvinus?' Anthus said when he joined me in the atrium. 'You're becoming a regular visitor.'

'So it seems,' I said. Interesting how freedom and the right to wear a freedman's cap affects behaviour: the old guy was much more relaxed, much chattier now than he had been when I'd first met him as a slave, even though that had only been a couple of days before. It's very easy to forget that the bought help are people, too, with their own thoughts and feelings. Too easy, maybe.

Mind you, I couldn't quite see him behind the counter of a baker's shop, hefting trays of rolls and passing the time of day with some chatty housewife over her morning Campanian Cob. That didn't really seem the guy's bag, somehow. Still, if he'd taken up with a baker's widow in the first place he must have another facet to his personality, so maybe it wouldn't be an issue.

'Did you talk to Lucius Ampudius?' he said. 'About the old master's will?'

'Yeah. He was very helpful, and like you

said everything seems to be above board there. No problems.'

'Then why this visit, sir?'

'I was just wondering if you could tell me a bit more about the old man himself.'

Anthus gave me a puzzled look. 'I scarcely see why that should be relevant to the master's murder,' he said. 'Particularly since Master Marcus has been dead for eleven years now.'

'Maybe not. Still, there is a chance that there's a connection. If you can fill in a few gaps for me I'd be very grateful.'

'Then of course I'll give you any information I can. Ask away.'

'You were major-domo here when he was alive, right?'

'Yes, sir. Of course. I've held the post for over thirty years now, and I'd been with the family all my life before that. In fact, I was born in this house.'

'According to Ampudius he was, uh, failing mentally and physically in his latter years. Including the time he made the will disinheriting his son.'

'Oh, no, sir. You must have misunderstood. As Lucius Ampudius will have told you, I expect, he was certainly showing some signs of frailty, both physical and mental, when he made the will, but he was in complete command of his faculties, at least where his powers of judgement were concerned. The real decline set in later, a year or two before his death, and it was very rapid, particularly in the final months.'

Yeah, well, that chimed with what Ampudius had said, right enough. Bugger. Still...

'At the time he made the will, your master Quintus Caesius was managing the family's business interests, is that so?'

'Yes, sir. At the old master's specific request. The interests were fairly widespread, and at times rather complicated. He was an intelligent man, Valerius Corvinus; he knew he was failing and he was unsure how far he could trust himself where matters of finance were concerned. Also, naturally, by that time Master Quintus was in his prime and an excellent, experienced man of business in his own right. Old Master Marcus decided that things were better left in his hands completely, and he never had cause to regret his decision.'

'Uh-huh. Ah ... Lucius Ampudius also said that your master eventually had his father certified. That true?'

'Yes, indeed he did. Rightly so. He postponed things as long as he could, but in the end, regrettably, he had no choice; in fact, if anything he left it too late. As I said, the old master's eventual decline was very rapid; in his final year he was unable to perform even the most basic of physical functions without help, and his mind had almost completely gone. The power of attorney which Master Quintus had been exercising for several years previously was only ever an ad hoc arrangement; it had no legal basis. By that time, of course, it was impossible to set it on a legal footing because old Master Marcus was beyond completing the paperwork involved, or even understanding what was required of him. So to avoid any possible legal complications my master's lawyer Publius Novius advised formal certifying. It was only a technicality, making no difference whatever to the existing situation, and as I say the old master died shortly afterwards.' He gave me a straight look. 'There was nothing there, Valerius Corvinus, which should arouse your suspicions, should you be entertaining any. Everything my master did, he did reluctantly, as a last resort, and for the most honourable reasons. He was the most excellent of men.'

Yeah, well, that more or less put the lid on it, and to be truthful under the circumstances I hadn't really expected anything else. So scrap the coercion theory. Bugger again.

'Thanks, Anthus,' I said. 'Again, you've been a great help.'

'I'm glad, sir.' He hesitated. 'Was there anything else? About the missing figurine, for example? You've talked to Quintus Baebius and raised the matter with him, I suppose?'

He was smart, Anthus, and no fool; but I already knew that.

'Yeah,' I said. 'It seems they were going to do some sort of deal the day your master died involving a part-exchange – a physical part-exchange – but it fell through. When he went out that evening, is it possible he had the figurine on him?'

'Very possible, sir. But if he did, as I told you, I wasn't aware of it. You have no idea where it could have gone?'

'No. No clear one, anyway. It's still a mystery. If it does turn up you'll let me know, right? You can always contact me through Silius Nerva. Or of course send direct to my son-in-law's villa outside Castrimoenium.'

'I'll do that. Although it isn't likely, I'm afraid.'

'No, I don't suppose it is.' I held out my hand. 'Thanks again, pal, for all your help. And if I don't see you before your marriage, give my regards to your wife.'

'Certainly.' We shook. 'As always, the best of luck to you, sir. I hope you bring the killer to justice.'

'Yeah, well, I'll try.'

I left. Enough for today; *really* enough.

Home.

Perilla was alone in the atrium when I got back, reading.

'Oh, hello, dear,' she said, putting the book

down. 'Back early again? You're doing well.'

'Yeah.' I kissed her and lay down on the couch opposite. 'Early-ish, anyway. No Clarus and Marilla?'

'They're both out. Marilla's walking Placida and Clarus was called away into town about an hour ago to set a broken arm. They'll be back in time for dinner. So how are things going?'

'Pretty well, really.' Bathyllus came in with the wine tray. 'Thanks, little guy. Everything still fine below stairs?'

'Yes, sir. Lupercus and I seem to have reached an acceptable *modus vivendi*, as I outlined to you.'

'That's great. Keep up the good work.' He poured and buttled out. 'I've solved the business of the fire in the wool store, anyway, lady. It was deliberate theft and arson right enough, and Manlius and Canidius were behind it.' I gave her the details.

'But, Marcus, that's dreadful!' she said when I'd finished. 'You can't be letting them get away with it, surely?'

I shrugged. 'That side of things has nothing to do with me. As far as their getting away with it is concerned the cover-up is going to cost them an arm and a leg, and with guys like those two that'll really hurt. Mind you, they'll get their names on the plaque above the door of the new public hall they're going to build and be well ahead on brownie points for elections in future, so they can't complain they've been too hard done by.'

'So you don't think they were responsible, then? For the murder?'

I shook my head. 'Uh-uh, lady, that's a separate issue. What it does confirm is that they had a genuine motive. They needed to stop the enquiry, the only way that was going to happen was if Caesius wasn't around in a month's time to push it through the senate, and now both of them are firmly on the hook where opportunity's concerned, too. At any rate, neither has a valid alibi for the time Caesius was killed. Canidius claimed that they were together at Manlius's place for a business dinner until midnight, but according to the major-domo he left the house well before sunset. Which means he, at least, could've been anywhere at all that evening. Manlius too, because instead of providing a genuine alibi for himself, if he had one, he backed up his pal's story.'

'Why should he do that if he knew it wasn't true?'

'Maybe just out of solidarity, because from what I can see Canidius is the brains of the pair, the cool head, and Manlius just follows his lead. On the other hand, maybe it suited him.'

'You mean he was elsewhere himself?'

'Yeah.' I sipped my wine. 'It's a possibility,

anyway. I didn't want to push things with the major-domo by asking if he'd gone out after Canidius had left, because he'd probably just have got suspicious and clammed up, or worse blown the whistle on me to his master. As it is, chances are that they don't know they've been sussed. Definitely sussed, that is. So like I say the upshot is that at the time of the murder both Manlius and Canidius, together or separately, were running loose.'

'You think they are likely prospects? Really?'

'Really, lady, I don't know. They're a proper pair of chancers, no arguments there, crooks to the core, and for guys from their background like you said yourself the threat of exposure and the social disgrace involved might swing things, sure. For Canidius, certainly; that is one cool, calculating bastard. Given the opportunity, and if he thought there was no way he'd be found out, I reckon Canidius could and would've done it. Manlius, now, I doubt if he'd have either the brains or the guts. Not on his own, and not with premeditation. Still, they're both in there with a shout, particularly after the fake alibi business.'

'All right.' She moved the cushion on her couch and settled herself more comfortably. 'So what else did you get? Did you speak to the rival collector, what was his name, Baebius?'

'Yeah.' I took another swallow of the Alban and topped up the cup from the jug. 'Turns out he'd had a clandestine meeting arranged with Caesius for that evening at sunset, at the old wool store, practically right next door to the brothel. Only Caesius never showed.'

'From what Baebius told you, you mean.'

I grinned. 'Come on, Perilla! I'm not stupid! He could've been lying about that, sure, but the details checked out with what his door slave said, and him I believed. Plus, whatever the truth of the meeting story was, Baebius couldn't have done the killing because at the time Caesius left the brothel he was safely back home up by the Alban Lake Gate.'

'Again, according to his slave.'

'The boy had no cause to lie, under the circumstances. And like I say, I believed him. If he was acting and telling porkies then he was damn good at it.'

'So what was the meeting about?'

'That's the odd thing. You know that figurine they quarrelled over, that all the fuss was about originally? The little bronze of the Runner? Seemingly Caesius offered to do an exchange, a partial exchange, for a similar piece they'd wrangled over in the past, and he was going to bring the figurine along with him. Which, presumably, he did, because it's gone missing.'

'What?' Perilla said sharply.

'Yeah. His major-domo Anthus hasn't seen it since the day his master died. And Baebius denies all knowledge.'

'Again, he could be lying.'

'Why would he bother? He's off the hook for the murder, and although the whole business of the clandestine meeting was a bit silly the deal itself was perfectly legal, none of anyone's business but his and Caesius's. If Caesius turned up and it went ahead, why complicate the issue? Besides, I'm pretty sure he was telling the truth there, at least. And the bronze was worth at least twenty thousand. If Caesius had it on him when he was killed – and I'd bet that he did, because where else could it have gone – then the simplest explanation is that the murderer took it himself.'

'Or herself. What about the brothel owner?'

'*Andromeda?* Perilla, that is crazy! Why should Opilia Andromeda murder Caesius?'

'For the figurine, of course. Just for that. If it was worth twenty thousand sesterces it would be a motive in itself.'

'Jupiter, lady! How would she know he had it? And it might be worth twenty thousand to a collector, but she'd still have to find one prepared to buy it. That wouldn't be too easy out here in the sticks. Besides, there'd be the question of provenance. Any reputable collector she approached would want to know how she'd got her hands on it in the first place. He might even recognize it for what it was, in which case she'd be properly up the creek.'

'I can't see any reason why either of these objections should be valid, dear. She did let Caesius in herself that evening, didn't she? Why shouldn't she have seen the statuette in the process, if he had it with him? Then, of course, it would have been easy to hit him from behind as he went out, steal it, close the door and leave the body to be found in the morning.'

'She's a woman, for the gods' sakes!'

'Petite? On the small, fragile side?'

'No, not at all, in fact, but—'

'Then it's a tenable theory. And you can always ask Clarus if it would be physically possible when he comes in. As far as selling the thing is concerned, well, Rome's not all that far away; there are plenty of art dealers in the city, not all of whom are scrupulous, and I'm sure the lady would be quite capable of mounting any deception she felt was necessary. Or don't you agree?'

I was staring at her. Shit! It was possible, at that. It was even plausible: Andromeda was no fluff-ball; she was smart and ambitious, and if she was building up a business and looking to go upmarket then twenty thousand sesterces would buy a hell of a lot of prime interior decorating. And certainly where opportunity was concerned she'd've had that far more than most. Maybe I should have another word, see which way she jumped. If she jumped.

'OK,' I said cautiously. 'Andromeda is a possibility, I'll give you that. Albeit an outside one. Proving it would be another matter, though.'

'Very well.' Perilla shifted on her couch. 'Let's move on. The brother, Lucius, and the nephew. Anything new there?'

'Not a lot, no. At least, nothing positive. As far as Lucius being behind the killing is concerned, sure, he's still very much our front runner, both in terms of motive and opportunity. Particularly if you bracket him with Roscius as the actual perp supplying the muscle and assume the murder wasn't premeditated. Marilla was right about that; it's the simplest explanation and it was something I hadn't thought of. Oh, I would've got round to it soon enough, but the kid was there first.' I glanced at Perilla over the rim of my wine cup. 'She's got a good brain in her head, that girl.'

Perilla sniffed. 'I'm not denying it, dear. All I'm saying is that encouraging her to use it in theorizing about who committed a murder and how and why they did it is perhaps not such a good idea at her time of life and in her position.'

'Yeah. Like I did with you.'

'*What?*'

'Come on, lady! You know what I mean! How old were you when you asked me to sub for you in getting your stepfather's ashes back from Tomi? Twenty, was it? Twenty-one, tops. More or less the same age Marilla is now, anyway. And I seem to remember you didn't have all that many scruples about getting involved with the case yourself at the time. Quite the reverse.'

'Marcus, that is simply not fair!'

'Sure it's fair. And relevant.'

'The situation was completely different! I had a vested interest!' I just grinned at her, until finally she ducked her head and smiled. 'Very well, dear, you have made your point; we won't quibble. And you're right; she does seem to have an aptitude. Unfortunately. Carry on. What about Mettius? Did you find out anything else on the will side of things?'

I hesitated. 'Mettius is still a puzzle,' I said. 'The guy's got secrets, that's certain, and he's dishonest as a Suburan horse trader. No arguments there. But that's "dishonest", not "crooked"; he's no Manlius, let alone a Canidius. He may be an outsider who plays by his own rules, but my gut feeling is that he plays fair and more for the sake of the game than anything else. That's what his pal Ulpius said, the guy who moved the wool bales for our two upright magistrate friends, and I'd say it was a pretty fair assessment.'

Perilla smiled. 'You like him, don't you?'

'Liking has nothing to do with it. I've liked guys who've turned out to be murderers before, and as far as motive goes – probably opportunity too – he's still well within the frame. But as far as the business with the will is concerned, I'm afraid that's a complete washout. I talked to the old guy who witnessed it, and he was adamant that it was genuine.'

'He was sure? It wasn't just an opinion?'

'Uh-uh. Marcus Caesius himself told him at the time that he was disinheriting his son, and he read the document before the old man signed it.'

'Damn!'

I grinned. 'Yeah. That's what I thought. Naturally, it blows that part of the case against Mettius to hell. If there was no skulduggery between Caesius and Publius Novius then he'd no grounds for blackmailing them, and in that case they'd no need to trump up a fake embezzlement charge to get rid of him.'

'So you think that was genuine, then?' Perilla was twisting a lock of her hair.

'It looks that way, sure. Like I say, Mettius is hardly squeaky-clean in the honesty department, and the only evidence to the contrary – if you can call it evidence – is his own claim that he was set up. On the other hand, everything I hear about Caesius confirms that he was straight where the law and business was concerned. Hard, yes, but straight. And by his own admission Mettius hated his uncle, there's no getting past that.'

'So where does that leave us?'

'I don't know, lady.' I sighed. 'He certainly went out of his way to finger Manlius and Canidius for me, which is suspicious in itself.'

'That isn't quite enough to make him a potential murderer, dear.'

'Yeah. Agreed. And it might well've been that he had a personal axe to grind. According to Ulpius again, Manlius's father was the aedile on the bench who sentenced him to relegation. Plus, he's got a definite down on Bovillae's Great and Good in general, so he could've done it simply out of pure devilment. That I'd believe, too.' I took a morose swallow of wine. 'Hell. Leave it for now. It'll all work out eventually, no doubt.'

'Hmm.' Perilla frowned, then said, 'Oh, by the way, we've had word from your mother and Priscus. They've decided to come early, so they should be here in three days' time.'

Oh, great. Joy in the morning. Only a scant four days left of not being told I drank too much and not being bored to death on the subject of Etruscan modal verbs.

'That's nice,' I said.

'Don't be sarcastic, Marcus. Personally, I'm looking forward to it.'

202

Yeah, sure; the lady had never been a good liar, and there was just a tinge of red in her cheeks.

Still, maybe there'd be another murder that'd keep me out of the house. I could always hope. Meanwhile, I reckoned sleuthing had had its whack out of me for the present and I was owed a bit of quality time doing bugger all. There was enough of the day left before dinner to stroll down the road to Pontius's wine shop in the village for a quiet cup or two and a gossip with the locals.

So that's what I did.

FOURTEEN

Pontius's is in Castrimoenium's main square, which sounds a lot more impressive than it is, because the place isn't all that big; maybe 'village' is overstating things a bit, but it's only half the size of Bovillae, if that, and Pontius's is the only wine shop on offer. Not that I'm complaining: Pontius himself is a good lad, he serves a more-than-decent jug of wine, and in general his regular customers are an OK bunch. All in all, as an occasional home-from-home and a relaxing watering hole for when we come down to the villa, I couldn't ask for better.

It didn't look like I was going to be shooting the inconsequential breeze with Pontius's other drinkers after all, mind. Maybe it was something to do with the weather – we were getting wintry showers turning to hail again, and the regulars had probably decided to stick by their own hearths – but the place was almost deserted, the only punter in evidence being Gabba, the barfly's barfly and Castrimoenium's leading opportunistic entrepreneur, whom neither wind nor hail nor gloom of night could deter from getting his daily skinful. The gods knew what the bastard did when he wasn't propping up Pontius's counter, which by my reckoning had to cover a good ten hours out of the daylight twelve, but if he was central to the local Alban Hills economy then rural Italy was in serious financial trouble. Apart from the retail wine trade, naturally.

'Hey, Corvinus.' He raised his cup as I walked in. 'I heard you were back. Good to see you again. How's the lad?'

'OK,' I said, easing myself on to a stool: all that unaccustomed horse-riding to Bovillae and back was taking its toll. 'Make it half a jug of the usual, Pontius. And a small plate of your cheese and olives.' It wasn't all that long until dinner, but I'd had an energetic day, and a few preliminary nibbles wouldn't hurt.

'Holidays again, is it?' Gabba topped up his own wine cup as Pontius filled my half jug from the flask behind the counter. 'All right for some. Ready for the festival, are you?'

'More or less. Yourself?'

'Looking forward to it, consul, looking forward to it. As ever. The wife takes the kids off to her mother's in Caba, so I get a bit of peace and quiet for a change.'

'Is that so, now?' Like I said, Gabba spent most of his day perched on one of Pontius's bar stools, so he couldn't've seen much of his wife under normal circumstances in any case. Me, I was surprised that they'd had the time and opportunity to have kids in the first place.

'Indeed it is.' He took a swig of his wine and smacked his lips. 'Best and sweetest time of the year, this. So. How's things up at the big house? You bring that fancy chef of yours with you?'

'Meton? No. He's back in Rome.' Pontius put the wine and nibbles down on the counter in front of me. 'Staying there, too,' I added pointedly.

'Pity. He's got talent, that boy, and it needs proper handling. Since them talks on cooking he gave last year I've had quite a few of the local ladies at me asking about a follow-up.' He winked. 'He could do pretty well for himself there, particularly this time of year when the little darlings're looking for something a bit special to put on the table.'

'Gabba, I've got enough trouble keeping Meton's ego within manageable proportions without you agenting for the bastard, right? Trust me. As far as celebrity cheffing goes, the world just isn't ready.' I took a large swig of my wine; not the best name that the Alban Hills could offer, Castrimoenian, by any means, but it had its merits, and Pontius's was top of the range.

Gabba shrugged. 'Suit yourself, Corvinus.

206

Your loss. But it's a crying shame.' He reached over and took an olive from my saucer.
'Oh, by the way, I hear you're mixed up with
another murder, over in Bovillae.'

'Where did you get that from?' I said
sharply.

'Word gets around. No particular secret, is
it?'

'No, but...'

'There you are, then.'

'One of the nobs, wasn't he?' Like he often
did when it was quiet, Pontius filled a wine
cup of his own, came round to the front of
the counter, pulled up a stool and sat down.
'Senator, magistrate or some such?'

I sighed. Well, I supposed it was fair
enough, and out here in the sticks you had to
make your own amusement, which included
milking any gobbet of current scandal for
what it was worth. And a murder was scandal in spades.

'Yeah,' I said. 'An old guy by the name of
Quintus Caesius. The censor-elect. He was–'

The door opened, and we turned round.

'Oh, bugger!' The newcomer was staring at
me like Perseus must've stared at Medusa,
but without the benefit of the polished
shield. '*Corvinus?* What the hell are you
doing here?'

After the initial shock of recognition, I was
grinning. 'Hi, Crispus,' I said. 'I could say
the same. Lovely to see you again, pal. Small

world, isn't it?'

'Bloody microscopic, seemingly. And none the better for that, either.' Caelius Crispus, upwardly mobile foreign judges' rep and Rome's foremost authority on the top five hundred's communal dirty linen basket, closed the door carefully behind him like it was made of glass. 'I asked first. Just answer the question, OK?'

'I'm practically one of the locals,' I said. 'Been coming here for years.'

'Oh, fuck.' Crispus hadn't taken his eyes off me. 'You're kidding, right? *Please* say you're kidding.'

'Why should I do that? Cross my heart, hope to die. Perilla's Aunt Marcia had the villa just up the road, and our adopted daughter and her husband have it now. You can ask Pontius here, or Gabba, if you don't believe me.'

'He's right, squire,' Gabba said. 'Back and forward all the time. I hate to say it, myself, because I'm no fan of purple-stripers, but there you are.'

'She here as well? That wife of yours?'

'Perilla? Of course she is. Wouldn't go any-where without her.'

'Shit.' Crispus moved across to the counter like he was a ghost walking on eggs and sat down. 'Double shit.'

'What can I get you, sir?' Pontius said.

'A carriage back to Rome would be favourite. Failing that, slip some arsenic into this bastard's drink.'

'He doesn't mean it.' I was still grinning. 'Me and Crispus, we go way back. Been friends for years.' An overstatement, if you like: if I died I suspected he'd quite cheerfully piss in my urn. Even so, our paths had crossed professionally quite a few times since I'd saved him a couple of years pre-Perilla from a boyfriend's irate daddy with a very sharp knife hell-bent on cutting his bollocks off, and we'd developed a cautious respect for each other based – on his side, at least – on scrupulous avoidance. He was OK at root, was Crispus, and, like I say, where the dubious alleyways of upper-class Roman society were concerned, the expert's expert. 'Give him a cup of your best Alban, Pontius. My tab. Come on, Crispus! It's not as bad as that.'

'Yes it is. Worse. If I'd known that you and that hellcat'd be staying anywhere near me I'd never've bought the sodding place.'

Aha! The penny dropped. 'So,' I said. 'You're the civil service bigwig who's bought the Satellius estate, right? My son-in-law was talking about that a day or so back. Pushing the boat out a bit, aren't you?'

'Certainly not.' He glared at me. 'I have a position to keep up, remember. These days, a small country *pied-à-terre* close to Rome where one can entertain friends and professional acquaintances in proper civilized comfort is practically *de rigueur* for a public figure.'

Yeah, right; I'd forgotten that our erstwhile sleazy scumbag of a gossip trader had been working seriously at his social transformation from plebeian duckling on the make into upper-class swan. Even so. '"Small" isn't what I heard, pal,' I said. 'We're talking major renovations here, on top of the original purchase price. And that wouldn't've been peanuts, either. Where did you get the cash?'

He sniffed. 'That is none of your business.'

True. And I probably wouldn't want to know, either: Crispus's private sources of income were murky at best, and if the guy hadn't made sure that he was triple-ring-fenced life insurance-wise he would've been drifting down the Tiber with a knife in his back years ago. Several knives, all with aristocratic crests on them. The Satellian villa with all the improvements to it that Clarus had mentioned probably represented the profits from a whole warehouseful of family skeletons prised from their cupboards and kept under wraps for a consideration mutually agreed on between Crispus and their owners.

Pontius set the cup of Alban down on the counter, and Crispus sank it in a oner. Yeah, well, seeing me away from the context of the praetors' offices in Rome where he usually hung out must've come as a shock, at that, but at least he was looking a bit brighter now. Or a bit less grey, at least. I motioned to Pontius to give him a refill: his best Alban wasn't cheap, but Crispus was a guest, in a way, and he needed it. Besides, it was the festival.

'So, pal,' I said. 'How's the department? Keeping you busy, are they?'

'Busy enough, thank you,' he said stiffly.

'Work for the government, do you, sir?' Pontius hefted the jar of Alban. 'There's nice. Finance, would it be?'

'Crispus here's attached to the foreign praetors' office,' I explained. 'Travelling rep.'

'It's good to have friends,' Gabba said. He pushed over his cup. 'Especially if they're buying.'

'Nice try, Gabba.' I reached for my own cup and took a swallow. 'Bugger off.'

'You'll be involved with the murder case, then,' Pontius said, sipping his own drink. 'When they catch whoever's responsible.'

'What murder case?' Crispus said suspiciously.

'Over in Bovillae. They've got Corvinus here looking into it for them. That's right, isn't it, Corvinus?'

'Yeah, well, I...'

'Nothing to do with me.' Crispus set the empty cup down. 'And I'll tell you now, you conniving bastard—' this to me – 'it won't be,

211

either. You won't get me mixed up in one of your investigations, not this time. It's the festival, I'm on holiday, and moving in or not, now I know you're here if you and that fury of a wife of yours even *think* about dropping round for a housewarming I'll set the dogs on you. In fact, I'll buy in an extra lot just in case. I might even invest in a leopard.' He stood up. 'Clear?'

'Oh, come on, pal! Aren't we overreacting just a tad?'

'No.' He made a move for the door. 'Thanks for the wine, have a good Festival, give my regards to the hellcat. And now just stay out of my life until hell freezes, OK?'

Well, I'd tried to be nice. Perilla would've been impressed. The wine hadn't been cheap, either. 'Suit yourself,' I said. 'I'll see you around.'

'Not if I see you first.'

I turned back to my drink. The door opened.

'So, Corvinus,' Gabba said. 'What about this Quintus Caesius, then?'

The door closed, slowly.

'Caesius?' Crispus said from behind me. 'That who the dead man was?'

I turned round again. 'Yeah,' I said. 'You know him?'

'If it's the same person.' He was looking sick. 'It's not a common name. Oldish guy? Silver hair, mid-sixties, thereabouts?'

'That's him.'

'Jupiter! We were talking just a few days ago. Well, maybe a bit longer now. Makes you think, doesn't it?'

He came back over to the counter and sat down.

'Where was this?' I said sharply.

'Rome, of course. At one of the clubs I use. The Crimson Lotus.'

Yeah, well, it added up. Anthus had told me that Caesius went through to Rome pretty often on business, and if he was in the habit of using the local brothel in Bovillae then the odds were he wouldn't be averse to putting his feet up and letting his hair down in the far more salubrious fleshpots of Rome. The fact that he shared a club with Crispus, mind, came as a bit of a surprise, given Crispus's predilections, but there again any self-respecting Roman club of that nature would cater to a fairly wide clientele. Particularly in these experimental days, when said clientele as individuals would have pretty catholic tastes.

'So where's this Crimson Lotus, then?' I said.

'On Pallacina Road. Mars Field end.'

Between the Quirinal and the Pincian. Right. Good address. 'You, uh, knew him well?'

'Hardly at all. I only met him a couple of times. We chatted about property here in the

Alban Hills; in fact, he was the one who put me on to the Satellian estate originally. Nice man. Civilized. A cut above some of the riff-raff you get in these places.'

The barest sniff; there spoke our wannabe swan.

'Did you know he was from Bovillae? Or that he was a magistrate?'

'No. That he was only visiting Rome, certainly. But he didn't say, and of course I didn't ask.'

'No?'

'Certainly not. No more than I'd've acknowledged prior acquaintance with him if we'd ever met on his home ground, or he with me on mine. The club does have rules, you know, Corvinus, and some things just aren't done. And now, if you'll excuse me, I'll be getting along.'

Gods! *This* pillar of respectability was the Crispus we knew and loved? Yeah, well, tolerated, anyway. Evidently, he'd joined the milk-and-water, poker-rectumed Establishment with a bang. He'd be giving up muck-raking next, and we'd be looking up at herds of flying pigs.

'Come on, Crispus,' I said. 'Truce, OK? It's the festival. We'll split a fresh jug and I swear to you that neither me nor Perilla will go anywhere near your property. Especially when you're entertaining prats like the foreign judges' panel. Deal?'

He fizzed for a bit. Then he shrugged and held out his hand.

'OK,' he said. 'Deal. But only because it's the festival. And it doesn't apply outside the town limits.'

'Fine with me,' I said. I shook, and made a top-up sign to Pontius.

'That'll be a jug of the Alban, then, will it, Corvinus?' Pontius said.

I groaned. Bugger. Well, I couldn't weasel out without tarnishing the image. And he had given me a lead. Of sorts, anyway.

It might be an idea, for completeness' sake, to get a picture of Caesius off his home ground. I had to talk to Opilia Andromeda again, sure, but I didn't have much else planned where the case was concerned at present, and Rome wasn't far. Maybe a quick visit to the big city wouldn't go amiss, at that.

The Crimson Lotus it was.

FIFTEEN

Given decent weather and a lack of heavy traffic, once you hit the Appian Road it doesn't take long to get from the Alban Hills to Rome or vice versa – which, of course, is why the area's so popular with well-heeled businessmen and high-ranking public sector employees like Crispus who can afford to pay the increasingly ludicrous prices that property agents are asking for a rural retreat away from the stresses of urban life. Even travelling by snail-pace carriage, if he knocks off work early in the afternoon by the time the lamps are lit for dinner your lucky second-home owner can be sinking his first cup of Alban *in situ* and listening to the crickets chirping amid the bosky silence. Which meant that having left the villa on the stroke of dawn I was edging my horse through the minor traffic jam at the Appian Gate by just shy of mid-morning.

As ever, it was strange being back in the big city after the peace and quiet of the country-side, particularly in the run-up to the festival. Not unpleasantly so: maybe it's my imagination, sure, but from about the beginning of December onwards the streets of Rome seem much more crowded than they usually do, and whatever the weather – it was filthy that day, as it happened, mild and wet, with some of the narrower roads covered with half-liquid mud up to the top of the horse's hooves – there's a sort of deliberate, cheerful bustle about the place that you don't get at other times of year. Friendlier, too: even the juggernaut septuagenarian bag-ladies homeward bound from the market with the day's shopping will give you a cheery smile as they mow you down or force you into the gutter. Nearer the actual day, if you're lucky, they might even throw in a 'Happy Festival' over their shoulders for good measure.

So, anyway, there I was, back in the Queen of Cities and Pride of the Empire. There was no point in heading for the Crimson Lotus much before sundown: these places, catering as they do for the better-off professional with daytime commitments, tend to keep late hours. Bread-and-butter stuff first. I went round to the Caelian to unpack my overnight bag and seriously piss off the bought help, who with the family away – and more important Bathyllus, who ruled the place with a rod of iron – had no doubt loosened their collective corsets, got out the booze and nibbles, and put their feet up for the duration.

Which, naturally, involved breaking the glad news of my temporary return to our chef Meton, the grump's grump who if there'd been a competition for Mr Abrasive Personality of the Year would've won it hands down. Given the anarchic bastard's pathological insistence that, where meals were concerned, any change to the current arrangements should be communicated at least a day in advance, preferably in writing and accompanied by a grovelling apology, I wasn't looking forward to it. Nor had I any intention of making the first move by going through to the kitchen: the first rule of warfare is never to meet the enemy on his home ground, and that would really have been taking my life in my hands. I had one of the skivvies roust me out a jug of wine, carried it through to the atrium, put my own feet up on the couch, took the first welcome sip, set the cup down, and closed my eyes for an hour or two of much-needed R&R...

'Corvinus?'

Oh, bugger. The joys of life are fleeting, and quickly sped; evidently, the skivvy had tattled. Well, it had to happen sometime, I supposed. I opened my eyes again.

'Uh ... hi, Meton,' I said cheerfully. 'How's the lad?'

'You're supposed to be in fucking Castrimoenium.'

218

'True. True.'

'So what're you doing back in Rome?'

Direct and to the point: not a sunny bunny, our Meton, at the best of times, and currently the guy could've posed for an artist's sketch of Polyphemus coming home to his cave and finding Ulysses in residence. He was glaring at me under his shaggy eyebrows, his huge hairy paws flexing spasmodically.

'Ah ... slight change of plan, pal,' I said. 'Nothing to worry about, it's only temporary. I'll be heading back tomorrow.'

'Sod that. What about dinner? Got nothing in, have I?'

'That's OK,' I said. 'No problem. I'll make do with something from the store cupboard. Or I could eat out.' The glaring and flexing went up a notch: to a simple soul like Meton, patronizing cookshops was only a small step up from rooting through the garbage heaps. And even then it'd have to be a pretty good cookshop, one with named meat, for a start. 'There again—'

'Fuck that. Only it means I have to go all the way over to the market, doesn't it? And all the best stuff'll've disappeared by this time. Some people really have no fucking consideration.'

'Uh ... right. Right.' I was beginning to sweat. 'Well, I'm sure you can manage to whip something up. I'm not fussy, pal, keep

it simple. In any case it'll have to be something quick because I'll be going out this
evening.'

'You'll be *what*?'

'Ah ... yeah. Just before sunset, in actual
fact. So I won't have much time for...'

But I was already talking to his back.

Hell. That had gone down like a fart at a
funeral. Still, I hadn't expected anything else.
Maybe I should just've camped out under
Tiber Bridge and saved myself the hassle.

Domestics.

Dinner, when it came, was lavish: a wide
range of starters, broiled pork liver with
bacon slices and a reduced wine sauce, truf-
fles with lovage, and a honey omelette to
finish; evidently we were talking coals of fire
here. Still, I wasn't complaining: with Meton
in seriously-put-upon mode, I'd been expecting bread and cheese – yesterday's bread,
and cheese liberated from the mousetrap, at
that – while after several days of Euclidus's
adequate but pedestrian cooking I reckoned
I could overlook the display of artistic tem-
perament. Surly, foul-mouthed bastard the
guy might be, but Meton was a professional
to his badly-pared fingernails.

It was past sunset when I set out for
the Lotus. I took a couple of skivvies with
torches along with me, plus one of the
heavier well-muscled bought help. Pallacina

Road's a good neighbourhood, sure, but the stretch between it and the Caelian can get pretty hairy after dark, particularly when the weather's bad and there aren't too many punters on the go barring opportunist muggers, and I'd stocked up my belt pouch from the strongbox in the study in case – as was very probable, because anywhere Crispus patronized was bound to be exclusive – the admission charge cost me an arm and a leg. Upmarket clubs aren't cheap.

In the end, it wasn't all that easy to find, which may've been deliberate: these exclusive places don't encourage passing trade. I finally tracked it down to a quiet cul-de-sac off the road itself, so clean that the flagstones that paved it must've been scrubbed. Even so, the only indication that this was the place was a small marble plaque showing the eponymous flower next to an expensively panelled and metal-grilled door whose brass fittings gleamed in the light of the two torches burning in equally highly-polished brackets.

I knocked, and a hatch behind the metal grille slid back.

'Good evening, sir.' The plummy voice could've belonged to a top-notch private major-domo, or maybe a professor of rhetoric. 'Are you a member?'

'Uh ... no. No, I'm afraid not,' I said. 'But I'm a friend of Caelius Crispus. He gave me the address.'

I had the uncomfortable feeling that whoever was on the other side of the grille was
vetting me, and I was glad I'd put on a fresh
cloak and brought a respectable retinue of
skivvies.

'That's quite satisfactory, sir,' he said at
last. 'If you'll just wait a moment?' The door
opened with a rattle of bolts, revealing a big
Nubian in a flowing embroidered kaftan.
Not so much major-domo or professor of
rhetoric as moonlighting Parthian ambassador with all the trimmings. 'Do come in.'

I left the bought help to twiddle their
communal thumbs – luckily for them the
rain had stopped – and went inside.

'Your cloak, sir?'

I undid the pin, handed it over and looked
around. Upmarket was right: large, open
lobby with coloured marble panelling and
flooring, a pool with an ornamental fountain
made up of stone dolphins, and dominating
it all on one of the walls a large fresco showing the appropriate scene from the Odyssey
of a tastefully manicured garden with figures
lolling about on the flower-studded grass,
lotuses in their hands, attended by scantily-
clad nymphs and satyrs. There were some
very nice bronzes, too. I sniffed: the air was
perfumed, but there were overtones of what
I recognized from past experience as the
scent of burning *qef*. Unusual, sure, but may-

222

be not too unexpected, given the name of the place name and the doorman's eastern get-up. We were definitely talking Parthian decadence here, and Parthia and *qef* went together like fish sauce on tunny steaks. Evidently not just an upmarket club, the Lotus, but a *themed* upmarket club: they were getting more common these days, together with the themed upmarket wine shops. Ah, well, decadent times, right enough.

'I'm Rhadames, sir.' The guy had folded my cloak over his arm like it belonged to royalty. 'The prospective members' fee is five gold pieces set against the final amount, payable in advance and extra to the cost of any services or beverages enjoyed during your visit. I trust that is in order?'

I swallowed, opened my belt purse, and handed over the coins. Shit! Prices had certainly gone up since I was last in a place like this. Not that that had been too often, mind, even in my wilder pre-Perilla days: you didn't get many clubs in Rome of the standard of the Lotus. I was glad I'd raided the strongbox before I'd left. This could've been embarrassing.

'Thank you.' My ambassador pal pocketed the cash. 'Now. If you'd care to follow me into the common room you can make your wishes known to the house staff at your leisure. Have a pleasant evening.'

'Ah – just a moment, friend,' I said.

That got me a poached-egg, jaundiced look.

'Yes, sir.'

'Actually, I only wanted to ask a few questions about one of your members. A Quintus Caesius?'

Make that a freezing stare. Well, it was only to be expected. Still...

'Could I enquire where you got the gentleman's name from, sir?'

'What?'

'Who told you, sir, that Quintus Caesius was a member?'

'Uh ... that was Caelius Crispus. The friend I mentioned before I came in? He's a member too.'

'Indeed, sir,' he said. 'But I'm afraid in any case your request cannot be complied with. House rules. We do not discuss any given member with another, let alone with prospective ones.'

Spoken like a King's Eye from Persepolis itself. Even so...

'The guy's dead,' I said. 'Murdered down in Bovillae. I'm looking into things on behalf of the senate there.'

'*Murdered*, sir?' A smidgeon of distaste; habitués of the Lotus evidently didn't get themselves murdered. Or if they did they kept it politely to themselves.

'Yeah. He had his head beaten in a few days back behind the town brothel.'

He closed his eyes briefly. 'Oh, shit.'

I blinked: not just at the language, but the accent had been pure Aventine Roman. Expat Parthian, my King's Eye.

'So, uh, if I could just have a word with the boss?' I went on. 'Discreetly, of course.'

'You'll have to hang on until I've asked, won't you? You can wait in the common room.'

I followed him through a marble arch. They hadn't tried to recreate the bucolic conditions of the fresco, but this was the urban equivalent: a large room that must've covered most of the club's ground floor, with a high coffered ceiling and a railed balcony running round creating a mezzanine level. There were two or three big chandeliers fitted out with crystals that spread the light of the beeswax candles at their centre – candles, unusually, not lamps – but the lighting mostly consisted of bronze candelabra scattered throughout the room, creating little islands of brightness, each with its own couch or group of couches. Some of these – not very many – were occupied by the real-life equivalent of the fresco's lotus eaters, wearing not mantles or tunics but loose woollen or silk kaftans, and I noticed on most of the low tables beside them the little dish of smoking *qef* that was probably responsible for the soporific atmosphere that seemed to be the place's main feature. Soft-footed slaves padded from island to island, tending the burning *qef* or exchanging a few murmured words with the punters. As I looked, one of these got up and followed the slave towards the staircase at the end of the room leading up to the mezzanine.

'If you'd care to make yourself comfortable, then, sir, I'll tell the owner that you're here.' 'Rhadames' was back in character, I noticed. Half the trick in these places is the razzmatazz, and it's what the customers are paying for, after all. 'Can I get you some refreshment?'

'A large cup of wine would be good, pal,' I said. It'd probably cost the earth, but what the hell, case or not I was on holiday. 'Straight wine, nothing fancy.' I could feel my head spinning with the *qef* fumes already. Passive smoking's always a drawback where *qef*'s concerned.

'Certainly. I'll have one of the boys bring it to you.'

He left, and I lay down on the nearest couch. Oriental luxury there as well: in addition to the thickly padded upholstery there were half-a-dozen cushions that felt like they were filled with lambs' wool. One of the peripatetic slaves brought over a dish of *qef*, but I waved him away.

The wine came a couple of minutes later: a small silver flask, bedded in snow, with a matching cup and a plateful of stuffed dates and miniature pastries. I poured and sipped. It went down like liquid silk: *echt* Caecuban, and top of the range.

I was on my third pastry – they were as good as Meton could make, which is saying something – when 'Rhadames' came back.

'The owner will see you in his office, sir,' he said. 'If you'll come this way? The boy will bring your wine.' He snapped his fingers, and one of the ministering slaves came over and picked up the tray.

I followed him through another arch, this one hidden behind a curtain, and down a short corridor to the door at the end. 'Rhadames' knocked and opened it. No oriental luxury here, just a standard office with document cubbies and behind the desk a greying business type busy with a wax tablet and stylus.

'I'll be with you in a moment,' he said without looking up. 'Come in and make yourself comfortable.'

There was a chair beside the desk; not a stool, one of these Gallic wickerwork things you sometimes get. I pulled it up and sat. The slave with the wine tray moved a small table over, set the tray down on it, and went out, closing the door behind him. The guy wrote down a few more words, closed the tablet and raised his head.

'Now,' he said. 'I'm sorry, I wasn't given your name.'

'Corvinus. Valerius Corvinus.'

He was still holding the pen. 'And what is it precisely that I can do for you, Valerius Corvinus?'

'I'm looking into the murder of one of your members on behalf of the senate down in Bovillae. A Quintus Caesius.'

'Yes. So Publius told me.'

'Publius?'

'Rhadames.' Not the trace of a smile; it didn't look like I was going to get his name in return, either. 'That may well be. I can't see, though, that it's any concern of mine. This is Rome, not the Alban Hills.'

'Yeah. Yeah, I know. I'm just covering the angles. I was hoping you might be able to give me some information about him.'

'Such as what?'

'Was he a regular? He was back and forward on business quite a lot, so it would seem likely.'

'Hmm.' The sharp, abacus eyes rested on me for a good half minute, assessing. Then he put the pen down. 'We've only been open for two or three months,' he said, 'so the question doesn't really arise. But in any case, I'm afraid I couldn't tell you much. That's couldn't *and* wouldn't, by the way. The gentleman may be dead, but that doesn't mean I can breach confidentiality. Particularly since, as I say, his death is totally unconnected with the Lotus.'

Yeah, well, I supposed that was fair enough, and not unexpected, either. 'So what can you tell me?'

'Only what you know already, and only *because* you know it: that he was a member. Fairly typical of the clientele we get here, well-off, good background, not particularly young any more.' He hesitated. 'Let's be clear about this, Corvinus, because given the circumstances as reported to me by Publius I'm sure you're thinking along those lines. The Lotus is emphatically not a brothel. Oh, yes, of course, we can and do cater for our members' sexual interests. But we are, primarily, what we say we are: a gentlemen's club, providing a home from home, especially for businessmen from out of town. Most of the customers, as you no doubt saw, come here simply to relax. As I said, Quintus Caesius was fairly typical in that regard.'

'He have any particular friends here? Among the rest of the members, I mean?'

A long silence. 'That I don't know, and if I did I'm afraid I wouldn't tell you,' he said. You could've used his tone to replace the snow in the wine cooler.

I blinked. 'Uh ... come again?'

'You saw our common room, of course?'

'Yeah. Yeah, very nice.'

'We pride ourselves on it. Our members are a mixture, very much individuals. Some are more gregarious than others, and the common room is designed deliberately to allow someone to circulate freely but anonymously as much or as little as he pleases, with the proviso that any exchanges of personal details that result be confined within the walls of the club. But that is emphatically their concern, not mine or my staff's.'

'Come on, pal! It was a harmless question!'

That got me another long, cold stare. 'Was it, indeed?' he said finally. 'That may be. Nevertheless, I can only repeat: any member, while he is within these four walls, is guaranteed absolute anonymity. That is the Lotus's strongest selling point. He can be totally sure that what he does or says while he is our guest here will go no further. And that stricture, as I said, is binding on our members as well as us. Which, incidentally, raises the issue of your own presence here.'

'Yeah? In what way?'

'You were told originally, I understand, that Quintus Caesius belonged to this club by a friend of yours.'

'Yeah, that's right. Uh ... Caelius Crispus. Not so much a friend as—'

'Then I'm afraid under the first and most important rule of the club we shall have to reconsider Crispus's own membership.'

'*What?*'

'"No member shall for any reason divulge the name or personal details of a fellow member to a third party, or give any account

230

of transactions between them outside club premises, subject to the summary removal of their own name from the club's membership roll.'" He picked up the stylus again and reached for another tablet. 'Perhaps you could inform your friend the next time you see him. And now I'm afraid I'm extremely busy. Publius will show you out and under the circumstances your entry fee will be returned. Just tell him that I have so instructed.'

'Now wait just a minute!'

'That's all, Valerius Corvinus. A pleasure to have met you. Have a nice Festival.'

He opened the tablet and began to read. Interview, obviously, well and truly over.

Bugger! Crispus would kill me! Still, it was done now, and he wouldn't find out until our pal Rhadames gave him the bum's rush the next time he dropped by. I'd just have to hope our paths didn't cross in the remotely foreseeable future.

On my way through to the lobby, escorted by the gentleman in question, I happened to glance over towards the far wall of the common room, just as a ministering slave bent over to talk to the punter lying on the single couch next to one of the candelabra. The man turned his head, and the light caught his face clearly.

It was Quintus Baebius.

Well, well, well.

SIXTEEN

When I checked on the weather for the ride back next morning it had taken a turn for the worse: a gusting wind with snow on its boots straight out of the north, with a mixture of rain and hail thrown in for good measure. Me, I'm no masochist – there's no fun in spending three or four hours on horseback getting soaked to the skin and frozen – so I put off going until the day after in the hopes that things might settle down.

Which, for a marvel, they did late in the afternoon, when the wind suddenly died, the sun came out, and Jupiter gave us what was left of a fine December day. Even so, it made for a late start. Worse, I'd only got about half way to Bovillae when the weather changed again with a vengeance. By the time I'd reached it and covered the last four miles to Castrimoenium it was long past dinner and I was long past caring. I had a much-needed steam in the villa's baths and lugged my shattered carcass upstairs to bed.

Not that I felt too bad next morning; grouses aside, all that riding exercise I'd been putting in between the villa and Bovillae recently seemed to be paying off. When I came down to breakfast – as usual, I'd left Perilla snoring away and dead to the world – the only one in the dining room was Clarus.

'Morning, pal,' I said, lying down on the couch. 'Where's the Princess?'

'Been and gone,' he said. 'Out with Placida. How was Rome?'

Ah, the joys of owning a pet with a daily need to roll in and then consume the remains and excreta of the local wildlife. 'Still there.'

'Successful time?'

'Not a complete waste, in the end,' I said. 'Tell you later.'

Lupercus buttled in. 'Good morning, sir,' he said. 'Would you like an omelette?'

'No. Bread and honey'll do fine, pal.' Me, I'm not normally a breakfast person, unlike Perilla, who can really shift it, or the Princess who can eat as much as both of us combined, and although I'd missed dinner the night before, a day and a half of Meton's cooking had set me up nicely. 'No Bathyllus? I thought that was part of this silly deal of yours.'

'Ah ... Bathyllus is slightly incapacitated this morning, sir.'

'You mean he's ill?'

'Not exactly, no.'

I looked up at him. The guy had an angry-looking bruise on his forehead. 'You have an accident, Lupercus?'

'It's nothing serious, sir. I bumped into a door.'

Clarus's full attention was focused on his omelette. No eye contact, no reaction. Lupercus might as well not have existed. There was definitely something screwy here.

I sighed.

'OK,' I said. 'Wheel him in.'

'Wheel who in, sir?' Lupercus said. I just looked at him. 'Really, there's absolutely no need to—'

'Just do it. Spit spot, if you will. Breakfast can wait.'

Lupercus went out.

'You know anything about this, Clarus?' I said.

'Not in any detail, no.' Clarus was still not looking at me. 'I was careful not to ask.'

'Bugger that.'

Lupercus came in with Bathyllus tagging along behind. The little guy had a beautiful shiner which was rapidly turning purple.

'Good morning, sir,' he said. 'Did you have a good trip?'

'Never mind the trip, sunshine,' I said wearily. 'Let's get this over with. And I won't believe a repeat of the door story, either. Who threw the first punch?'

Bathyllus fizzed for a moment. Then he said: 'Actually, sir, it was a pot of metal polish. I happened to be holding it at the time.' I goggled at him. 'In my defence I have to say that he called me a superannuated fossil.'

'What the hell is a fossil?'

'Only after *he* called *me* a talentless whippersnapper,' Lupercus said.

'I did not!'

'You did!'

'I did not say "talentless". The word I used was "incompetent".'

'That's even—'

Gods alive! *'Will you both shut up!'* I shouted. They subsided. 'You're acting like five-year-olds, the pair of you! Bathyllus, you especially. What started all this in the first place?'

'Your mother, sir. The Lady Vipsania. And Helvius Priscus,' Bathyllus said stiffly. 'They're arriving tomorrow.'

'Yeah. So?'

'I've always looked after them when our visits here coincide. You know that. They expect it.'

Gods give me patience! I took a deep breath. 'Sure you have, Bathyllus, so far,' I said carefully. 'No arguments. But that was while the Lady Marcia was alive, and only because she sent Laertes down to Baiae to visit his sister for the duration. Marcia's gone, and so has Laertes. The household's got its own major-domo now.'

'That's exactly what *I* told him, sir!' Lupercus said. 'But he wouldn't listen!'

'Hold on, pal.' I held up a hand. 'Just leave this to me, OK? Bathyllus?'

'The Lady Vipsania and her husband are family, sir, and as such according to our agreement–' he gave Lupercus a fifty-candelabra glare – 'they fall within my area of responsibility.'

Lupercus glared back at him. 'Look,' he said. 'I've told you a dozen times, they are *not* family, they are fu—' He caught himself. 'They are *guests*. Guests are my affair.' He turned to Clarus. 'Isn't that right, sir?'

Jupiter! 'Just hang on a minute, Clarus,' I said. 'This is easily enough settled. Bathyllus, pack your things.'

He stared at me. 'I beg your pardon, sir?'

'Toothbrush and smalls, please, straight away. I warned you. Lupercus is absolutely right. If you can't get along with him – which you obviously can't – then you can go back to Rome.'

'But...'

'No buts. It's the Winter Festival in a few days, and nobody wants squabbling and temper tantrums then. No doubt there'll be a cart going through at some time or other today. See that you're on it. I'll talk to you when we get back.'

'But you can't...'

'Oh, yes, I can. Watch and marvel.'

He drew himself up for a bit more self-righteous fizzing, then caught my eye. Finally, teeth firmly clenched, he said: 'Yes, sir. Will that be all?'

'Yeah, Bathyllus. That's about it. Put some raw steak on that eye.'

'Yes, sir.'

'You can go too, Lupercus,' Clarus said.

They left.

Clarus looked at me. 'Come on, Corvinus,' he said.

'Come on, what?'

'Like you said, it's the festival in a few days. Bathyllus was looking forward to it. You can't send him back to Rome now.'

'Sometimes you've just got to be firm. And he is acting like a five-year-old.'

'Granted. Still, do you want me to have a quiet talk with him? Maybe let Marilla weigh in? And I'll have a word with Lupercus too. See if I can patch things up.'

'Suit yourself, pal. But make it clear that it ends now.' I got up. 'I think I'll skip breakfast after all. I can have an early lunch in Bovillae.'

Bugger. First Meton and now Bathyllus. Slaves. They're as much trouble as kids sometimes.

It was mid-morning by the time I arrived. I went straight round to the brothel for another talk with Opilia Andromeda.

237

'Hi, uh, Carillus, wasn't it?' I said when the slave opened the door for me.

'Yes, sir.'

'The mistress about?'

'No, sir, not yet. But she's usually down at around this time, so she shouldn't be long, if you can wait.'

'No problem, pal.' I took off my cloak – it had been raining again, and the ride over from Castrimoenium had been pretty damp – and hung it on one of the lobby pegs. 'She lives over the shop, then?'

'Yes, sir. She has a separate flat on the floor above.' Right; that explained the external staircase on the alley side of the back door. 'But you can use her sitting room, if you like. I'm sure she won't mind.'

'That'd be fine.' I paused. 'Just out of interest, have you been with her long? I mean, did you know her before she came to Bovillae?'

'No, I was the previous owner's slave, sir. Rutilia Tyche. I came as part of the property when she transferred the ownership. That would've been about fourteen months ago.'

'So you don't know anything about her? Prior to then, that is?'

'No, sir. Apart from the fact that she worked in a similar establishment in Tibur.'

'Right.' I followed him along the corridor to Andromeda's room. He opened the door and stood aside. 'Ah ... One more question. Aulus Mettius. He come here often?'

'On occasion, sir.' Guarded: well, given what Andromeda had said about confidentiality that was fair enough.

'Friendly with him, is she? I mean, outside professional contact, as it were?'

'I'm sorry, I really couldn't say.' *Guarded* had gone up a couple of notches to *stiff as hell*.

'So you wouldn't know whether, for example, he was here the night of the murder?'

'No, sir, I wouldn't. Now if there's nothing else I'll get on with my duties.'

'Sure.' Well, it'd been worth a try. 'Thanks, pal.'

He left, closing the door behind him.

I wouldn't get a better chance than this to take a proper nosey around. Book cubby, small but bursting to the gunnels with a fair collection of books, mostly philosophy, in the original and translation, but also including a copy of Herodotus's 'Histories', Xenophon's 'Memorabilia' and a couple of Sophoclean dramas. Serious stuff again, no Alexandrian bodice rippers. And, more to the point, no pricey bronze figurines squirrelled away under the couch, either. Well, it had been a possibility, although if Andromeda did have it then it'd be far more likely to be in her private flat upstairs than in her relatively public sitting room.

Apropos of which...

There was a curtain on the far wall that

turned out, when I moved it aside, to be covering a flight of steps. So, the upstairs flat was accessible by an internal staircase as well as by the external one. It was odd that I couldn't hear anyone moving about in the room above, mind, particularly since from the light showing between the boards the sitting-room ceiling was also the room's actual floor. But then maybe Andromeda was a late riser.

I sat down on the stool to wait for her. Half an hour or so later, I heard the sound of footsteps on the ceiling boards, then on the stairs, and Andromeda came through the curtain.

She stopped dead. For a moment she looked … Fazed? Frightened? Guilty? I wasn't sure which, if any. Flustered, certainly, like she'd been caught out somehow. And white as a ghost.

'Valerius Corvinus,' she said. 'You gave me quite a start.'

'I'm sorry,' I said. 'Carillus told me you wouldn't mind me waiting for you in here.'

'No. No, of course I don't.' She lay down on the couch and tried a smile that didn't quite work. 'But I am rather busy this morning, as it happens. Or will have to be, shortly, with house matters. What can I do for you?'

'Just a couple more questions. When he was here that night, did Caesius have a small bronze with him? The figurine of a runner?'

Was that a blink? It might've been, but I couldn't be sure. In any case, she answered calmly enough.

'I don't know. He may have done. He was wearing his cloak when I let him in, so if the bronze was a very small one I wouldn't have noticed. Why do you ask?'

'Just checking possibilities. The chances are that he had it when he left home, and it's gone missing. It was pretty valuable.'

'Was it, indeed? It seems a strange thing to be carrying around, then. Would he have had a reason?'

'Yeah. Seemingly he had a deal going with someone involving an exchange. Before he came here. But the deal fell through, so he'd still have it on him.'

'Well, I'm afraid I can't help you. All I can say is that I didn't see it.'

'How about his partner? Lydia? Would she know? Maybe I could talk to her again?'

'Lydia isn't here at present,' she said short-ly. 'Her time of the month. She's spending a few days with her mother and small son in Castra Albana.'

'That's pretty generous of you, lady. I didn't think the girls in these places got days off.'

She shrugged. 'She can't work. Obviously. Castra Albana is close by. And I've been one of these "girls" myself, Corvinus; I know how valuable free time is to them, particularly if they have children, as many of them do. If you can't accept that explanation then put it down to a purely mercenary desire to save the cost of a few days' rations and lamp oil. Now, if you have no more questions, as I said I have work to do, so...'

'Marcus Manlius. Would he be a customer of yours, by any chance? Or Sextus Canidius, maybe?'

It was a shot in the dark, but this time she really did blink. She hesitated before replying.

'Both of them, yes, as it happens,' she said. 'But that information is given to you in the strictest confidence. Both are married – happily, as far as I'm aware – and they're only occasional visitors.'

'Either of them here the night of the murder?'

Again, the hesitation. Then she said: 'Canidius did drop in. Briefly. His visits are always brief. He's quite a cold fish, according to the girls.'

'When would that be? When Caesius was here?'

'They overlapped, yes. But Canidius arrived after Caesius and left before him.'

'They ever meet at all? Here, face to face, I mean?'

'Not that I'm aware of, and we do everything we can where the special guests are concerned to avoid that happening. That's always a possibility, of course, and if it had happened it would have been embarrassing for both parties. But as I told you last time Caesius generally went with Lydia, so unless Canidius – or, indeed, Manlius on another occasion – happened to come along the corridor as Caesius was actually entering or leaving by the back door then the situation wouldn't have arisen. Naturally, if it did, none of them would have mentioned it to me.'

'One last question, lady.' I indicated the scarf round her neck. 'The bootmaker in the alleyway outside said you'd been in a fire in Tibur, before you took over here. That so?'

'Valerius Corvinus!' She sat up on the couch and glared at me. 'That can have nothing whatsoever to do with your investigation, and it is certainly none of your business otherwise!'

'True. You're right, and I was just interested. Only it was quite a lucky break, wasn't it? That's what the bootmaker said, anyway. Got you your freedom and the sub to buy this place.'

'Indeed.'

'There wouldn't be much to spare, though, would there? I mean, money-wise. It must've taken quite a sizeable lump sum, and however grateful she was, your ex-mistress could not have been all that generous. After all, what with the fire and everything, she'd have

243

her own losses to recoup.'

She was getting angry, and trying not to show it. 'Corvinus, I repeat: that is none of your business. For your information, she gave me part of the money as a loan, in exchange for a share of the profits. A perfectly normal business arrangement between an ex-owner and her freed slave, which I was and am.'

'Yeah, right. Only that'd shave your profit margins even further, wouldn't it? And from the looks of things the place could do with some serious capital investment.'

She flushed. 'What exactly is your point, please? If you think I murdered Quintus Caesius and stole this statuette you claim he had with him, then—'

'I was just wondering where you got the spare cash for that pricey perfume you're wearing. Not to mention a Coan silk scarf, a wig that must've come from one of the best couturiers in Rome, and a fair-sized specialist library. Book copying doesn't come cheap. Believe me, I know.'

That fazed her; for a moment, she looked blank.

'What?'

'Of course, they might've been presents from a rich boyfriend. Me, I was wondering about Aulus Mettius.'

She stood up. She was quivering with rage, sure, but there was something else there, in her eyes and her expression and her whole body language. 'Valerius Corvinus, you will leave now, please!' she snapped. 'My private life is none of your concern!'

I stood as well. 'Fair enough,' I said. 'Thanks for your time.'

I left her still glaring. Cage nicely rattled.

Anger, yeah, I'd been expecting that, but there'd been that flash of something else when I mentioned Mettius. Even fear wasn't putting it strongly enough. Unless I missed my guess, the lady was terrified.

Interesting.

OK, time for that early lunch. I went back to the main drag and turned right towards the market square and my usual wine shop. I was just passing the square and about to cross the road when someone shouted my name. I turned: Silius Nerva was hurrying towards me.

'Corvinus, thank goodness!' he said. 'I'm glad I've caught you myself. I've had men out looking for you.'

'Yeah?' I said. 'What about?'

He was looking grave. 'There've been ... developments.'

'What kind of developments?'

'Aulus Mettius has been found dead. Murdered.'

'*What?*' I stared at him. 'When?'

'About an hour ago. The finding, anyway.'

Gods! 'Where did this happen?'

'At the edge of his property, just outside town on the Castrimoenium side. His mother sent one of their slaves to tell me.'

'The Castrimoenium side? You mean near Quintus Roscius's place?'

'Indeed. They're close neighbours. As a matter of fact, it was Roscius who found the body.'

'*Roscius* found it?'

'Yes. He was out hunting, seemingly. Mettius was lying in a clearing between the two farms. His head had been beaten in.' Sweet Jupiter! I remembered hoping, when Perilla had said that Mother and Priscus were arriving early, that there'd be another murder to take me out of the house. Be careful what you wish for, because it might come true. And this I hadn't expected. 'You'll want to go over, naturally.'

'Sure.' My brain had gone numb. 'The body's still there?'

'No. Vatinia Secunda – that's his mother, of course – had it carried back to the villa. Corvinus, this business is dreadful! Simply dreadful!'

'Yeah.' I frowned. 'OK, I'll collect my horse and get over to the villa now. Where exactly is it?'

'I'll have my slave take you.' He glanced round at the slave who had followed him and was waiting just within earshot. 'Tertius.

246

Take Valerius Corvinus to the Mettius villa. Stay with him as long as you're needed.'

'Yes, sir.' The slave touched his forelock.

'Hang on,' I said to Nerva. 'You think you could send someone over to Castrimoenium to ask Cornelius Clarus if he'd join me?'

'The doctor?' He looked nonplussed. 'It's a little late for that, surely.'

'I just thought he might be able to help, that's all.'

'Well, if you think he'd be useful, of course I'll see to it at once.'

'Thanks.'

He went off, leaving me sorely puzzled. Who would want to kill Aulus Mettius? And why?

SEVENTEEN

Slaves were already outside the entrance to the Mettius villa hanging up the branches of funeral pine and myrtle. Before I'd got as far as the door one of them had gone into the house and reappeared with the major-domo.

'Valerius Corvinus?' he said.

'Yeah,' I said as I dismounted. 'Look, I'm sorry to disturb you, but Silius Nerva said—'

'No, that's all right, sir. It was the mistress who asked him to send you straight over if he could. This way, please.'

I left Nerva's Tertius to look after the horse and followed him inside. I thought, as with Caesius, they might've laid the corpse out in the atrium, but maybe it was too soon even for that, and they were waiting for the undertakers. In any case, the room was empty apart from an elderly woman in a mourning mantle sitting in a chair. Vatinia, presumably – Mettius's mother and Quintus Caesius's sister-in-law. She looked up when I came in.

'Valerius Corvinus, madam,' the major-domo said.

'Thank you, Phrontis. Bring a stool over for him, please, and then you can go.' Her eyes were fixed on a point to the left of my shoulder. They were covered with a white film, and I realized she was blind. 'It's good of you to come so quickly.'

'I was in town anyway, and I bumped into Silius Nerva in the street,' I said. 'I'm sorry for your loss, Vatinia. You're, uh, sure you want to talk to me now? I mean...'

'I'll grieve later, Valerius Corvinus. At present, the fact of Aulus's death hasn't really sunk in. I'd rather I talked to you now, if I must, before it does.'

The major-domo brought the stool, bowed, and left. I sat down.

'Very well,' I said. 'Can you tell me anything about what happened? Anything at all?'

'No. I keep mostly to my own room these days, even for meals. Aulus was a good son, in some ways at least, but although we occupied the same house we lived quite separate lives. According to Phrontis – and you can confirm this with him yourself, of course – he went out shortly after breakfast, which was the last time anyone saw him. Our neighbour Quintus Roscius came round about two hours later to say that he'd found his body in the grove of pines up beyond our topmost vineyard. That's really all I can tell you.'

'Your son didn't say where he was going? Whether he was meeting someone, for example?'

'Not to me, certainly. I hadn't talked to him since he came to my room yesterday evening to say goodnight, as he usually did when he was sleeping at home. But Phrontis would know.'

'He, uh, spent his nights elsewhere on occasions, then?'

Vatinia smiled. 'Aulus wasn't a child, Corvinus. And nor am I. Yes, quite frequently, although to my knowledge he never brought the woman to the house. That would have upset me greatly, and he knew it.'

'"The woman"? A particular one?'

'The freedwoman. Andromeda. I hear she runs a brothel now in the town. I've nothing against that in itself – she must live, after all – but I was sorry he'd taken up with her again after all these years. I'd hoped, when he came back home, he'd marry a girl of his own class and settle down properly. But then that wasn't Aulus's way.'

'"Again"? They knew each other before she moved here?'

'Oh, yes. When she was my brother-in-law's slave. It was quite the family scandal. We expected, when he got rid of her to a woman in Tibur, that to be the end of the affair. As, at the time, it was.'

'Andromeda was Quintus Caesius's slave?'

250

'Indeed. Many years ago now, of course. Aulus could only have been seventeen, and the girl was about the same age, or slightly younger. You didn't know?'

'No.' Holy gods alive! 'No, I didn't.'

'Aulus always was wild. His father died when he was seven, but even before that he had a mind of his own, and he was constantly getting into trouble. My brother-in-law did his best to help the boy, of course, out of duty to the family, but even I realized that it was a losing battle. Worse: it was through his association with Quintus that he became involved with the slave girl. And then there was the business of the missing money and his relegation. I thought that might bring him to his senses, but it wasn't to be. When the woman got her freedom and moved back into the neighbourhood he took up with her again straight away. He was quite besotted.'

Sweet Jupiter! I remembered the lack of any sound from Andromeda's flat above her sitting room. Oh, sure, she could've been in bed until just before she came down, but it was equally possible that the flat had been empty, that she hadn't been upstairs at all, and that she'd just come in via the outside stair. It would explain why she was flustered when she'd found me there, too. 'He could-n't've been seeing her today, could he?' I said. 'Arranged a meeting for this morning, I

251

mean?'

'It's possible, although I wouldn't have thought so, certainly not here. Why should he? He always went to her; she has a flat above her place of business. But as I said I don't know.'

I was thinking hard. I agreed with the lady that an arranged early-morning meeting out here in the sticks – particularly since it wouldn't have been at the villa itself – was pretty unlikely on the face of it, but it was still definitely something to check up on, because if that had been the way of things then it raised some very interesting possibilities indeed. The major-domo Phrontis might be able to shed some light. Plus, like I said, there was the distinct probability that she'd been out and about that morning before I talked to her, so she must've gone somewhere. A meeting with her boyfriend was as good a solution as any. I didn't know how exactly it would fit in with Mettius's death, mind – if they'd been lovers, as they obviously had been, then why she'd want to kill him I couldn't think – but where Quintus Caesius's murder was concerned the undisclosed past connection between the two combined with the opportunity factor put her squarely on the most-likely suspects list. Pretty well near the top of it, at that.

Whatever the truth of the matter, I would sure as hell be having another word with the lady herself before she was much older.

'Is there anything else you can tell me, Vatinia?' I said. 'About your son's recent activities? Any names he's mentioned in the last few days, and so on, that might be a clue to why he died? Anything at all, really, however trivial.'

'No, I'm afraid not. As I said, Aulus led his own life. Talk to Phrontis. He may be able to help you more.'

'Yeah,' I said. 'Yes, I'll do that.' I stood up. 'Thank you. Again, I'm terribly sorry.'

She nodded acknowledgement. 'He was a good boy at heart, you know,' she said. 'He had his faults, as do we all, perhaps more than most, but he didn't deserve to die for them. Certainly not in the way that he did. Find his killer for me. Please.'

I got up and left the room. The major-domo was waiting for me in the lobby.

'Would you like to see the young master, sir?' he said. 'Or perhaps the place where he was found? I'll have one of the slaves take you.'

'Yeah,' I said. 'Both. But I'll wait for my son-in-law, if you don't mind. He should be coming over from Castrimoenium.'

'Your son-in-law?'

'Cornelius Clarus. The doctor. I asked Silius Nerva to send for him. Meanwhile I was wondering if you had anything you could tell me yourself.'

He frowned. 'Not really, sir.'

'Your master didn't say where he was going, or why? That he'd arranged a meeting with someone, for example?'

'No. He left with hardly a word, just after breakfast. I assumed he was going into town.'

'On foot?'

'It isn't far. And he usually walked, whatever the weather.'

'Was he carrying anything?'

'Such as what, sir?'

'A small bronze statuette, for example?'

'I don't think so. But then if he had been I probably wouldn't have noticed. It was raining, and he was wearing his heavy cloak.'

Yeah. Fair enough. 'Uh ... Does the name Quintus Baebius ring any bells with you, by any chance?'

'I know the gentleman exists, certainly, but the master never mentioned him.'

'What about Opilia Andromeda?'

Phrontis's lips set in a tight line. 'That lady, sir, I do know. Unfortunately. And of course the master mentioned *her* frequently.'

'They were having an affair, right?'

'Gentlemen of the master's standing do not have affairs with ex-slaves, sir. There was a relationship, yes.'

I grinned, mentally: I've never yet met a major-domo who doesn't have a higher regard for what's done and not done than the guy who owns him. Social snobbery is built in with the bricks. 'OK, pal,' I said. '"Relationship" will do fine. They saw a lot of each other, certainly.'

'Yes, sir. Or so I assume. She's never set foot in this house, of course. The mistress would never have allowed it, and to be fair to him the master respected her wishes.'

'The place where the body was found – the pine grove – that in the direction of anywhere in particular?'

'No, sir. It's well away from the road, on the edge of our property where it adjoins Quintus Roscius's farm.'

'So your master would've been going there specifically? To the grove, I mean?'

'Yes. At least, that's a logical assumption.'

'Could there've been any particular reason for that? Under normal circumstances, that is.'

'No, sir. None that I can think of.'

'Did he know Roscius at all? Socially, I mean.'

Phrontis sniffed: pure Bathyllus. 'The families don't mix socially,' he said. 'He knew him as a neighbour, of course. But whether he did any more than speak to him in passing, I can't say.'

'So they'd no contact? Social or business? As far as you're aware?'

'No, sir. None.'

The answer had come out flat. Well, that

was pretty final. Still...

'OK, Phrontis,' I said. 'I might just—'

'Hello, Corvinus. You wanted me?'

I turned. Clarus was coming in through the front door.

'Oh, hi, pal,' I said. 'I wasn't expecting you for another half hour, at least.'

'I was visiting a patient this side of Castrimoenium. Nerva's messenger caught me on the road. What's going on? The man said Aulus Mettius has been found murdered.'

'That's right,' I said. 'I thought you might want to show off. Save me a bit of bother and just tell me who did it.'

He grinned. 'I'll do my best. But I don't perform miracles, Corvinus, and sleuthing's your department.'

'Fair enough.' I turned to Phrontis. 'This is my son-in-law. Do you think we could see your master's body now?'

'Certainly, sir.' The major-domo was frowning at Clarus: doctors tend to come pretty low in the social pecking order, and doctors visiting dead patients rank even lower. 'If you'd like to follow me?'

They'd put him on the bed in his room, just as they'd brought him in, on a makeshift stretcher. The way he was lying, like with Caesius, there was no sign of the wound, and what I noticed most of all was the look of surprise on his face.

'We're waiting for the undertakers to come

from town,' Phrontis said quietly. 'They shouldn't be long. Would you like me to stay?'

'No, that's fine. We'll come back out when we've finished. If you could arrange to have someone show us to where he was found?'

'Yes, sir. I'll do that.'

'Oh, and maybe send someone over to the Roscius place, ask Quintus Roscius if he'd meet us there to give us the details. Nerva's slave Tertius would do. He came over here with me.'

'Yes, sir. Of course.'

He left.

'OK, Clarus,' I said, stepping back. 'Do your stuff.'

I waited while he examined the body. Me, I'm OK with corpses, but like the last time I'd watched him do it I found his brisk detachment chilling. Finally, he pulled the bed well away from the wall, moved round into the space behind it, and put his hands beneath the corpse's armpits.

'Take a hold of his head for a second, will you, Corvinus?' he said. 'Don't let it droop.'

'*What?*'

'I need to see the wound. Unless we roll him over – which I don't want to do, because he's beginning to stiffen – I have to pull him clear of the stretcher so I can get underneath. Do it quickly, please, in case anyone comes.'

I moved in and took Mettius's head in both hands, supporting it, while Clarus heaved the body backwards.

'That should do it,' he said. 'Don't let go, right? Rigor's setting in quite fast, and we might not be able to get it to go back the way it is now.'

Gods!

He took a metal stylus from his tunic pouch, knelt down and peered up at the wound, prodding it. Finally, he grunted with satisfaction.

'OK, that's enough,' he said, straightening and moving back to the corpse's feet. 'Hang on for a bit longer while I pull him back on to the stretcher.'

He did. Then we moved the bed into its original position.

'Well?' I said.

'He's been dead three or four hours, but you knew that already, I suppose. Killed by a single blow to the back of the skull. From the shape of the wound, the weapon was about an inch and a half thick at its striking point. Possibly a club of some kind, but because the angle and the position suggest a lateral blow rather than a downward one, more probably a longish weighted stick. That'd account for the severity of the damage, too. The bones of the skull aren't just broken at the point of impact; they're completely shattered and driven into the base of the brain itself. My guess is a double-handed swipe with a lot of force behind it and plenty of leverage.'

'So the murderer was probably a man?'

'No, not necessarily. A strong woman in good health could've done it, easy. Given, as I say, a long, heavy stick and plenty of room to swing it.'

I sighed. 'So we've narrowed it down to the murderer being either a man or a woman, right?'

'More or less.'

'Great. Score one for science. You're not helping much here, pal.'

'I warned you, Corvinus, I don't do miracles. I can tell you at least that you're not looking for a one-armed midget. Whoever hit him was as tall as he was, or not all that much shorter. Unless he was kneeling down when he got clouted, of course, in which case all bets are off.'

'Very useful,' I said sourly. 'Thanks a bunch.' The bottom line was that none of it ruled out any of the likely suspects – including Andromeda – barring maybe Brother Lucius, who probably couldn't have mustered up the requisite strength. But then if Marilla's theory was right – and it was the best one going, under the circumstances – he wouldn't be doing his own dirty work in any case, would he?

Hell.

Mind you, the long, heavy stick side of things was interesting. Who did we know whose everyday job involved carrying a long, heavy stick and knowing how to use it offensively?

Right.

'OK,' I said. 'If you're finished then we'll go and take a look at the scene of the crime.'

It wasn't far, just out of sight of the villa complex where the cultivated land stopped and nature took over, a dip in the landscape made even more secluded by a close-packed grove of pine trees with thick, man-high bushes growing between them. The perfect place for a clandestine meeting.

A good place for a murder, too.

'Where exactly was your master found, pal?' I asked the slave who'd brought us.

He pointed to a patch of flattened grass just inside the clearing. 'Just there, sir.'

Yeah. That fitted. The way things were arranged, the killer could've hidden behind the screen of foliage and scrub, waited for his victim to pass or turn his back, then come out and let him have it. Which is what I reckoned had happened. It'd been raining, but not heavily, and there were still clear splashes of blood on the ground.

'Which way's the Roscius property?' I said.

'We're on the edge of it, sir. The farmhouse is over there.' The slave pointed again, to the

260

right. 'About two or three hundred yards.'

'Uh-huh.' I looked round. Clarus was poking about in the undergrowth. 'You find anything?'

'No. Nothing that could've been the murder weapon, anyway,' he said.

'See if you can...' I began, then stopped. Quintus Roscius was coming through the trees from the direction of his farm. 'Ah. Hi, Roscius. Thanks for coming over.'

'No problem.' I noticed he very carefully wasn't looking at the spot where the body had been. 'There isn't much I can tell you, though.'

'Just what you've got will be enough, pal,' I said easily. 'So what's the story?'

He shrugged. 'I was hunting. When the dog led me down here I thought she was following a scent. Mettius was lying face down, with the back of his head all bloody. I went down to the villa and raised the alarm. That's all there is.'

'You usually hunt in this part?'

'Sure. Technically, this is my land, although that wouldn't matter much because it's useless ground and no one around here gets uptight about things like that. You get a few deer coming down into the fields, particularly in the winter when food's scarce. I usually leave some vegetable scraps lying around to attract them and take a walk up this way when I'm out after the small stuff. Sometimes I get lucky.'

Yeah; now he came to mention it there was a pile of old cabbage leaves and a few rotting carrots at the edge of the clearing. Fair enough. 'Did Mettius do any hunting?' I said.

'Nah. Never took any interest in it. He was a town boy, and the family's well enough off not to have to bother about keeping their larder stocked personally. They get their bailiff to set a few snares and limed twigs, sure, but that's about it.'

'So why would he be up here?'

He shrugged again. 'Search me. Why not? It's a free country, and like I say no one bothers about boundaries.'

'You didn't see anyone else around?'

'Not a soul. But then again, I wasn't looking.'

'You'd been out for long?'

'Not very. An hour or so.'

'Close by to here?'

He was frowning. 'No. The other side of my property, as it happens. There wasn't much doing over that way, so I thought I'd try in this direction. Like I say, there was always the chance of a deer. Corvinus, what is this?'

'Just getting the facts straight, that's all, pal,' I said. 'So you, uh, didn't have much contact with Mettius? As a neighbour, I mean.'

'We passed the time of day occasionally, sure. He was OK, friendly enough, not stuck up like a lot of the nobs around here, and the family's old Bovillae, like mine is. But like I said, he was a townie, not a farmer. We didn't have much in common.'

'Fair enough.' I looked round. Clarus was chatting to the slave, obviously intentionally keeping a low profile while I talked to Roscius. 'You done, pal?' I said to him.

'Yes. Not a lot I can do for you here, Corvinus.'

'We'll get going, then. Clarus is my son-in-law,' I explained to Roscius. 'He's the de facto doctor over in Castrimoenium.' They nodded to each other. 'Oh, by the way, how's the business with the farm going? You get that loan problem sorted out?'

'Yeah,' he said guardedly. 'Yeah, that's all fine now. More or less.'

'So you managed to square things with Lucius Caesius?'

'He's given me a year's extension, and he's happy to go beyond that if it's necessary. I told you, old Lucius is all right, and he isn't exactly pressed for cash himself now.'

'I suppose it helps, him being a drinking crony of yours, doesn't it?'

'I wouldn't exactly call him a drinking crony. We see each other around, that's all.'

'Like on the night of the murder? When you split a jug or two in the wine shop near the back of the brothel and left together an hour or so after sunset?'

Long silence; he was staring at me. 'Who told you that?' he said.

'You mean it isn't true?'

'Sure it's true, as it happens. So what?'

'So why did you lie when I asked you where you were that night?'

'Wouldn't you? Come on, Corvinus! It didn't matter. I know I didn't kill the guy, and it'd only have complicated things.'

Yeah, well; the jury was still seriously out where that was concerned. Still, I let it go unremarked. 'You go straight home?' I said.

'Of course I did! I'd work to do in the morning.'

'So you didn't happen to bump into Caesius at all on the way, then? You and good old Lucius?'

I thought he was going to hit me; certainly his fists balled, and his whole body tensed. Then, abruptly and without another word, he turned and walked away, back the way he'd come. At the edge of the trees, he turned again and levelled a finger.

'You fuck off, Corvinus!' he said. 'You just keep the fuck out of my sight from now on! Is that clear?'

'Yeah.' I nodded. 'Yeah, it's clear. Thanks for your help, Roscius.'

Hmm.

EIGHTEEN

I let Clarus get on with his rounds, collected
my horse from the villa and headed back
into town for another word with Opilia
Andromeda. Me, I don't go for coincidences
as a rule, and the lady turning up late for
work and flustered a scant couple of hours
after her lover had had his head bashed in,
with every evidence that she'd been away
from home, was too coincidental for comfort. Particularly since at that point Mettius's death hadn't been reported, so she
couldn't have known about it and it couldn't
have been a factor.

Unless, of course, one way or the other she
did.

I'd been thinking things over on the ride
into town, and my bet was that the business
in the pine grove had been an arranged
meeting that had gone wrong. As far as I
could see, there were two possibilities that
fitted the circumstances, the first being that
the meeting was between Mettius and Andromeda, pure and simple. Possible though
that scenario might be, circumstantially

speaking, it didn't make any sense: as Vatinia had said, Andromeda never came near the villa, and when the pair got together it was in the comfort of the lady's flat. So why, if Mettius had wanted to meet his girlfriend or vice versa, should either of them faff around by changing the usual arrangement for something a lot less convenient and, given the weather conditions, a hell of a lot less comfortable? While if there'd been some skulduggery involved on Andromeda's part – which was hard to credit in itself – surely that would unnecessarily invite her boy-friend's suspicion.

The second possibility was a lot more likely. My guess was that the meeting had been by arrangement between the two of them on one side and the killer on the other. In which case we were left with the obvious questions of *who* and *why*. I could theorize, sure – Roscius, as being practically on the spot, Baebius, because of the missing statu-ette, and Manlius's rod man regarding the weapon used were prime contenders, albeit for different reasons flawed ones – but the simplest way of getting answers was to ask Andromeda herself.

So to the brothel I went. The front door was open, and this time I didn't stop to knock. I was heading along the corridor to-wards the lady's sitting room when Carillus materialized and intercepted me.

'Can I help you, sir?' he said.

'No,' I said. 'Not this time, pal. No problem, I was hoping to have another word with the boss, that's all.' I made as if to go past him, but he moved directly in front of me, blocking the way.

'I'm sorry, but you can't do that,' he said firmly. 'The mistress has gone out.'

Right; and I was Cleopatra's grandmother. I pushed past him without another word, carried on down the corridor, and opened the sitting-room door.

The room was empty. I turned to find Carillus glaring at me.

'There, sir,' he said. 'You see?'

Sure I did, for what it was worth: she'd probably nipped upstairs when she heard my voice and would now be lying low. Even so, I couldn't bet on it, and in any case, however urgent the matter ostensibly was, forcing my way into her private flat would've been taking things too far.

Bugger. Well, we might as well play the game through to the end, if only for appearances' sake.

'You any idea where she's gone?' I said. 'Or when she'll be back?'

'None whatsoever, sir.' *And you can take a running jump*, Carillus's tone said.

'OK. Fine.' I moved towards the exit. 'When you see her again, just tell her I called to say that Aulus Mettius has been murdered, will you?'

'*What?*' He was staring at me. 'When?'

'Early this morning, near his villa.' I kept on going. 'No hassle, pal, and no doubt she'll get the news from someone else in any case, if she hasn't heard it already. I only thought she might be interested, that's all.'

I left him gawping, shut the door behind me, and walked off in the direction of the market square.

What now? If we were to discount a talk with Andromeda, at least for the time being, it came down to the mechanics of checking alibis, particularly – because I knew about Roscius's already, or rather his lack of one – Marcus Manlius's rod man's. Clarus hadn't seen the wound that killed Caesius, sure, so I couldn't be certain, but I'd bet a gallon of Alban to a busted sandal strap that the two of them would've matched. That didn't automatically make Rod the killer, mind, but like I said where your ordinary everyday rod man's concerned the weighted stick is the weapon of choice. I didn't have any problem with likelihood, either: rod men are all bloody-minded thugs with a penchant for GBH as it is, or they wouldn't be doing the job in the first place, while Rod – Decimus, that was his proper name, wasn't it? – had already been involved criminally up to his neck in the wool store business. He'd simply be the muscle, sure, with Manlius being the one who gave the orders, but I reckoned in theory at least that that horse would run: Manlius already owed Mettius for blowing the whistle on him and his chum over the wool scam, while if they were behind Caesius's murder, leaving a loose barrel like Mettius rolling around just wouldn't be safe.

Yeah, I fancied Manlius, certainly as a comfortable side bet. Particularly with Canidius in the background as an *éminence grise*.

Maybe, though, if I was pushing that angle I should rope in Silius Nerva. I wasn't exactly *persona grata* with Bovillae's aedile, and I certainly wasn't going to ask him straight out if his tame gorilla had zeroed Mettius: Nerva could arrange things more subtly, and with a better chance of a satisfactory result. Besides, the bastard was getting his penny's worth of effort out of me where this case was concerned as it was.

So. First stop the town offices. If Nerva wasn't there – which as an ordinary senator he probably wouldn't be – the public clerk would be able to point me in the right direction.

In the event, I didn't have to bother looking for him: Nerva was in the square itself, chatting to a guy in a sharp plain mantle who had his back to me. I went over.

'Ah, Corvinus,' he said. 'How did things go at the Mettius villa?'

The other guy turned round. Canidius.

'Uh, OK,' I said. 'Do you have a moment to spare? In private?'

'Of course.' He frowned and turned to Canidius. 'I'll talk to you later, Sextus, if that's convenient. But tomorrow evening should be fine. We'll call it a date, shall we?'

Canidius was giving me a jaundiced stare, which after the circumstances of our last meeting wasn't surprising.

'The Mettius villa?' he said.

Nerva hesitated, and glanced sideways at me. 'Poor Aulus Mettius has ... met with an accident,' he said. 'A fatal accident. You hadn't heard?'

'No, I hadn't.' Canidius didn't seem too surprised, mind. Or all that shocked, or even interested. 'Oh, dear. What a pity. Tomorrow evening it is, then, Publius. I look forward to it. Corvinus.' He gave me the briefest of nods and moved off.

I watched him go. 'So what's happening tomorrow evening?' I said to Nerva.

'Just a dinner invitation. He and his wife are coming over for a meal.' Yeah, of course: in a small town like Bovillae, the Great and the Good of the social network would be in and out of each other's houses all the time, particularly in the festival period. Still, it was a salutary reminder that I couldn't be absolutely sure of even Nerva's objectivity. 'Now, Corvinus, what can I do for you?'

'I was wondering if you could check on

270

something,' I said. 'Manlius's rod man, or one of them. Would anyone know whether he was doing anything in particular earlier this morning?'

Nerva frowned again. 'Do you have a reason for asking?'

'Just checking, like I say. Mettius had his head beaten in, as you know. My son-in-law Clarus says it could've been done with some sort of long, weighted stick. The kind that rod men carry.'

'And you think this man might have been responsible?'

'It's ... a possibility,' I said cautiously. 'If he was elsewhere at the time it'd definitely rule him out.'

'But why on earth would Marcus Manlius's rod man want to kill Aulus Mettius?' Nerva asked. I said nothing. Nerva sighed. 'Very well, I won't pry. You're dealing with the case; you have your reasons for suspecting him, no doubt, and presumably you think they're valid, or sufficiently so. But as I told you, it's a bad business.' He patted my arm. 'Still. As far as checking on the fellow's whereabouts is concerned, we can find those out easily enough, in fact we'll do it now. The lictors are public servants. The clerk over at the town offices should be able to say whether he was on duty today. Follow me.'

The offices were just the other side of the square. We crossed over through the crowd and I followed Nerva up the steps and inside.

'Ah, Salvius,' he said to the slave on the desk. 'This is Valerius Corvinus. He wants to know if one of Aedile Manlius's lictors by the name of...?' He glanced at me interrogatively.

'Decimus,' I said.

'By the name of Decimus had any formal duties this morning.'

'No, sir,' the slave said. 'Not today. The aedile was at home, so he wasn't needed.'

Nerva grunted and turned back to me. 'There you are, Corvinus,' he said. 'Question answered. Of course, Manlius might have told him otherwise, as he has a perfect right to do. If he's at home at present we can always go over and check. It wouldn't take long; he doesn't live far away.'

'No, that's OK,' I said. There was no point: if Decimus had been moonlighting on instructions from his boss, Manlius wasn't likely to admit it just for the asking, was he? I turned to the clerk. 'One more thing, pal, while I'm here. You know the night the censor-elect was murdered? Could you happen to tell me if the guy was on duty then?'

'That'd be after sunset, sir, so no, he wouldn't be, definitely not. Under normal circumstances, a lictor's duties fall only between sunrise and sunset.'

Under normal circumstances. Right.

272

'Thanks,' I said, turning away.

'Well, Corvinus,' Nerva said as we left. 'So your "possibility" is still possible. For what it's worth, I'm compelled to say.'

'Yeah, it seems so. Still, it's only one of several.' I glanced up at the sky, to where the sun was peeking through the clouds. Getting towards the middle of the afternoon. Well, there wasn't anything to keep me in Bovillae for the moment, not if Carillus over at the brothel was acting watchdog for his mistress. I really, really needed to talk to her, but it seemed that was going to be difficult now. I just hoped she hadn't skipped town altogether, which was a distinct possibility. 'Thanks for your help, Nerva. We'll leave it there for the present.'

'I'll be getting home, then,' Nerva said. 'Good luck with the continued investigation. Libanius was quite right to suggest contacting you. You appear to be doing very well.'

Uh-huh. It didn't exactly feel like that from my side; in fact I'd describe my progress as like wading through glue. The usual problem: too many theories, not enough hard evidence. Still, glue or not we were moving forwards, and at least I was able now to make a case for Decimus the rod man being a possible perp for both murders, with his boss – and, by implication, Canidius – the guiding brains.

Unless, of course, the killer had been

Roscius, who together with Brother Lucius was equally if not a hell of a lot more possible where motive and opportunity went. Or Opilia Andromeda, using the second murder of her lover as a cover-up for the first. Then again, ignoring the alibi his door slave had given him, there was always Quintus Baebius...

Glue, pure and simple. Sod it. I was going home, too.

Bathyllus met me in the villa's entrance lobby with the wine tray, his black eye very much in evidence.

'Here you are, sir,' he said, handing me the welcome-home cup of wine. 'And let me just say I have given my solemn, binding promise to Master Clarus and Mistress Marilla that if I am allowed to stay for the duration of your visit you will have no further cause for complaint. Lupercus has given his word, too. Will that be satisfactory?'

I grinned. 'Yeah, OK, Bathyllus. You're off the hook, pal. It is the Winter Festival, after all, and so long as you and Lupercus behave yourselves and get along nicely that's all I ask. But you're on strict probation, right?'

'"Share", sir, shall henceforth be my watchword.'

'Good.' I kept my face straight and made a move towards the atrium. 'See you keep it that way.'

'Ah ... sir?'

I turned. 'Yeah, Bathyllus? Was there something else?'

'I should tell you that your mother and Helvius Priscus have just arrived. About ten minutes ago, in fact.'

Bugger! *Already?* 'That's ... good news, little guy,' I said.

'And that they have brought their chef with them.'

I stopped. 'They have *what*?'

'Phormio, sir, is one of the party. Dinner will be in an hour, should you wish to change.'

Oh, hell! Hell and bloody damnation! I carried on into the atrium. The bought help had brought in a couple of high-backed chairs, which Mother and Priscus were occupying. As usual, she looked stunning, even after the thirty-odd-mile coach trip, perfectly made-up and coiffured, and a good twenty years short of her actual age, while Priscus was doing his normal wrinkled-prune older-than-God impression. Perilla was on one of the room's three couches, and Marilla and Clarus were sharing another. I set my wine cup on the small table beside the unoccupied third and gave Perilla the usual kiss.

'Successful day, dear?' she said.

'Later,' I said, teeth gritted. I turned to Mother. 'Hi, Mother. Priscus. You're early.'

'The traffic was very light,' Mother said, putting her cheek up to be kissed. 'And it is Titus's birthday today, after all.'

Bugger! I'd thought it was tomorrow. But then I always get birthdays wrong. 'Happy birthday, Priscus,' I said.

'*Mmmaa!* Thank you, Marcus.'

I settled down on the couch and tried to keep my voice neutral. 'Ah ... Bathyllus says you've brought Phormio with you.'

Mother gave me her best dazzling smile. 'Yes. Oh, I know what we agreed, dear, but I didn't have the heart to leave him behind. And he has such *marvellous* plans for the Winter Festival dinner! You'll be amazed!'

I glanced at Clarus and Marilla. Obviously, from the looks on their faces, this was news to them, too. Not good news, either, to put it mildly, which came as no surprise. No one wants to spend the Winter Festival spewing their guts out, and with Phormio doing the cooking it'd be practically a dead cert.

Stopping Mother in her tracks, however, was a task about as easy as all twelve of Hercules' labours rolled into one and doubled. Fuck. Double fuck.

'Vipsania, we do have a perfectly good chef of our own, you know,' Marilla said.

'Of course you do, darling!' The smile shifted to her and Clarus. 'And I'm sure Euclidus is simply marvellous, for the every-day stuff, at least. But Phormio has just got

276

this frankly *unbelievable* book of recipes from a correspondent of his in Palmyra, who had it from a friend at the other end of the spice route.' She turned to Perilla. 'So terribly exciting for him! He really does take his cooking *seriously*, the lamb, and he's always on the lookout for anything just that little bit *outré.*'

'Yes,' Perilla said through tight lips. 'I know.'

'It's quite fortuitous, really. He's been waiting for the book to be copied and sent for almost two years now. And the special ingredients the recipes call for, of course, because most of these you can't find here. Those were even more difficult. We had to arrange for them to be imported on an almost individual basis, and you would not *believe* how much time and trouble that involves. Not to mention the expense.'

'Ah ... just exactly what would these ingredients be, Mother?' I said.

'Oh, really, *I* don't know, dear. Lots of things. You'd have to ask Phormio, although I doubt if even he could help. I don't actually think the majority have names in Latin at all. Or even in Greek, for that matter, which was why Phormio's Palmyran friend took so long to send the book in the first place. Seemingly, finding a capable translator who knew both Greek and whatever language the poor dears beyond Parthia speak was *such* a trial you wouldn't credit. As I said, it's all very exciting.'

Oh, shit. Shit, shit, shit! This sounded bad. Being poisoned was one thing, but being poisoned by something that didn't even have a proper civilized name west of the Indus would be nothing short of fucking embarrassing.

'Uh ... maybe we should talk about this, Mother,' I said cautiously. 'I mean, the Winter Festival meal's no time for experiments, is it?' Not sodding Phormio's kind of experiments, anyway, even if we did have a doctor on hand. Which wouldn't be much help if Clarus was down in the latrine or bent over a bucket along with the rest of us.

'Oh, don't be so boring, Marcus! You're such a fuddy-duddy traditionalist! It'll be an experience, I promise you.'

Right. Well, I was ready to go along with her on that score, certainly. And personally I'd rather spend the festival as a fuddy-duddy traditionalist with all his digestive organs still intact and functioning than an avant-garde gourmet who had to wear his running shoes to bed. Still, we'd a few days' grace before Phormio had his evil way with us. Maybe a solution would present itself.

Time for tact, and a change of subject.

'Incidentally, Priscus,' I said. 'I've a present for you.' The ivory plaque was still in my belt pouch. I took it out and handed it to him.

'Look and marvel.'

'*Mmaa!*' He held the thing up to the light and examined it. 'Oh, how very nice! Thank you, Marcus. You really shouldn't have. What an interesting design.'

'Yeah. It's Sicilian. About a century and a half old, the guy in the shop said.'

'Oh, no. The original may have been Sicilian – the design certainly is, Archimedes lecturing, I think – but this is a copy.'

'*What?*'

'*Mmaaa!* You didn't know? Well, it really doesn't matter; it's the thought that counts. Representations of Archimedes are quite common in Sicilian minor art of the period, particularly, naturally, that of Syracuse. Possibly as a covert expression of contemporary anti-Roman feeling, since of course he was quite the local hero and his death at the hands of the – in Greek eyes – philistine Roman captors of the city was viewed by its citizens as—'

'Hang on a minute, Priscus,' I said. 'Are you saying the thing's a fake?'

'But of course it is.'

Jupiter! 'You sure?'

'*Mwahahaha!*' He chuckled; not a pretty sight or sound. 'Oh, come now, really, my dear boy! You only have to look at the patina! It's obvious!'

Yeah, well, maybe it was, to your average antiquarian nut who could deliver an impromptu lecture on hundred-and-fifty-year-old Sicilian minor art at the drop of a hat. Me, I'd just have said that the thing was yellow.

'So, *mwahahaha*, you bought it as genuine, then?'

'Yeah, I did. From a shop in Bovillae.'

'Oh, dear, oh dear! *Mwahahaha!* In that case, Marcus, I shouldn't patronize it again, if I were you. The owner obviously doesn't know a thing about what he's selling. Or, of course, you've been sold a pup.'

'Guy by the name of Baebius. Ring any bells?'

'Quintus Baebius?' He blinked at me. 'Indeed it does, my boy, indeed it does! Quite a loud one. We've met on occasion, in the Saepta and at auctions.'

'He know his stuff?'

'Certainly! *Mmmaaa!* Oh, he's an expert, all right, quite the aficionado. Alexandrian period, if I remember, specialising in the Asian cities. But from what I've heard he's – *mmmaa* – not quite pukka, shall we say. Hairy in the hoof and too ready to take the main chance when it's offered, that's about the fellow's measure. What today's youngsters would no doubt call – *mmmaa* – a bit of a wide boy.'

Would they, indeed? 'Is that so, now?' I said. 'Thanks, Priscus.'

'*Mmmaaaa*. A nice enough piece in itself,

280

though. Thank you.'

'You're welcome.' I was thinking hard. Passing off a fake antique as genuine didn't exactly rank as the crime of the century; not when it could only have brought in a couple of extra gold pieces, max. And, if I believed his door slave, which I did, Baebius couldn't have committed at least the first of the two murders. However, the guy evidently wasn't the honest, solid citizen he pretended to be, and we still had a quite genuinely valuable figurine to account for, which the chances were that Caesius had had on him the evening that he died. Me, I wouldn't trust the bastard's word that he hadn't got it now if he swore blind by every god in the pantheon. Plus the fact that we had the coincidence of him and the murdered man being members of the same club in Rome to consider.

Shit; weren't *any* of these guys straight?

I'd have another talk with Quintus bloody Baebius tomorrow.

NINETEEN

I left it later than usual to make the trip into
Bovillae, intentionally so, setting off a good
hour after breakfast. Which, I was glad to
note, despite Mother and Priscus being in
evidence, was blessedly free of Phormio's
gunk. Over dinner the previous evening
Clarus, with uncharacteristic firmness, had
ignored Mother's strident protests that as a
medical man himself he should be encouraging his guests to eat a healthy breakfast and
put his foot down on that score: Phormio
had been barred from using the kitchen to so
much as boil an egg pro tem, which, considering that the bastard's eggs of choice
came from crocodiles and had been shipped
over from Egypt in jars of sand, made it a
reasonable place to start. Where that left us
vis-à-vis the actual Winter Festival dinner,
mind, was still a moot point: it'd take a much
braver man than Clarus – or me, for that
matter – to go head-to-head with Mother
when she was dead set on something, and
that particular sword of Damocles was still
hanging. We'd just have to hope for divine

intervention. Or maybe a major earthquake.

So. Since he lived in the top part of town, it had to be Baebius first. The guy had questions to answer, not only in regard to the dodgy plaque his freedman had sold me but also as to why he hadn't mentioned the fact that he and Caesius shared membership of a Roman club. I dumped my horse as usual at the Tiburtine Gate water trough and went straight round to his house, only to be told that that he was out.

'You know where he might be at all?' I asked the young door slave who seemed to double as his major-domo. 'It's pretty important.'

'He could've gone to the shop he owns, sir,' he said. 'You could try it, anyway. The one selling antiques and curios, in the street opposite the market square.'

'Yeah, I know where it is,' I said. 'I'll do that. Thanks.'

I was cutting through market square on the way to the shop when I felt a hand on my arm. I turned to find Tertius, Silius Nerva's slave who'd taken me out to Mettius's villa.

'Yeah, pal, what can I do for you?' I said.

He glanced over his shoulder before answering. Then he said quietly: 'The master told me to keep an eye out for you, sir. I was to say you should go over to the brothel straight away.'

'I was planning to do that anyway later,' I

said. 'Any special reason for the hurry?'

He swallowed and lowered his voice still further: like I say, we were in the middle of the square, and as usual at that time of day you couldn't get anywhere in town less private. 'There, ah, seems to have been another suspicious death, sir. The owner, Opilia Andromeda.'

'*Andromeda?*' Oh, shit. I stared at him. 'When the hell was this?'

'I don't know, sir. I don't know any of the details. But the slave Carillus reported it to the master about an hour ago. He's instructed that nothing be done until you were contacted.'

Gods alive! First Mettius dead, now his girlfriend. How many more bodies were we going to get before we were finished? Still, I should've seen this one coming: if my second theory about the meeting was right – that Mettius and Andromeda had met the killer together – it was a murder waiting to happen.

Fool! Mind you, it wasn't altogether my fault. I'd tried to talk to her, after all, and she'd ducked out.

'OK,' I said. 'I'll go over there now. Same procedure as last time. Send to Castrimoenium for Clarus as soon as you can manage it, right?'

'Yes, sir,' he said. 'I'll go myself straight away.'

'Fine.' Yeah, well, there was one plus, if you could call it that: being dead let Andromeda off the hook as a suspect pretty spectacularly. Like I said, though, I should've been expecting it after Mettius had been killed. If the two of them had been an item – and I knew now for certain from Vatinia that they were – then they must have had something cooking between them. Something, naturally, involving the murderer and prompting that meeting in the pine grove. And whatever it was, it'd done for them both.

I went round to the brothel. The door was locked this time, but when I knocked Carillus opened it for me. Barely after the first couple of raps, too: I wondered if the guy had been standing in the lobby right behind it, just waiting for me to arrive, maybe even for the whole time since he'd called in the death.

He looked old, older than he even had a right to look, and his face was grey as an unwashed rag. He was also, very obviously, still in shock. When I stepped past him he closed and locked the door again behind me.

'I'm sorry,' he said. 'Master Nerva gave strict instructions that no one be let in except you. And I've told the girls to stay in their rooms.'

'That's fine, pal,' I said. 'Now tell me what happened, OK? At your own pace, slowly and clearly.'

'Yes, sir.' He took a deep breath. 'The mistress didn't come down at her usual time. Normally I would just have waited until she did and had rung for me, but one of the local tradesmen arrived with a bill that had to be settled urgently, so I thought it was best to let her know at once. She wasn't in her sitting room, so I called up the stairs and got no answer. I went up to the flat and ... found her. She was ... She...' He stopped and stood shaking. 'I was very fond of the mistress, sir, even though I'd only known her for a short time. She was a good person. She didn't deserve to die like that.'

'OK, Carillus,' I said gently. 'I'll go up. You want to stay here?'

'No, sir, I'll come. You'll have more questions for me, no doubt.'

'Fine,' I said. 'Lead the way, then.'

We went through the sitting room and up the internal stairs. The flat was a single room, sparsely furnished with a bed, a clothes chest and another book cubby packed with book-rolls. Andromeda was lying on the bed. She was wearing a sleeping tunic, and her head and the mattress beneath it were a mess of blood. Barring a cursory look, I didn't touch her: that was Clarus's department, and I was familiar enough now with the way he worked not to disturb things.

Or not to disturb the body, at least; there was still the question of the missing statuette. It hadn't been in her sitting room downstairs when I'd looked, but there was just a chance that it was up here. I crossed over to the clothes chest and opened the lid. Nothing but clothes all the way down. There wasn't anything that shouldn't be there squirrelled away in the book cubby, either, or underneath the bed. Of course, the murderer could've seen and taken it, but still...

I went to the door that led to the outside staircase and lifted the latch. The door opened.

'This wasn't locked?' I said.

Carillus was carefully not looking at the body. 'No, sir,' he said. 'There's no key. It went missing in Rutilia Tyche's time, and the mistress didn't bother to replace it. There was no need, really. We don't have much crime in Bovillae.'

I almost smiled to myself. Yeah, right; barring three murders, an arson scam and a dodgy antiques business, at the very least. But I knew what the old guy meant.

'She'd arranged for a locksmith to come round to fit a new lock and a set of bolts, though.'

'Oh? When did she do that?' I asked.

'Yesterday, sir. I told you when you called that she'd gone out. The man was going to do it this afternoon.'

So he hadn't been lying after all, except about not knowing where she'd gone; which might just – if he had pointed me in the right direction – have saved her life, because then we might've had our second talk that day after all. Not that I'd even hint at that to Carillus; he was upset enough already without adding guilt to the mix. Still, the fact that she'd been updating the flat's security arrangements as a matter of urgency was significant: Andromeda had known she was a target, and she was frightened. Which almost certainly meant that, when she'd talked to me only a few hours previously, she'd known perfectly well who murdered Caesius – and more, that he'd just nailed her lover Mettius.

Gods! Why the hell hadn't she told me then?

Unless, of course, she'd had a guilty secret of her own to keep. Which would make all kinds of sense...

'You know that she used to be Quintus Caesius's slave?' I said to Carillus.

His surprise was obvious. 'No, sir. I didn't. That she'd been a slave, certainly, but as far as I knew she'd always belonged to the brothel owner Opilia Lucinda over in Tibur.'

'This would've been before that. Twenty years or so back.' Shit; there was something there, I just knew it. 'Listen, pal, this is important. Is there anything you're not saying? About your mistress and Caesius's death?'

His face was set. 'No, sir. Nothing.'

288

He was lying, that I was sure of. Still, putting the pressure on at this point wouldn't do any good: the guy was tottering on the edge already. Past it.

'Fine, I'll take your word for it,' I said. 'But if you do think of something you've forgotten, you let me know, right? No comeback, I promise, and it can't harm anyone now, can it?' He didn't answer. I sighed. 'OK. Is there anything else you can tell me? About Andromeda's death, I mean?'

'No, sir.'

'You wouldn't happen to know something about a small bronze, would you? Pretty old? The figure of a runner? You ever see your mistress with that? Or Aulus Mettius, maybe?'

'No, sir.'

He was beginning to clam up. Well, like I said, twisting arms wouldn't help. We'd just have to let him think things over and hope that he changed his mind.

'OK,' I said. 'That's about all I can do for the present. My son-in-law Clarus should be here later on. He's a doctor over in Castrimoenium, and he'll want to look at the body. You fine with that?'

'You mean I have to just leave her as she is, sir? That I can't contact the undertakers and have her taken care of? That's not decent.'

'Clarus shouldn't be long. And he'll be pretty quick. But it's important that nothing's disturbed before he gets here.'

'Yes, those were Master Nerva's instructions too. I understand. Very well, I'll do as you ask.'

'Fine.' I turned to go.

'Valerius Corvinus?'

I turned back. 'Yeah?'

'Perhaps it's not the time to raise the question, but the girls will be asking me. What will happen to the house now? With the mistress dead, I mean?'

Shit; you don't think of these mundane things at a time like this. Unless, of course, you're a slave and part of the property, to be disposed of as such. Then they rank pretty high.

'I don't know, pal,' I said gently. 'You'd better ask Nerva.'

'I'll do that, sir. Thank you.'

I left.

OK, I could talk to Clarus about the how and when of Andromeda's death later, back at the villa. Meanwhile I'd carry on with the original plan of getting Baebius by the throat regarding the probably totally minor issue of the fake birthday present, plus a follow-up on the missing bronze front and the business of the Lotus. After that – and, ancient history or not, I'd a gut feeling that this was anything but minor – I might chase up the connection between Andromeda and Quintus Caesius, particularly in terms of why he'd sold her on to a brothel owner in Tibur. Anthus would be gone by now, sure, off to start his new life with his baker fiancée, but although I could probably get an address for him easily enough I suspected he wouldn't be too forthcoming on the subject: when I'd talked to her, Caesius's sister-in-law Vatinia had used the phrase 'family scandal' in connection with it, and I'd bet that the old guy would balk about repeating any story that showed his ex-master in a dishonourable light. Which, from all the indications, it would. So Vatinia herself it had to be.

Onwards and upwards. I found the antiques shop and went in. No Baebius in evidence, but the old freedman (Nausiphanes, wasn't it?) was sitting behind the counter.

'Good morning, sir,' he said, getting up. 'Back again?'

'Yeah,' I said. 'Actually, I wanted to have a word with your boss. His door slave said he might be here.'

'I'm afraid not. He hasn't been in today at all; in fact I didn't know he was back from a trip to Rome. Is there anything I can do for you? No problems with the plaque I sold you, I hope.'

There was no point in bawling out the hired help. 'No, my stepfather was delighted with it,' I said, which in its way was perfectly

291

true. 'It's about something else entirely. So you wouldn't know where I'd be likely to find him?'

'No, I'm sorry. I can take a message, of course, if you'd like to leave one. He's bound to drop by sooner or later.'

'It doesn't matter, pal. No hurry. Oh, by the way, though, while I'm in. That little bronze you talked about last time. The one of the runner, from what's-his-name's estate. The Roman ex-governor.'

'Plautius Silvanus, sir. That's right. What about it?'

'How much would it have been worth?'

'The going price on the open market would've been about twenty thousand, sir. It was, as I said, a very nice piece, although certainly not unique. Why do you ask?'

'Just curiosity.' Well, that checked with what Baebius himself had told me. And it cleared up one possibility, that the statuette was worth far more than he'd said it was. That would've upped the ante on how desperate he was to get his hands on it and provided him with a viable motive for at least the latest two murders, which, as the only one of the suspects with an acknowledged interest in the Runner, he might well have had. Twenty thousand was a large slice of cash, sure, but not enough for a guy in Baebius's position to kill for, and if the bronze wasn't a major collector's item in itself, that side of things was a non-starter, too. If I was looking for a reason to finger Baebius as the perp, I'd have to do better than the missing Runner. 'Thanks, Nausiphanes. I'll see you around.'

'Any time, sir. Have a good festival.'

So. Up to the Tiburtine Gate to collect my horse, and on to Mettius's villa for another talk with his mother. I reckoned that would just about do me for the day. Besides, by the time I'd finished there, Clarus might be back to put in his report on the latest corpse.

At least this time I'd managed to avoid the slightly gut-churning forensic examination. That I could do without.

As she had been before, Vatinia was sitting in the atrium.

'Valerius Corvinus,' she said when the slave had shown me in and I'd sat down. 'I didn't expect you back so soon. Have you any news?'

'No, I'm afraid not. Or not about your son's death, anyway.' I hesitated. 'Opilia Andromeda. She was found dead this morning. Murdered.'

Her blank eyes stared at me. 'Sweet Juno!' she whispered. 'The poor woman! I'd no liking for her, as you know, but I wouldn't have wished her ill. What happened?'

'From the looks of things, she was killed while she slept. By a blow to the head.'

'Like Aulus, you mean?'

'Yeah, more or less.'

'Was there a connection?' She frowned. 'Forgive me, that was a silly question; of course, there must have been. And with poor Quintus's death, too.'

'Yeah. Actually, that's what I came to ask you about,' I said. 'When we talked yesterday you mentioned something about a family scandal involving her. When she was your brother-in-law's slave.'

Her lips tightened. 'I was referring to her liaison with my son, of course,' she said. 'As you well know.'

'Right. Right. Only I have the feeling, now, that maybe that wasn't all there was to it.'

Her chin went up. 'Where you got that impression from, Valerius Corvinus, I really can't think. Certainly not from me.'

'So I was wondering if you could sort of give me more of the background details. If you don't mind, that is.'

'I'm afraid that I do mind. I've told you all I can. Certainly as much as it is your business to know.'

There was something screwy here, I was absolutely sure of it: the lady was being far too defensive, and she had no reason to be, not if she was being straight.

'You see,' I said, 'I was wondering if it wasn't all a bit too over-the-top, under the circumstances. After all, Andromeda was just a slave, so fair game for any red-blooded young member of the family to play about with. There couldn't have been any question of your son marrying her; that would've been legally impossible, for a start, and anything less shouldn't really have mattered. Only your brother-in-law not only goes and sells her; he sells her to a brothel-keeper twenty miles away. And your son hates him so much even now that he won't refer to him as "uncle" and goes to his funeral just for the pleasure of seeing him burn. Me, I find all that curious. Certainly when you lump it all together.'

'I told you, Corvinus.' Vatinia was obviously keeping herself in check only with an effort: her colour was mounting. 'Aulus always was wild, a law to himself. The legal aspect of things wouldn't have mattered to him. Oh, the girl wouldn't have had the title of wife, but if he could have engineered it she would have had the position.'

'I'm sorry, lady,' I said, 'but that's nonsense. She was Caesius's property, pure and simple. If your son had tried to remove her, taken her to live with him, it would've been straightforward theft, and the law would've been down on him like a ton of bricks. He would've known that, and so would Caesius. So why the over-reaction? What else had she done to deserve it?'

And Vatinia's face ... shut. There was no

other word to describe it. She stood up and shouted: *'Phrontis!'*

The major-domo came hurrying in. 'Yes, madam?'

'This gentleman is leaving. Now. And he is not to be readmitted on any future occasion. Not for any reason. Is that clear?'

'Yes, madam.' He was glaring at me. 'Sir? If you would, please?'

Well, so much for that, then. I stood up.

'Sure. No problem.'

He led me out without a word, and the front door closed behind me.

Jupiter! I'd touched a nerve there, and no mistake. Though what the fuck it was I couldn't think.

One thing was certain, though: I needed to find out more about what exactly had happened twenty years back. With Andromeda herself dead, there was only one way to do that now, if it was possible at all: talk to the woman Caesius had sold her to. Which meant, having just ridden all the way to Rome and back, joy of joys, I now had to go to Tibur.

Bugger!

TWENTY

I set off early next morning.

Well, at least it got me away from Mother for the day and a half that I'd allowed for the round trip, which was a definite plus. The lady being the card-carrying militant non-drinker that she is, where the wine was concerned I'd been pretty abstemious at dinner the previous evening. Even so, I'd still got the glare and pointed sniff of disapproval over the duck with saffron nut sauce every time I topped up my cup, with the result that Aunt Marcia's best reserve Alban had tended to slip past my tonsils like third-rate Veientanum. Priscus, I noticed, had been ostentatiously mixing extra water from the water-jug into his ration; except when, between the main course and the dessert, Mother went out to powder her nose, at which point he'd poured himself a surreptitious whopper and downed most of it in one. He'd been putting away Euclidus's veal cutlets with fennel like there was no tomorrow, too, and considering Mother usually fed the poor old bugger on groats and alfalfa, it wasn't surprising.

Yeah, well, no doubt his married life had its balancing compensations. Not that, at his age, they could've been very strenuous or exciting.

Anyway, there I was in Tibur. It'd been an easy enough ride, good weather all the way, and although the road connecting it with Castrimoenium is gravel-surfaced rather than paved I'd covered the twenty-odd miles in fairly good time, certainly a lot less than I'd budgeted for. It wasn't a place I'd ever been to before; a pleasant little town about the same size as Bovillae, maybe a tad bigger, with a setting high above the plain that's impressive as hell if you like your scenery to be on the rugged side, don't suffer from vertigo, and don't mind streets that you practically have to wear pitons to climb.

Luckily, though, the house belonging to the guy I was (hopefully) going to be staying with – a doctor friend of Clarus's father – was near the gate I came in through. No problems there, fortunately: Clarus had given me clear directions plus a letter of introduction, while the old doctor turned out to be a widower desperate for company and only too pleased to put me up for the night. I got a pretty funny look when I asked him where I'd find the local brothel, mind.

I found stabling for my horse and then went straight round to the address he'd given me. The place was in a narrow street off the centre of the lower town, appropriately enough near the main meat market. I pushed open the door...

'Good afternoon, sir!' A youngish slave in a natty mauve tunic who'd been sitting on a bench in the small entrance lobby sprang to his feet.

'Uh, hi, pal,' I said, closing the door behind me. 'A good afternoon to you. I was wondering if—'

'Of course you were, sir. And the answer is *yes.*'

'Ah ... pardon me?'

'A stranger in town, are you? Or perhaps you've just heard of our amazing two-for-one pre-festival offer?'

'Your *what?*' Jupiter! I didn't believe this! 'Hang on a minute, sunshine; just let me finish, OK? I only wanted to—'

'Quite natural! And believe me, we can cater! If you'll take a moment to read our extremely comprehensive and reasonably priced list of staff and services displayed on the wall to your left I'm sure we can accommodate you.'

Sod this for a game of soldiers. I reached out and grabbed him by the neck of his tunic, and he froze, goggling. 'Now look,' I said. 'I only want to talk to the boss, OK? Strictly business. She around at present?'

'Ah...' He swallowed. 'Possibly. If you'd

care to wait I'll enquire.'

'Fine, pal. You do that small thing.' I let him go, and he scuttled off. Gods, I hate this modern high-pressure salesmanship.

I looked round. The place, or the lobby, at least, was a bit cramped, but not bad for a provincial town, and streets ahead of its equivalent in Bovillae. The decoration – mini-fresco of badly drawn nymphs and satyrs partying in a sylvan landscape, plus a surround on all four walls of painted rectangles representing wooden panelling – looked new, for a start, which I supposed was fair enough: it could only have been eighteen months or so since the fire that had given Andromeda her freedom, and the brothel had almost certainly moved to different premises. Mind you, if the front man was anything to go by the general laid-back ethos of these places had certainly changed a lot since my young day, that's for sure. Ah, well, you couldn't stop progress.

Mauve-tunic came back. 'If you'd like to follow me, sir,' he said stiffly. I did, along a short corridor. He opened a door and stepped aside.

I'd been expecting a sitting room like Andromeda's, but what I got was a functional office with a desk and document cubbies. Not that that had been its original purpose: the building must've been a private house at one time, and quite a swish one, because the room was pretty big and its far end looked out on to a peristyle court with a small garden. The result was that at this time of year it was cold as an icebox, despite two sizeable charcoal braziers. I was glad I'd kept my cloak on.

'Thank you, Publius,' said the woman sitting behind the desk. 'Off you go, dear.' Mauve-tunic closed the door behind me, and I took stock. Sixties, easy, but made-up to the nines. Auburn wig that would've made two of the normal variety, with a fair bit left over. Nose like the business end of a trireme and earrings that, if they moved, would clank rather than tinkle. Not exactly a subtle dresser, was Andromeda's ex-mistress.

She didn't look all that friendly, either. The eyes above the trireme's beak were as frosty as the air in the room.

'Well?' she said. 'What do you want?'

'Opilia?'

'Opilia Lucinda, yes.'

'Valerius Corvinus. I'm looking into a couple of murders on behalf of the senate over in Bovillae.'

'Are you, now?' The heavily made-up eyebrows went up a notch, and she smiled. 'That's nice. So?'

'One of them was your freedwoman. Andromeda. She was found dead yesterday morning. In her flat above the brothel.'

The smile disappeared and the expression

on her face under its inch or so of powder and rouge suddenly went blank. There was a cup of what looked like neat wine on the desk beside her. She picked it up, drained it at a swallow and closed her eyes. I waited.

'Holy Mother Juno!' she murmured. 'Oh, the poor little bleeder!' She opened her eyes again. 'Who did it?'

'I don't know,' I said. 'That's what I'm trying to find out. I wondered if you could help.'

She shook her head. 'Not me, dear, I'm sorry. I haven't seen her for over a year now.'

'Yeah, right, I understand that. I was hoping, though, that you could fill in a bit of her background for me. About the time before she came to Bovillae. Before she came here, even.'

'Park yourself.' There was a stool to one side of the desk. I pulled it up and sat. She took a deep breath. 'What did you want to know?'

'You bought her from a guy named Quintus Caesius. About twenty years back.'

'Seventeen. Which was her age at the time too. Lovely girl, she was. Clever, also.'

'You happen to know why he sold her?'

'There was a bit of trouble over a young man. One of the family. Her master wanted rid of her.'

'Was that all?'

'All that the gentleman told me, lovey.'

Bugger! My heart sank; it looked like I'd had a wasted journey. 'Not that I asked for more, mind, because I was lucky to get her, particularly at the price. She was a good little worker, Andromeda, took a real interest in the job. Customers appreciate that. And she kept her looks, until we had the fire. That doesn't happen with many in the trade, not past thirty. You'll know about the fire, I suppose?'

'Yeah.'

'Dreadful, that was, and I wouldn't be here now if it wasn't for her, none of us would. She kept her head, and she got us out, all of us, me and the girls. Got herself badly burned doing it, too, the silly cow.'

'That was why you freed her, right?' I said.

She nodded. 'It was the least I could do, and she was finished in the trade. Scarring's a proper turn-off for the punters.' She frowned. 'And now she's dead, holy Juno rest her bones. What a bloody waste.'

'So there isn't anything else you can tell me?' I said. 'About her life before you bought her?'

'No. I'm sorry, dear, but I can't.' Hell. 'Mind you, you could always ask Galla. She might know more.'

'Galla?'

'One of the girls. They were very thick together, her and Andromeda. Galla was ... you could call her a protégée, if you were being fancy.'

'You think I could do that now?'

'No reason why not. We're quiet at the moment. Pre-festival's always a quiet time; the punters tend to have other things on their minds. And I'm sure Galla will help you if she can.'

'That'd be great. Thanks.'

She stood up: the chair she'd been sitting on must've been raised, because she was tiny. 'You just stay here and I'll get her, then,' she said. 'But give me a minute or two to break the news to the little bitch myself, because it'll come as a bit of a shock. All right?'

'Sure. No problem.'

She went out, and I waited. It was a good quarter of an hour before the door opened again and a girl came in. Reddish hair, probably dyed (which would explain her name), late teens, pretty, thin face. She'd obviously been crying.

I got up. 'You like to sit down, Galla?' I said.

She sat on the stool, while I perched on the edge of the desk.

'How did she die?' Quiet voice, clear vowels. I could see why she and Andromeda had got on so well. Or maybe if she'd been Andromeda's protégée she'd used the older woman as a model.

The kid was upset enough already. I hesitated before I answered.

'Uh ... does that matter?' I said gently.

'No. Not really. But I'd like to know, please.' She was sitting prim as a well-brought-up schoolgirl, knees pressed together under her short tunic and hands folded in her lap. She sounded like one, as well. I wondered, fleetingly, what her own background was.

'Someone hit her on the head,' I said. 'Probably while she was sleeping. At least, that's what my son-in-law told me. He's a doctor. He said she wouldn't have known anything about it.' Actually, when we'd had our talk about the when and how of Andromeda's death, Clarus had said nothing of the kind. But a lie about a thing like that doesn't do any harm.

She nodded; just once, but there was a sort of satisfied finality to the movement. 'The mistress said you'd questions to ask me,' she said. 'About her life before she came here.'

'Yeah. That's right. It might be important.'

'Do you know about Gratillus?'

'Who?'

'Gratillus. Her brother.'

'Andromeda had a brother?'

'Yes. He was seven years younger than her.'

'Is that so, now?' I said, trying to keep my voice level. 'OK. Tell me about Gratillus.'

'He ... her master – Caesius, that was – used him.'

'Used him?'

'You know.' She shrugged. 'Bed, like. Finally he ran away. Only they caught him and brought him back. Caesius had him sent to the mines, and a month later, he was dead. A tunnel collapsed.'

Shit! I was staring at her. 'And this happened just before Andromeda was sold, yes?'

'Yes. One day, she took a knife and ... Caesius wasn't hurt, not even scratched, but Andromeda said it gave him a fright. She thought he'd have her killed, or mutilated at least as a punishment. She wouldn't've minded either, if only she'd managed to stab him first. But Caesius sold her to the mistress instead. He said he was being merciful. That's the word he used, merciful. On account of the circumstances. He believed it too, she said.' She looked straight at me. 'Andromeda hated that man.'

Yeah; I'd bet she did. Gods! 'Was that why when she got her freedom she chose to move back to Bovillae?' I said.

Galla nodded. 'Even though she knew there wasn't anything she could do to hurt him, she thought if she waited long enough there might be a chance.'

'Of killing him, you mean?'

A slight shake of the head and a frown; not a denial, more like she hadn't been clear and was annoyed with herself. 'Destroying him. That was the word she always used. Death wasn't bad enough; she wanted him to suffer first. Oh, she would've settled for second best, killed him outright if she could. In any case, what other way was there? The law wouldn't help. Her brother was a slave. Caesius could do whatever he liked with him.'

True. Only it was truth with a qualification: the law's one thing, sure, but society's another. Caesius might've been within his legal rights, but if the respectable voters of Bovillae had found out that one of their great and good was in the habit of screwing ten-year-old slave boys the bastard's political career would've been finished, and no one would've touched him socially with a barge pole. No wonder he'd got rid of her.

And she'd destroyed him right enough, in the end, or as near to it as she could manage. When he'd been found dead behind the brothel, Caesius's carefully built reputation had taken a real hammering...

Something was nagging at the back of my mind. I reached for it, but it was gone.

'Surely she could've said something,' I said. 'Told someone. When she came back to the town.'

Galla just looked at me; not a schoolgirl's look this time, not within a hundred miles of it. 'Who'd listen to an ex-slave who ran a brothel and who'd been a whore herself for the past seventeen years?' she said. 'Particularly since she'd another reason for bearing a grudge. You know about the nephew? The one who was sweet on her and got relegated?'

'Mettius? Yeah, I do. He's...' I stopped myself.

'He's what?'

'Never mind, it isn't important.' Telling her that Mettius was dead as well would only have complicated things. 'Did he know? About Gratillus?'

'Oh, yes.'

Said like it was obvious, which I supposed it was. Well, judging from Galla's story everything added up, certainly. The only problem was that the result didn't make sense. 'So,' I said. 'The first opportunity she gets Andromeda kills Caesius. Probably with Mettius's help. That's what she said she'd do from the beginning, why she went back to Bovillae in the first place. Yes?'

'She'd certainly have tried. But...' Galla stopped. 'Wait a moment. Are you saying that Caesius is dead too?'

'Yeah. That was what started all this.'

She was frowning. 'But in that case who killed Andromeda? And why?'

'Right.' I sighed, and stood up. 'Good question. The answer is I don't know, or not yet. But thank you, Galla. You've helped me a lot.'

'Good,' she said simply. 'Can I get back to

work, now? I've a customer waiting.'

Schoolgirl again, asking permission.

'Yeah. Yeah, sure,' I said.

She paused at the door, and turned.

'I'm glad Caesius is dead,' she said. 'Andromeda will be pleased.'

She left, and I watched her go.

I needed to think.

I was in front of the shoe shop in the alleyway behind Andromeda's brothel, trying to fit a pair of hobnail boots on to Marilla's donkey Corydon, and getting more and more frustrated by the second because they wouldn't go on over his hooves. Suddenly, there was Lucius Caesius, looking down at me, arms folded and laughing.

'What's up with you, pal?' I snapped at him. 'Never seen a donkey wearing boots before?'

He shook his head and laughed even harder. 'You just don't listen, do you, Corvinus?' he said. 'I told you, you idiot. He's no donkey, he's a mule. You'll never get boots on a mule. He's the wrong kind of animal.'

...And then I woke up. I was lying on the truckle bed in Clarus's father's pal's spare room, bedclothes everywhere, soaked with sweat. Which was absolutely fine by me, because I'd got it all now, the whole boiling: *in somno veritas*, right enough. The details were still to come, sure, but they could wait until I'd had another heart-to-heart with Carillus.

Gods! I'd been an idiot, like the guy had said. Right from the beginning. Lucius – the real Lucius – had blown the whole case wide open that day in the wine shop; he had given me the key on a silver platter, practically in words of one syllable, and I'd ignored him.

Fool!

Oh, I knew who the murderer was now, sure I did; that much was obvious from the dream-Lucius's crack about a mule being the wrong kind of animal. The why ... well, that I could only make an intelligent guess at, but it'd come in time, no doubt, along with the rest of the fine detail.

It was just after sun-up, but luckily my host was an early riser. I ate a quick breakfast, left as hurriedly as politeness would allow me to, collected my horse from the stable, and headed back down the road to Castrimoenium and Bovillae.

TWENTY-ONE

I didn't bother stopping off at the villa in passing: Bovillae was only another four miles, it was barely noon, and I might as well finish this now.

Confirmation first. There was a hackney stables next to the Tiburtine Gate itself and it'd been a long hard ride, so instead of leaving my horse as usual at the water-trough to drink himself sick I took him in there for a rub-down and a well-earned rest with a full nosebag while I carried on to the brothel.

This time the door was open, although there was a sign on the door saying the place was closed for business due to a bereavement, and the posts and lintel were hung with cypress. I didn't bother to knock.

Carillus met me in the lobby. He must've read my face, because he stopped himself from saying whatever he'd been going to say, and just stood there with an expression like a patient waiting for the surgeon's knife, or a sacrificial bull for the hammer.

Ah, hell. Get it over with.

'Caesius was never in here at all,' I said.

'Not while he was alive, anyway. Not on the night he died, not at any time. That whole side of things was an invention from beginning to end.'

Carillus closed his eyes briefly, swallowed, and then nodded.

'Yes,' he said. 'How did you know?'

'It's the only answer that makes sense, pal. Why should the guy visit a brothel? One that only provided female partners, anyway. He didn't like women, everything points to that. There was the business with your mistress's brother Gratillus seventeen years back, and his own brother Lucius dropped enough hints about his relationship or lack of one with his wife for it to be obvious to anyone but a cloth-eared idiot like me. Oh, he had a wife, he was married, sure; but it was a marriage of convenience, on his side at least, and for him not being married wasn't an option. Not if he wanted to get on. Bovillae's pretty strait-laced. The good townsfolk expect their representatives to be solid family men with solid, dutiful wives in the background, even if the marriage does turn out to be childless. And there was his wife's income from her first marriage, which would've helped bankroll a political career. His major-domo was in on the secret, of course: you can't keep things from your major-domo, and he'd been with Caesius all his life. His wife and sister-in-law, too. But they were all on Caesius's side, as it were: they wanted his reputation kept intact.'

'He wasn't a bad man, sir,' Carillus said. 'Oh, I know my mistress hated him, and she had good reason. But he was honest enough by his own lights, and he served the town well.'

'Yeah. Agreed.' That was part of the tragedy: even the Gratillus affair was at least understandable, given the social and moral code the guy had been brought up with. That we're all brought up with, to be fair: slaves aren't real people, they're property, and like Galla had said, he had genuinely believed it when he'd claimed he'd been merciful. 'No argument there. So. That's the background. Let's cut to the chase, shall we? What happened that night was that he died elsewhere and Andromeda and Mettius brought him here, yes?'

'Yes.'

'How did they know? That he'd been murdered, I mean?'

'That was Dossenus. He's—'

'Yeah,' I said. 'I've met Dossenus.' Fuck; another piece of the puzzle slipped into place. 'The vagrant, right?'

'Yes. My mistress kept an eye out for him, saw he didn't starve. He had a soft spot for her. Dossenus was the one who found the body. He came and told her.'

'This would be inside the old wool ware-

313

house, or what's left of it, further down the street, wouldn't it?'

'Yes. It's where he sleeps, usually.'

'Did he see the actual murder?'

'That I don't know. Very probably, but he didn't say. He was frightened to death, barely coherent.'

'So then Mettius and your mistress went and collected the corpse and brought it back here?'

He hesitated. 'The mistress, no, sir. That was no job for a woman. She stayed here, to keep watch, and Mettius and I carried it between us. Caesius was still wearing his cloak and hood, and we made sure his head was covered. If we'd met anyone we'd have said he was drunk, but fortunately that didn't happen.'

'Fair enough. You took him into Andromeda's sitting room?'

'Yes. It was just after sunset. The mistress told us to wait for an hour so she could pretend later that he'd been with one of the girls, then to carry him out the back door and dump him in the alleyway. Which is what we did.'

'Lydia. The girl he was supposed to be with. How did you square her?'

Carillus smiled. 'Oh, Lydia wasn't any trouble, and she was glad to help. She's a very intelligent girl, the brightest we have, and the mistress coached her carefully. I

314

don't think she would've told you much. Did she?'

'No. No, she didn't.' Right; well, that would teach me not to go by first impressions, wouldn't it? 'So in effect Andromeda created a scenario from whole cloth that she could give when the body was found the next day: not only had Caesius been tomcatting that evening, but he was a regular customer. She couldn't kill him herself now, because he was dead already, but she could destroy his reputation. Or at least give it her best shot.'

'Yes, sir. That's it exactly.'

Ironic, really, that she'd had to go for a fake way of doing that when there was a genuine one to hand, and after the business with her brother she must've at least suspected the truth. But there again Caesius had been careful to save that side of things for his trips to Rome; where his life in Bovillae was concerned he was as squeaky clean as everyone thought he was. Andromeda would've had to make the best use of what she'd got within the time available, and she'd managed that pretty well. Like I said, she'd been a smart cookie, that lady.

'What about the figurine?' I said.

Carillus frowned. 'What figurine, sir?'

'The little bronze Caesius had with him. The runner.' He was still looking blank. 'Aulus Mettius didn't take it?'

315

'He picked something up from beside the body and put it in his cloak pocket, sir. But I didn't see what it was.'

'Never mind, pal. It doesn't matter.' Sure it mattered: it had killed him, and Andromeda too. But Carillus didn't need to know that. I stood up. 'Thanks. Oh, one more thing. Dossenus. Your mistress – or Mettius, possibly – warned him against talking, right?'

'Yes. It was hardly necessary, because as I said he was frightened out of his wits, or what he has of them. But Mettius told him that if the news got out that Caesius had died inside the wool store he would be the obvious suspect. That was quite enough.'

Yeah, I thought grimly, it would be: when he'd talked to me as the guy officially empowered to point the final finger the poor bugger had desperately wanted to make it absolutely clear that he hadn't been involved. It did mean, though, that we had another witness to what happened, if we needed one. And he might just have seen the murder, after all, which would be a definite plus.

Which brought me to the next part, the nasty bit. I'd have to pay a call on Silius Nerva, explain the situation, borrow a couple of the town's rod men for muscle, and then confront the murderer.

Not a job for the day before the start of the Winter Festival, but it had to be done.

★ ★ ★

316

I knocked on the front door, and Baebius's young slave opened it. He frowned when he saw the two rod men – one of them, by an ironic twist of fate, was Manlius's pal Decimus – but said nothing.

'You think we could see the master?' I said.

'Yes, sir. Of course.' He stepped aside. 'He's in the study. If you wouldn't mind waiting, I'll—'

'No, that's OK. We'll go straight through.'

The frown deepened. He opened his mouth to speak, but then obviously thought better of it.

'As you wish, sir.'

He led us through the atrium, stopped outside a panelled door, and knocked.

'Come in.'

'That's fine, pal,' I said before the slave could open the door. 'We can take it from here. Just leave us in private, right?'

He gave me a scared, sideways look and went back down the corridor.

I went in. Baebius was sitting at his desk, writing. His eyes narrowed when he saw the rod men, and he put the pen down.

'Corvinus,' he said. 'This is a surprise. And why the lictors? I didn't know you'd been promoted to aedile.'

'They're just helping out,' I said. 'Forget they're here.'

'Rather difficult, but I'll do my best.' He sat back. 'Well, no matter. What can I do

317

for you?'

'Let's start with the bronze,' I said. 'The Runner. You have got it, haven't you?'

He stared at me, his face expressionless. Then he stood up, went across to a cupboard in the wall and opened it.

'There you are,' he said, taking out the figurine inside and holding it up. 'I'm sorry for lying to you, but you can understand why I did it. If I'd admitted that Caesius had actually turned up for our rendezvous it might have placed me in a very difficult situation.'

'So you had it all the time?'

'Yes, of course. I said: the agreement was that Caesius would exchange it for a similar piece plus a sum of money. Everything happened as I told you, except for the fact that the exchange was made after all.'

'In that case, what happened to the replacement and the cash?'

'I've no idea. He certainly had both when he left me. Presumably they were taken from him by whoever killed him.'

'Behind the brothel.'

'Naturally. Or inside it, or wherever.'

'There's only one problem with that, pal,' I said. 'Caesius wasn't killed behind the brothel. He didn't go near the place. He was killed where you met him, at the wool store. And he was killed much earlier than everyone believed, around sunset, at the time you said you were meeting him.'

The silence lengthened, and I heard the two rod men shifting their weight behind me. Baebius glanced at them, moved back to the desk, carefully set the figurine down, and resumed his seat.

'Is that so, now?' he said.

'You want to tell me what actually happened? Or shall I tell you?'

'Go ahead. I'd be most interested.'

There was a stool next to the desk. I pulled it up and sat down.

'Fine,' I said. 'First of all, there was no exchange. Or at least, you never got your hands on the bronze. Not then, anyway.'

'So when did I, if I have it now?'

'My guess is that you set the meeting up intending to kill Caesius from the start. Only when you'd done it something went wrong. You found that you were being watched, by the vagrant who sleeps there, a guy by the name of Dossenus. So you panicked and ran, leaving the bronze behind.'

'Corvinus, please! The thing's worth, what, twenty thousand sesterces, yes? A large amount of money, agreed, but I'm a wealthy man with a position to think of, and beautiful though it is, it's scarcely a unique piece. I'm hardly likely to plan and commit a murder for a trivial reason like that, am I?'

'Yeah, well,' I said. 'As far as motive's concerned, we'll leave that side of it for now.

But that's the way it happened; like I said, there was a witness who saw the whole thing.' I gave him the lie straight, without blinking – it might even be true. 'Anyway, Dossenus goes to Opilia Andromeda and tells her the whole story. Her boyfriend Mettius, who's spending the night in her flat, picks up the body and takes it inside, together with the statuette. Then, sometime over the next couple of days, being the crook he is and having no particular reason to see his uncle's killer brought to justice, he decides to do a bit of business on his own account. Just for the fun of it rather than the actual profit, although where Andromeda's concerned the cash'll be very welcome. He comes to you, tells you he knows what you have done, and promises to keep his mouth shut for an appreciable consideration. He's an honest crook, though, as crooks go, and not a proper thief *per se*, so he says he'll throw in the Runner as a gesture of good faith. You agree to meet him in the pine grove above his villa to complete the deal. I'm not sure about this bit, but the chances are that Andromeda was waiting close by, to see how things turned out, and she was the one to find her boyfriend's body, well before Quintus Roscius happened along.' Baebius hadn't moved, or reacted in any way since he'd last spoken, but now he smiled. 'Anyway, when Mettius turns up carrying the bronze to fulfil his part of the bargain you kill him instead. Then, the following night, just to make sure your secret's safe, you go to his girlfriend's flat above the brothel and kill her as well.' I paused. 'OK. So how am I doing?'

'It wasn't murder,' he said quietly. 'Not the first death. You were wrong about that. Caesius's death was an accident.'

Joy in the morning!

'Fine,' I said. 'You want to tell me?'

'Why not? You have most of it. You may as well get your facts right. And I'm no killer, not by nature. Mettius and the woman – well, they were necessary. Besides, as you say, one was a crook and the other was a whore.'

Delivery cold as hell. If I'd had any sympathy for him – which I didn't, really – that's when it would've vanished.

Baebius picked up the statuette and turned it over in his hands. He didn't look at me.

'I was in Rome halfway through last month,' he said. 'There was a new club I'd heard of which had recently opened, and I wanted to look it over. A gentleman's club, very private, very expensive.'

'The Crimson Lotus. In Pallacina Road.'

His eyes came up, and for the first time they showed genuine surprise. 'Now how the *hell* did you know that?' he said.

'You were there a few days ago. I saw you

321

myself.'

There was a long silence. Baebius's eyes were still locked with mine. Then he shrugged and dropped his gaze.

'Evidently you're a darker horse than I took you for, Corvinus,' he said. 'Interesting. But it's of no great matter. As you'll no doubt know, then, if you've been there, the Lotus ... specializes. Young slaves like Clitus, who let you in. Anyway, as I say I was there about a month ago and I happened to bump into Quintus Caesius. He was with a little Ethiopian boy of no more than nine or ten. *With* being the operative word. I was shocked.' He smiled. 'I didn't know, you see. Up to then, I'd never even considered the possibility. No one had, no one did. Like me, he'd been very careful to keep that side of his life a secret, by indulging his inclinations only in Rome, and with slaves whose job it was to cater for him. Unlike me, though, to him the secrecy mattered. I hide things only out of politeness. Bovillans are very provincial, in all the senses of the word. If they discovered that I consorted with young men – rather than, as at present, simply suspected it – my friends and acquaintances would find the fact at the very least embarrassing, and although I'm not at all ashamed of what I am I have no wish to cause them pain. However, to me, personally, it would not be of great importance.'

'But to Caesius it would,' I said.

He nodded. 'Very much so. Particularly since his penchant was for the pre-adolescent variety. He was a highly respected public figure who had just been elected censor. A position in which he would be exercising moral judgement over the citizen body. Even the rumour that he was a practising paedophile would have ruined him completely.'

'So you decided to blackmail him.'

He was still holding the bronze. He set it down carefully before answering.

'I'd put it differently,' he said. 'For all he was no friend of mine, I had the utmost respect for Quintus Caesius. He may have played rough at times as a rival collector, but we were both self-confessed fanatics in that field; you must expect these things and exercise a certain give-and-take. Also, he was an extremely hard-headed businessman, one possibly not too averse to cutting corners, so long as he was acting within the law. However, as far as I know, in his public dealings he was scrupulously honest. Uniquely so, in fact. I'd no wish to damage him there.'

'So asking for the Runner in exchange for your silence was a one-off?'

Baebius nodded. 'There was a certain element of pique involved, I admit: when he'd stolen a march on me and bought it in advance of the auction it had been going a little too far, and I resented it out of all proportion to the thing's worth, both monetary and aesthetic. But that would've been the end of it; there would have been no later demands, I give you my word on that, as I gave it to him. As I saw it, he had cheated me and I was rectifying the situation. I even offered to give him back the money he had paid for it.'

'So what went wrong?'

'I'm not sure. I suspect that my continued silence was so important to him that he simply didn't believe me, or couldn't take the risk of trusting me. After all, we were long-standing enemies. In the event, at the meeting in the wool store while the transfer was being made he suddenly attacked me with a knife. There was a struggle, I got the upper hand, and he fell backwards, hitting his head on a lump of masonry. When I looked, he was obviously either dead or very seriously injured. I panicked and ran, stupidly forgetting to pick up the statuette. Then I went home. And that's all I know.' He looked at me. 'I didn't see your witness – Dossenus, was it? I didn't even know of his existence, until you told me just now. If I had, then I'm afraid I would have had to kill him too.'

Yeah, well, it all added up, I'd give him that. And whether he was actually telling the truth about Caesius attacking him was academic now. Me, I could see it happening: like he said, the guy must've been desperate, and perhaps it wasn't too much out of character, given the circumstances. The knife might still be there to find, or Dossenus might've taken it, which would prove things one way or the other, but that was no concern of mine. Let Silius Nerva and his oh-so-respectable cronies in the senate deal with their own dirty linen from here on in.

'One more thing,' I said. 'Not for me, but my son-in-law will be curious. The murder weapon. What did you use to kill Mettius and Andromeda? Presumably you took something with you.'

'Ah.' He went over to a stand of walking sticks in the corner. My two rod men shifted uneasily, and he glanced at me and smiled. 'May I?'

'Go ahead.'

He pulled out one of the sticks: ebony, with a silver head. 'I take it with me on my outings in Rome,' he said. 'For obvious reasons, I prefer to be accompanied only by a single torch slave on the nocturnal parts of these, and I find this very useful. The top six inches are filled with lead, and I'm quite proficient in its use.' He put the stick back, and I could hear the rod men relax. 'So. What happens now?'

'That's up to the authorities,' I said. 'These gentlemen' – I glanced over my shoulder at the two rod men – 'will take you to Nerva. Or whoever. Me, I'm out of it.'

'Job done?' There was just a trace of sarcasm in his voice. I ignored it.

'Yeah,' I said. 'Job done.' I turned to go. 'Oh, by the way. That ivory plaque you sold me. Or your freedman did, rather. It was a fake.'

'Was it really?' He didn't sound too surprised, or interested, which, given the events of the last ten minutes or so, was understandable. For someone who was looking at either exile or the strangler's noose, a little minor fraud wasn't going to weigh much. 'I'm sorry. Call in at the shop and tell Nausiphanes from me he's to refund the cost. You needn't return the plaque. Consider it a Festival gift.'

I nodded. 'Thanks.'

'You're very welcome. Happy Winter Festival.'

I didn't answer.

Like he'd said, job done. Not that the fact had left a very pleasant taste in my mouth, but then it seldom did. I left the rod men to it, and went home.

TWENTY-TWO

Winter Festival morning.

Like I said right at the start, the Winter Festival's really for the bought help, which is fair enough: the poor buggers have a pretty rotten time of it for most of the year, and it won't do the empire much lasting harm if they're allowed to let their hair down – within reason, of course – for three or four days in mid-December. Then, naturally, there's the tradition aspect, and that's for everyone to enjoy. Some things like the roast pork dinner, the gambling games, dressing up in party gear and being sick from overeating are pretty standard, but each family has its own traditions. We like to start the day with the presents, and Clarus and Marilla have followed suit.

So there we were, Perilla and me, plus the two youngsters, in the atrium with the Sack. No Mother or Priscus: Mother's convinced that if you show your face before the chill's properly off the morning the crow's-feet goblin will get you, while Priscus is just plain bone lazy. And, of course, there were the household staff, everyone from the two major-domos to the kitchen skivvy, lined up in the dinky little freedmen-caps that they're allowed to wear for the duration; faces washed, bright as buttons, hair neatly combed – except for Bathyllus, who as usual had polished his scalp specially for the occasion – and waiting with bated breath for the Sack to be opened.

'You want to do this, pal?' I whispered to Clarus. 'It's your house, and you're Head of Household.'

He was grinning. 'No, that's OK, Corvinus,' he said. 'Carry on.'

Fair enough. Like I said, I enjoy the Winter Festival, and the Sack is the best part. Everyone got a Festival doll, a wax candle and a little pouch of cash, which was traditional all over the empire – and as Head of Household Clarus had handed these out already – but the Sack was an extra.

'OK, then let's get started,' I said, taking out the first present and looking at the tag and raising my voice. 'Who's got number six?'

A hand went up: one of the stable lads.

'Congratulations, pal,' I said. 'You've got a bottle of scent.'

There were hoots from his mates, plus a couple of raspberries as he came up to collect it. He didn't look too disappointed, mind, which was understandable: no doubt he could work a deal out later to their mutual satisfaction with one of the maids.

'Next,' I said. 'Number eleven. Ex eye, ladies and gentlemen. Who's got eleven?'

That was better. The mouse-like kitchen skivvy crept back to her place proudly clutching a packet of Alexandrian honeyed dates.

'Five. The big vee.'

Five was a belt pouch with a couple of silver pieces in it. Always popular, that one. Euclidus the chef. I was glad it was him: the rest of the gang could enjoy their day off, but if we all wanted to eat then someone had to do the cooking.

'Vultures over the Palatine, number twelve.'

'That would be me, sir,' Bathyllus said, coming forward.

I grinned. Yeah, it would be: the little guy never did have much luck with raffles. 'It's, uh, a rather fetching little brush and comb set, Bathyllus.' Hoots and catcalls again as the assembled throng caught sight of them. Still, it was the Winter Festival, and you could take a joke too far. 'Never mind, pal. See me later and we'll arrange something different. OK, moving on rapidly. Number nine. All the Muses, number nine. Who's got nine?' Silence. 'Come on, people! Somebody must have it!'

'I think that might be Phormio's, sir,' Bathyllus said. 'He isn't here, I'm afraid.'

Yeah; now he came to mention it there wasn't any sign of Mother's lantern-jawed coconut-headed demon chef among the serried ranks. Currently speaking, the universe definitely had a Phormio-shaped hole in it. Not that we'd be grieving over this. Still, it was festival morning...

'So where the hell is he?' I said.

Bathyllus coughed discreetly. 'In the latrine, sir,' he said. 'Or so I'd imagine. He's been spending most of his time there ever since the small hours of this morning. If you give his present to me or to Lupercus we'll be very happy to pass it on when he re-emerges.'

'The latrine, eh?' I glanced at Clarus. 'Your department, I think, pal. A bit of medical research.' He nodded and went out. 'OK, Bathyllus. Here it is: a new pair of sandals.' Very appropriate, under the circumstances. 'Right. Number fourteen. One of each, ex eye vee. Who's got fourteen?'

And so it went on. The Sack emptied and was put away for another year. Ah, well. The ladies went off to bring our own presents hidden in clothes-chests and under the beds – Perilla always gives me a new mantle; surprise, surprise – while the bought help dispersed to the general revelry below stairs.

'Not you, sunshine,' I said to Bathyllus. 'Or you, Lupercus. Winter Festival or not, I want a word. Just twiddle your thumbs until

330

Clarus gets back, will you?'

They did, and he did, a few moments later. 'You found him?'

'Oh, yes. It's nothing serious. Just a bad case of the runs. Something he ate. I've given him a suspension that'll help, but he'll be out of things for the rest of the day.'

'Is that so, now?' I said. 'And I suppose this means that he won't be up to cooking this extra-special super-duper beyond-the-spice-route gourmet Winter Festival meal that Mother was talking about, does it?'

'I doubt it.' Clarus cleared his throat; I could see he was trying hard not to grin. 'We'll just have to fall back on Euclidus, I'm afraid.'

'Hmm.' I was looking at Bathyllus and Lupercus and getting two blank-eyeballed stares in return. 'Something he ate, right? And this would be last night, in the servants' hall, presumably. Together with the rest of the staff.'

'Probably,' Clarus said.

'Anyone else dumping his or her guts out downstairs in the small hours, Lupercus?'

'No, sir.'

'Not so much as a twinge?'

'Ah ... no, sir. Fortunately.'

'And it couldn't be self-inflicted, could it? The deal was that he was barred from doing any cheffing until the festival meal itself. Right, Bathyllus?'

'Yes, sir.'

'So it's odd, isn't it?' No answer. I turned to Clarus. 'Uh ... absolutely *apropos* of nothing whatsoever, pal, have you checked the contents of your medicine cupboard recently? For, say, your supply of purgatives?'

He'd twigged. He cleared his throat again. 'Oh, I'm sure that's not necessary, Corvinus. Lupercus here keeps the simple basics up to score. I've taught him how to prepare the non-harmful medicines I use a lot of, and I'm certain he'd make good any shortfall.'

'Right. Right.' I nodded. 'Well, it's a complete mystery, isn't it? Mother will be disappointed. As will we all. Still, it can't be helped. Never mind, better luck next year.'

'Will there be anything more, sir?' Bathyllus said. He was looking relieved.

'No, little guy, I think that just about does it. It's the festival: go and put your feet up, let your hair down or whatever. Oh, that reminds me' – I reached into my belt pouch – 'the replacement for that brush and comb set. I can't think of anything suitable at present, so you'll just have to make do with the cash equivalent.' I gave him a gold piece, and handed another one to Lupercus. 'Happy Winter Festival, pals. Don't spend it all in the one shop.'

They went to join what was no doubt by this time a staff knees-up in full swing. Minus, of course, Phormio, who wouldn't want to stray too far from the hole in the floor.

Ah, well. It was only once a year, and they deserved it.

Author's Note

Solid Citizens is completely fictional, of course, but what was interesting for me was that, uniquely and purely coincidentally, it was set at exactly the time it was written, in the lead-up to what would've been the Roman Winter Festival (Saturnalia), a week before our Christmas. *That* was quite an eerie experience, since I found for a lot of the time that I was sitting down at my laptop in December 2012 and mentally shifting back to precisely the same date in AD39. Even the weather outside my living-room window was the same – unfortunately, given my twice-a-day dog-walking duties. So despite all the murder and mayhem, for me at least the book has a definite Christmassy feel.

A word or two, for anyone who may be interested, concerning the Saturnalia itself. (I've already put some of this into the author's note for *Last Rites*, but never mind.) It was dedicated to the god Saturn, which explains a lot about its character. Saturn occupied a very special place in the Roman psyche; he was a benign, grandfatherly figure, as opposed to his more authoritarian son Jupiter, and he had presided over the First Age of Man when life was much simpler and kinder. The festival began according to different accounts on 16 or 17 December, and originally lasted for three days, although this was extended to five and longer in the AD years. Through no coincidence whatsoever (early Christianity exhibiting the plagiaristic features that it did), it had a great deal in common with our Christmas, particularly in the latter's mediaeval form: all public business was suspended, and the normal rigid social conventions – particularly those governing the relationship between slave and master – were relaxed or even reversed. It was a time for parties, when even the stuffiest Roman would let his hair down, swap his toga for a party mantle or indulge in a bit of cross-dressing *à la* pantomime dame; also for exchanging presents, particularly – by tradition – wax candles and dolls/puppets, which served the same purpose as our Christmas cards. Not the Sack, though; that is pure invention on my part, and just a bit of fun, because I thought it was something that Corvinus would enjoy, so I gave him his head at that point. As at the mediaeval Christmas, often an equivalent of the Lord of Misrule or King of the Bean was chosen by lot – slave or free – whose word for the duration was law.

The poet Catullus calls the Saturnalia *optimus dierum*, 'best of days', which more or less sums the thing up. *Very* un-Roman, in many ways – at least, as we think of the Romans – but none the worse for that.

A very merry Christmas to you, when it comes.